London Ever After

BOOK 9 IN THE LONDON ROMANCE SERIES

by Clare Lydon

First Edition February 2024
Published by Custard Books

ISBN: 978-1-912019-47-2

Cover Design: Kevin Pruitt
Editor: Cheyenne Blue
Typesetting: Adrian McLaughlin

Find out more at: www.clarelydon.co.uk
Follow me on Twitter: @clarelydon
Follow me on Instagram: @clarefic

This is a work of fiction. All characters and happenings
in this publication are fictitious and any resemblance
to real persons (living or dead), locales or events
is purely coincidental.

Also By Clare Lydon

London Romance Series

London Calling (Book One)
This London Love (Book Two)
A Girl Called London (Book Three)
The London Of Us (Book Four)
London, Actually (Book Five)
Made In London (Book Six)
Hot London Nights (Book Seven)
Big London Dreams (Book Eight)
London Ever After (Book Nine)

Standalone Novels

A Taste Of Love
Before You Say I Do
Change Of Heart
Christmas In Mistletoe
Hotshot
It Started With A Kiss
Nothing To Lose: A Lesbian Romance
Once Upon A Princess
One Golden Summer
The Christmas Catch
The Long Weekend
Twice In A Lifetime
You're My Kind

All I Want Series

Two novels and four novellas chart the course of one relationship over two years.

Boxsets

Available for both the London Romance series and the All I Want series for ultimate value. Check out my website for more: www.clarelydon.co.uk/books

Acknowledgements

I was scheduled to write *London Ever After* in 2022, the year after *Big London Dreams*. But then, family bereavement and major illness threw my whole year off course. I eventually wrote the book in 2023, and it's finally in your hands. The journey was long, but I hope you enjoy the end of this most precious, fabulous series, and that this book was worth the wait.

The London Romance series was what kicked off my whole writing career, so I will be forever grateful to Jess & Lucy, Kate & Meg, and the rest of the gang. I'll also be eternally thankful for the readers who loved the stories, too. You gave me the encouragement to keep writing, and see where it took me. In the case of this series, the answer was nine full-length novels over a decade.

With *London Ever After*, I hope it's a full-circle moment. The series began with *London Calling*, which saw Jess moving in with Kate in Shoreditch. It ends with Kate and Meg moving out, but Cordy and Hannah just getting started in East London. A changing of the guard; a passing of the baton. But the key element of finding someone you love remains the same. Lesbians and queers need and deserve love, too. That's what my books will always be about.

Where to start with my thanks for helping to get *London Ever After* out the door? First, to my early readers, Angela, Sophie, Becca and Kathy who gave me the initial thumbs up. Then to my stellar ARC team, who spot all the last-minute errors. Particularly the typo in the dedication. Don't worry, they're all fixed now (I hope).

Huge thanks to the drag kings I interviewed, particularly Carlos Al Dick and Phillippa, along with the oodles of inspiration from shows I saw put on by Pecs Drag Kings and Boi Box. A tip of the hat to Fran for her piano-teaching stories, too. Plus, a huge high five to the Vegas intervention that got this story back on track. Thanks to Sacha Black, JJ Arias and Lise Gold for the tequila and tough love.

Cheers to my talented trio of professionals who make sure my books look and read as best they can. Kevin for the ace cover (and tip-top series rebrand); Cheyenne for her eagle-eyed editing; and Adrian for his expert typesetting, and enthusiastic cheerleading. Thanks also to all the bloggers and readers who've shown such enthusiasm for this book in the run-up to launch. I hope you love it!

Bundles of roses and huge love to my wife, Yvonne. Our London love made me want to write the London Romance series in the first place. Ultimately, she's the reason you're holding this book.

Finally, and most importantly, thanks to you for coming on the London Romance journey with me and all the characters. I hope it kept you entertained, wrapped you in laughter and love, and that you felt seen. It's why I write lesbian and sapphic romance, because representation matters.

Expect more London-based books from me in the future,

and perhaps a new series. But for now, from the London Romance series, it's a final goodbye.

If you fancy getting in touch, you can do so using one of the methods below. I'm most active on Instagram.

Twitter: @ClareLydon
Facebook: www.facebook.com/clare.lydon
Instagram: @clarefic
Find out more at: www.clarelydon.co.uk
Contact: mail@clarelydon.co.uk

Thank you so much for reading!

This is for everyone who's ever
loved the London Romance series.
I hope you saw yourself included.

Chapter One

The first thing Cordy Starling noticed about the woman was her tits. Specifically, the flash of her cleavage, coy and charming like a Mona Lisa smile. Next, her eyes fell on the coppery, streaked skin beneath the wide rip on the knee of her jeans, so uneven it had to be from a bottle. Then Cordy eyed her stretched Asda Bag For Life, clearly not on its first outing, rammed with oranges.

The woman gripped the handle tight as she threw herself into the warm tube carriage, before lowering herself onto a seat, eyelids fluttering shut. Her cheeks were flushed candyfloss-pink, as if she'd been running, her thick black winter coat open, missing all but one button. Cordy dropped her gaze to the other bag the woman carried. She squinted at the logo on the side: *Fruity Tooty Juice Bar!* It was also filled with oranges. Someone ought to tell her they are not the only fruit.

The tube picked up speed as it vibrated away from Stratford. The metal door to Cordy's right rattled on its tracks, and she wondered, as she always did, if one had ever sprung open by mistake. After a couple of minutes, the train slowed, and then stopped. The classic tube signage told her they'd reached West Ham. The carriage doors beeped, then jerked open. A man got on, accompanied by a sandy-coloured cockapoo. A ball of fluff with two eyes.

"Sit, Nigel," the man instructed.

The dog obeyed. His owner sat in the spare seat next to Orange Lady. It turned out, Nigel was just as intrigued by the woman's fruit haul as Cordy. The cockapoo nudged its wet nose into the top of one of the bags, dislodging a single orange. It landed on the floor with a thud, then rolled across the aisle and settled between Cordy's scuffed blue-and-white Adidas.

Orange Lady shifted, her brown eyes wide. She pushed herself up, let go of the bag nearest Nigel, then leaned forward to grab the orange from between Cordy's feet before the tube jerked away.

Big mistake.

Fluff-pot Nigel saw his chance, and promptly stuck his nose inside the nearby bag. It toppled sideways.

Before Cordy or the woman could do anything to stop them, a stream of oranges rolled onto the carriage floor, thudding one by one, like the drum section of an experimental jazz track.

"Fuck!" was the first word Cordy heard from the woman's lips.

Beside Cordy, a teenage boy, headphones over ears, jolted as oranges pooled at his feet. He glanced down, frowned, then closed his eyes.

Orange Lady let out an exasperated noise, then sprang to her feet, letting go of her other bag.

More oranges cascaded left and right, banging into feet, bags, and poles.

That caused a mini-flurry of activity as people nearby

leaned down to rescue oranges. It was quite the scene. London was often thought to be a selfish capital city, but if the world could see this tube carriage, on a cold Friday in January when everyone just wanted the month to be over and to get paid because they were still skint from Christmas, they'd know that wasn't true. Meanwhile, having caused the kerfuffle in the first place, Nigel was now barking madly, tail wagging, clearly thinking this was the best game ever.

To Cordy's left, a baby with a shock of jet-black hair sat in a man's arms. Alarmed by Nigel's incessant barking, they began to wail a high-pitched holler.

This was not the relaxed tube journey Cordy had hoped for today. Her destination was only two stops away. But the woman opposite now wore a haunted look.

She couldn't leave her hanging. Not with oodles of oranges milling about the tube floor.

Cordy jumped up and started grabbing oranges, depositing them on her seat, then diving down for more like she was a contestant on a game show. *The most oranges collected in a minute wins an all-expenses-paid trip to London including a show and a meal!* Cordy would jump at the chance. She'd been in London for over three months and still hadn't been to a West End production, much to her gran's displeasure.

When she'd scooped up all the oranges within reach, she strode down the aisle and started collecting them from nearer the door, where customers were looking at their feet like they couldn't compute what they were seeing. She bent down and picked up one, two, three oranges. Then three more. She turned to walk back to her seat, just as the tube lurched to a hasty stop. Cordy reached out to steady herself on one of the yellow poles, and dropped all the oranges in her grasp. They bounced to the floor, one landing squarely on her foot.

"Ow!" She hopped on one foot, just as the tube lurched again. With nothing to hold onto and her balance compromised, she promptly toppled herself, landing on a bed of oranges and a bag of shopping, spilling some of its contents on the floor.

Cordy ignored the pain that skittered through her hip and elbow. She scrambled to her feet, picking up her crumpled dignity, noting what had fallen from the upturned shopping bag: a tube of lube and a packet of condoms, along with a box of Ferrero Rocher. Someone was in for a good night. The owner, a woman with exquisite eyelashes, blushed aubergine as she bent to pick them up. Cordy gave her a sympathetic smile.

The tube stopped at the next station, and passengers got off and on, stepping over oranges with hardly a blink. Did they think it was National Orange Day?

Cordy bent down to scoop up another fistful. She wasn't going to take too many this time. When she had them securely cradled in her right arm, and the train was on the move again, she looked up and came face to face with the owner of the oranges. The woman's eyes were hazel, but that was too flat a word to describe them. Gold and green danced in the brown. They were multi-layered. Was the woman who owned them the same?

"Thanks for helping," she muttered, cheeks still flushed. She pushed her hair from her forehead. It was the colour of burnt buttered toast. The woman had flawless skin, too. But even though she'd thanked Cordy, her tone didn't sound very thankful. She sounded pissed off. Which Cordy could understand, considering the past few minutes.

The tube lurched again, but this time, Cordy was holding on.

She squeezed past Orange Lady and put the fruit on her seat, then repeated her action, like she was in the weirdest relay of all time.

New passengers stepped through from the adjoining carriage. Laughter came from near the door as a group of teenage boys picked up three oranges, and one proceeded to juggle with them. If she had free hands, she might have applauded. She'd never mastered juggling, much to her frustration.

"Hey, they're my oranges!" Orange Lady pushed past Cordy, then grabbed the oranges from the juggler.

The three boys made a noise that showed she needed to lighten up.

She ignored them and dumped the oranges back in her bag, before doing the same with the mound of fruit on Cordy's seat.

Once clear, Cordy sat down. She caught the woman's gaze. She tried to keep her face neutral, and not judge this stranger. Who knew what had led up to her orange frenzy?

"Thank you, and sorry." The woman sighed. "It's just been quite the day." She grabbed a final orange from the floor, then steadied her Asda Bag For Life.

Cordy nodded. "Right." She had no idea what that meant.

"Actually, quite the week. Quite the last few months."

The tube pulled up at North Greenwich. Cordy's stop.

"Enjoy your oranges," she told the woman.

Finally, the hint of a smile.

As Cordy reached the tube door, she heard a yelp. When she turned, the baby had projectile vomited across the carriage, and the puke was now dripping from the top of the oranges.

Cordy got off the tube before Orange Lady had a complete meltdown.

Chapter Two

It had been a rugged, arm-wrestle of a day. Hannah Driver flung herself into her flat, closed the door, and sucked in a huge breath. Bad move. All she could smell was orange-tinged baby vomit. It wasn't a fragrance she planned to bottle anytime soon. In fact, she wanted to get rid of it, pronto.

She walked into her bathroom, tipped the oranges into the bath, then ran the cold water. She rinsed, adding hot water when her fingers couldn't take the temperature anymore, then stood with her hands on her hips, eyeing the fruit. There had to be at least 60, maybe more. What was she going to do with them?

She hadn't thought that part through before she'd stolen the fruit on the last day of her job at Fruity Tooty Juice Bar. The theft was a statement. A two-finger salute to her ex-employers. She couldn't possibly have foreseen how impossible oranges were to transport. She did now.

Thank goodness for the kind woman with the dyed red hair and the clickbait green gaze. Hannah was pretty sure she'd come over as ungrateful and gruff. But that was her survival mechanism kicking in. She couldn't accept the woman's help with grace. Somebody being so nice to her would have tipped her over the edge, made her fall apart.

Leaving the oranges to enjoy their bath, she threw her keys in the bowl by the front door, put her coat and bag on the hook, then finally allowed herself to relax as she walked down the hallway to her lounge. Soon to be her bedroom. On the wall was a photo of her and Lauren, grinning like idiots in front of the Eiffel Tower. Every time she passed it, it took her back and a spark of happiness ignited. Until she remembered.

Lauren had ended things just after Halloween, saying they were on "different paths". She'd disappeared from the flat the next day, and then from Hannah's life altogether. Eighteen months of togetherness, and then, boom! Hannah was surplus to requirements. A little like she had been in her job. This had not been a stellar few months.

She stared at the photo. Who pays for a trip to Paris, and then leaves three months later? It still made no sense at all. She'd thought they were destined. She reached out a hand and took the photo down. Then she walked through to the small kitchen the size of a postage stamp, and dropped the photo frame in the bin.

"What are you doing? At least save the frame, you might want it later!" Hannah's mum's voice echoed in her ears. She was very much about living life carefully. About doing the right thing. About living up to expectations. Which is where she and Hannah clashed a lot when it came to Hannah's career (or lack thereof), along with Hannah's sexuality.

Her third daughter being queer and wanting to be a performer wasn't something Polly Driver was keen on, despite the fact her mum had once been a performer. Or perhaps, that was *why*. Her mum was convinced that performing was a one-way ticket to poverty and disappointment. She'd been in a band, been ousted, then joined another, and her dreams had been dashed when her very strict parents found out and banned her from performing.

"Those were different times. You did what your parents told you to," she'd said.

However, Hannah had never forgotten that New Year when her mum had drunk one too many champagnes, and opened up about her time as a singer. She'd got a wistful look in her eye as she told them how it was the most exhilarating time of her life, how it unlocked a part of her she never knew was there. Then, when a Bowie track her band used to play came on the Spotify playlist, her mum had got up and spun around the room, completely taken over by the music. Hannah and her sisters had all exchanged stunned looks.

Their mum didn't sing anymore. She'd put that part of her life in a box and stowed it away. Got on with the job of having a steady career in finance and raising her three daughters, because that's what she was expected to do.

But Hannah knew the urge was still there.

That it never went away.

When Hannah performed, it took her somewhere special. She loved the drama, the power. But she wanted her performance to be more, to maybe wear a new costume.

Her mum knew the magic of performing, too.

As a daughter, Hannah was a letdown on many levels. Hence, it was best never to let her mum know how she was failing in other areas of her life. Love? Check. Job? Double-check. Plus, she might soon be homeless. Dammit, she hoped she could at least stave off that impending disaster. She could just imagine her mum's face if she didn't.

Her hand hovered over the bin. Should she rescue the frame as her mum would want? She shook her head. Polly might want it, but crucially, Hannah didn't. The frame was tarnished, and it was time to move on. To start thinking positively. Even if her one act of defiance had ended in a bathful of oranges.

For starters, she had three interviews for potential flatmates starting tomorrow. At least one had to be decent, right? Her financial situation dictated that even if they weren't, she'd have to accept one. But that was for tomorrow. Tonight, she was going to relax. To that end, Hannah opened the fridge, and pulled out the bottle of chardonnay she'd scored for a fiver. She poured herself a glass and smiled as she took the first sip. It tasted cheap, but it did the job.

In the lounge, she put her wine on her IKEA LACK coffee table, then did a lap of the room, removing any trace of Lauren. She should have done it weeks ago. One more photo of them at Lauren's friend's wedding, in dresses and heels, done up to the nines. She'd ended the night barefoot. Heels were a man-made construct to stop women being able to run, surely?

There was also a straw donkey they'd bought while on holiday in Spain that had to go. She contemplated giving the vase Lauren had bought to charity, but decided she liked it too much. She could fill it with gorgeous flowers, get over the association. She put the photo and the straw donkey in the bin, then returned, eyeing up the space where the dining table and chairs had sat. Lauren hadn't taken much, but she'd taken those. Now, Hannah was about to put a bed there. She shook her head. Life could change in the blink of an eye. But she wasn't going to get maudlin.

She sat forward and grasped the remote. It was sticky. She

held it up for closer inspection. What had she eaten before watching telly last? She licked her finger. Strawberry jam. Not bad. On the coffee table, her phone buzzed.

A message from Syd, head of the drag and burlesque collective she belonged to.

Can you slot in for Alicia tomorrow? Her mum's still sick.

She messaged him straight back to say yes. She needed all the work she could get now she'd lost her day job. The transformation from mundane, juice-bar manager covered in orange pith to burlesque dancer never failed to thrill her. But while she was happy doing burlesque (and she *definitely* needed the money), she'd seen a few drag kings perform lately, and wondered if she could do that, too. Create a character, maybe sing live. She had the time to do it now she was unemployed. She chewed her lip as a light bulb flickered in her mind.

At eight, she'd stomped around the house pretending to be a boy. At nine, she'd insisted on being called Han. At ten, she'd joined the football team and styled herself on David Beckham. And then hormones kicked in, and teenage years blurred the distinction, and she'd grown more comfortable in her skin. But the ache in her stomach never entirely went away. Maybe she could regain that strut, that other side of her, throw it into performance and make something different. Make *someone* different.

Burlesque felt like work, and she was good at it. Whereas, contemplating being a drag king stirred something far deeper inside her.

"I want to be a drag king." That was the first time she'd said those words out loud.

Hannah jolted as a spark ignited inside, then sucked in

a calming breath. She'd told hardly anyone about her night-time side hustle. Only Lauren, who'd hated that she performed burlesque. Could Hannah make doing both burlesque *and* drag work as her main gig?

She took another sip of her wine, and thought about her oranges. A ten-second Google returned a 20-minute video on how to make marmalade. Her enthusiasm died. It seemed like an awful lot of work. But if she didn't make marmalade, what was she going to do with them? Hannah didn't have a juicer, and she wasn't about to do it by hand.

A kernel of an idea lodged in her brain. She jumped up and checked the cupboard by the front door. The pink-and-white candy-striped paper bags she'd over-ordered for her cousin's wedding were still there. She walked back into her bathroom and eyed the oranges. She was going to dry them, bag them up and gift them to her neighbours. It was a way of introducing herself at least, something she'd been meaning to do ever since she moved in over a year ago.

Didn't they say that giving was better than receiving?

Hannah was going to put it to the test.

Chapter Three

"You know what I mean. How do I know if I've made the right move? I love living here, but I need to find my own space." Cordy tucked her dyed red hair behind her right ear and sat on the stool at her gran's kitchen island. Strictly speaking, it was Gran and Joan's kitchen island. Cordy wasn't sure what it said that her 80-year-old gran had more luck with the ladies than she had of late. Actually, she did know, but she didn't want to dwell on that sore point. She'd thought once she moved to London, doors would open and the world would be her oyster. So far, every oyster she'd encountered had stayed shut tight.

"For one, you don't give up so easily with the flat-share interviews." Her gran made the tea in her white china teapot, then grabbed a couple of mugs from the pegboard on the far wall. Her gran's wife, Joan, had an eye for design. No mug tree for them.

When and if Cordy ever had enough money to buy her own house (it seemed like a far-off pipe dream right now), she was definitely stealing some of Joan's ideas. The mug pegboard for one. The coffee station for two. Don't get her started on their enormous wine fridge, either.

Yes, she was living with her gran and Joan for the time

being, so she could enjoy these luxuries. However, it was a temporary solution. She was living in Joan's writing room that she'd cleared for her, and she wanted to give it back. Her housing situation was causing her sleepless nights and she had to sort it soon. She had her tenth flat-share interview tomorrow. The previous nine had all been unsuccessful.

"I know, I know." Cordy rubbed a teaspoon between her thumb and forefinger. "But nine rejections. Plus, tomorrow's place seems too good to be true. Close to my work, too cheap. Something has to be wrong with it. The ad said there was a catch, but that it would be revealed at the interview. Right now, I'm desperate enough to consider most things."

"You most certainly are not." Joan walked into the kitchen, giving her gran a smile that always made Cordy's heart sing. These two were young lovers in London 60 years ago, and after a lifetime apart, they'd recently reconnected. To say they were meant to be was an understatement. Cordy's heart ached they hadn't found each other earlier. But both her gran and Joan were adamant: they found each other again when they were meant to, and now they were going to make the most of the time they had left.

Cordy didn't like to dwell on that, either.

"You can stay here as long as you like, so you're not desperate in the slightest." Joan held up a hand that had seen life. Eighty years. Cordy could hardly comprehend it. "I know you want to be independent, but you should wait until the right place comes along. Your home is your sanctuary. Make sure you're comfortable there. Where's this one tomorrow?"

"Haggerston," Cordy replied.

Gran loaded the tea tray with Jaffa Cakes, her new addiction, then Cordy jumped up and carried it through to the lounge, placing it carefully on the marble coffee table. She was always petrified she was going to break it or scratch it, and nothing was going to stop that fear. Once she moved out, at least she wouldn't have that daily worry. She sat in the armchair to the left of the fireplace. Her gran and Joan sat in their usual positions, on the mustard sofa to her right.

Above the fireplace, in pride of place, was a photo of their wedding day just four months ago. The pair, photographed by a cool lesbian photographer named Heidi, were laughing, heads back, and it was the most gorgeous, natural photo. Their wedding had been a sumptuous day shared with close family and friends, including Cordy's mum and dad, her brother, Elliott, plus Joan's nephew Vincent and his husband, Gary. There had also been a gaggle of lesbians her gran had got to know when she found Joan again. Some of them had oozed style and glamour. They'd all been way out of Cordy's price bracket.

Yes, her gran knew more queer women in London than she did. It was another fact she had to turn around if she wanted to make a go of living here.

"I remember when you didn't go to Haggerston unless you were desperate. Is it desirable now?" Joan leaned forward and poured the tea from the bone-china pot.

"Depends who you ask." Cordy pressed the tip of her index finger to her chest. "To me, yes."

Joan gave her a knowing look. "First rule of flat-hunting: be laidback, and they'll come to you. Maybe you've been giving off an air of desperation."

Cordy had thought the same thing. She was going to

correct that, starting tomorrow. She glanced at the fruit bowl on the edge of the coffee table. The two oranges at the bottom made Cordy smile.

"Anyway, despite my rubbish flat situation, at least my day wasn't as bad as this woman on the tube who had two big bags of oranges, and proceeded to tip them all over the tube carriage."

"Oh my goodness, poor thing!" Gran's face creased with anxiety. "Did she manage to collect them back up?"

Cordy nodded. "Mostly. I gave her a hand. But she was flushed, to say the least." Also, grumpy. But with a great cleavage. But Cordy wasn't going to admit that to *this* audience. They'd jump on it and be relentless until she agreed to scour London for Orange Lady.

Cordy grabbed a mug of tea, along with a Jaffa Cake. Everything could be soothed by this combination.

"You know what, I've got a good feeling about tomorrow. You've got your job sorted. Your flat will fall into place soon. Then, you just need a girlfriend in your life."

Cordy spluttered. "You of all people know that's easier said than done."

Her gran tapped the side of her forehead. "Positive mental attitude, that's what you need. You're not going to find a woman without it. Picture the perfect woman in your mind, and maybe she might manifest into reality." Her gran was all about self-help and spirituality these days. She'd discovered podcasts since she'd moved to London, and now there was no holding her back.

Her perfect woman? Cordy's mind instantly conjured an image of Orange Lady. Difficult. Odd. Gorgeous. She was just Cordy's type. She pushed the picture from her brain. "Positive mental attitude. I'll make sure I'm wearing it head to toe tomorrow."

Chapter Four

Hannah knocked on the doors of all three of her immediate neighbours. One answered and refused the oranges, one wasn't in, while the other took the free fruit but his face told her he was waiting for the catch. Perhaps that whole 'making friends' vibe was going to be harder than she thought.

She bounded up the creaky, threadbare stairs to the next floor. Aromas of garlic and tomatoes wafted up her nose. Her stomach rumbled. She'd only eaten a tuna bagel today. Admittedly, it had been from Sylvie's Bagels, the boss of bagel shops, but it was still minimal food. Hannah was a regular customer, and Sylvie had admonished her, telling her, "she needed to eat more to stop looking like a rake". A rake with a rack, but a rake, nonetheless.

The next door she knocked on proved to be the owner of the delicious smells. A woman answered her knock almost before she finished it. She had styled afro hair and a cool apron that proclaimed, *Don't Fuck With Me, Or I'll Put You In My Soup*.

Hannah explained her oranges dilemma and the woman took two bags. Behind her, a man in Lycra wandered into the hallway.

"Alan!" the woman said, turning. "This is our neighbour.

Come and say hi. She's giving us free oranges that she nicked from her job today."

Alan grinned as he approached the doorway, carefully rounding his bike that was propped against the wall. "That's a sentence that can only be spoken in London, but we'll gratefully accept."

The woman dumped the oranges in Alan's arms. "I'm Bernice," she added. "You are?"

"Hannah." She paused. "And can I just say, the smell coming from your flat is insane. I want to lick the door."

Bernice grinned. "New recipe I'm working on. And no need to lick our door: very unhygienic I imagine. Come back in half an hour and I'll give you some. As a thank you for the oranges."

"You don't have to do that."

"I know, but I want to." She turned her head to Alan. "Wasn't I just saying to you recently that I want to be more neighbourly?"

Alan nodded. "She was. We've lived here for six months and don't know anybody."

"Have you got dinner for tonight?" Bernice asked.

"I've only had a bagel today," Hannah replied. "Too busy stealing oranges."

"In that case, it's settled. Knock for your dinner at six."

She gave them another bag of oranges, then turned her attention to the blood-red door opposite. The person who answered gave her a quizzical look.

Hannah fought not to give them one, too, because they had a five o'clock shadow painted on their face, their short dark hair swept up in a quiff. She'd found a drag king! Or at least, if they weren't a drag king, someone who was very good at makeup. Hannah had so many questions. Also, a mountain of oranges that came first. Hannah did her spiel, and the person accepted the oranges. She was about to leave, when her curiosity got the better of her.

"I have to ask. Your face paint. What's it for?"

The person puffed out their chest.

"For a performance later. I'm a drag king."

Excitement bubbled in Hannah's chest, like a year-ten chemistry experiment. "I'm a performer, too." She clenched her fist to stop her hand from shaking. "Currently burlesque, but I want to get into drag."

"Really?" They leaned forward and peered into Hannah's bag of oranges. "How many of those have you got, by the way?"

"Loads. Still a full bag downstairs."

"My mum makes marmalade and she could take the whole lot off your hands if you want to get rid of them. She'd be absolutely thrilled."

"That would be perfect." No more door knocking was the ideal scenario.

The person stood back. "Come in, and I'll message her your details. She should be able to swing by tomorrow. This will give me brownie points as I didn't make it for her birthday last weekend. I was working, and she hasn't forgiven me. I'm Theo, by the way."

"Hannah, good to meet you."

They shook hands, and exchanged a warm smile.

A few messages later, and it was arranged that Theo's mum would collect the oranges tomorrow. Hannah nipped back to her flat to get the rest of the fruit. When she returned, Theo was at their kitchen island, giant mirror on top, painting on a handlebar moustache. Hannah tried her hardest not to stare, but her fingers itched to paint one onto herself. She clenched her fists by her sides again.

"Burlesque to drag. Why the change?" Theo eyed her with curiosity.

Hannah shrugged, fighting hard to play it cool when she felt anything but. "They're not too dissimilar really. Just performances of different sorts."

"True, and I know plenty who do both. The want in people's eyes, when they're not sure if they want to be you or fuck you?" Theo grinned. "I like to stir things up. Drag stirs things up, apparently. Just ask right-wing politicians."

Theo finished painting one side of their moustache with the final swirl, then stepped back and assessed it from various angles. "What do you think? I'm trying out a new look."

"I think it looks good."

I think I want one, too.

Theo grinned, then licked their lips. "Have you done any drag yet?"

Hannah shook her head. Her heart thumped in her chest. "I figure I need to work up a drag name and persona first. It's what I did with burlesque."

"Then it seems like you knocked on the right door at the right time."

"I did?"

Theo nodded. "We're going to exchange numbers because I run drag workshops. Plus, I live upstairs from you. And what do they say about helping others out, paying it forward? You just gave me some oranges. You made my mum happy. This is good karma biting you on the bum." Theo paused. "Plus, you already do burlesque, so I assume you can perform?"

Hannah nodded. "I can. I have crowds who would agree."

"Getting up on stage is half the battle. You've already conquered that. Have a think about what you want to do drag-wise. Do you want to strip? Do comedy? Lip-sync? Live vocals? Make a statement with it all? There are so many options." Theo sat back on their stool, and put a hand over their heart. "But the best way to go is by doing what feels right. Be you in your immense power on stage. It might take trial and error, but once you find it, you can fully commit."

They pressed their finger to their chest. "For me, I've always loved dressy military outfits. I dreamt up an act to fit that. My drag name is Captain Von Strap."

Hannah grinned. "I fucking love that."

Theo matched her grin. "So do I. I sing modern songs with an ultra-masc vibe, and the crowds go wild for it. But it was always in me." They eyed Hannah. "What's always been in you? That's what you need to think about. It's what I teach on my course. I'm doing one this weekend. Come along. It'll give you some ideas, I promise. It's sold out, but I'll squeeze you in."

She wanted to hug Theo. And Hannah didn't voluntarily hug many people. "That would be epic, thank you so much." Could this be the break she'd been waiting for?

Theo handed over their phone. "Put your name and number in there and I'll message you the details."

Hannah took the phone and did as she was told. This was actually happening. Something positive, for a change.

"It's a great time to start drag, the scene's really hotting up, particularly for kings. Can you sing?"

Hannah gave the phone back, then nodded. "I was in a couple of productions at uni. I'd love to use my voice more. It's not really an option in burlesque."

"You're a step ahead, then. If you can do comedy or sing, you're going to get booked up. You should enter one of the competitions currently on in the clubs, too. It's a great way to get yourself noticed and booked." They offered their hand and Hannah shook it. "It was lovely to meet you. But now I have to get rid of you so I can finish getting ready." Theo walked her to the front door. "I reckon we met today for a reason, don't you? The universe working in mysterious ways. I'll be in touch about the weekend. Amanda says thanks for the oranges. That's my mum, by the way. I'll drop some marmalade around when it's made."

Theo shut the door and Hannah stared at it for a few seconds.

That was what she'd call a success. She'd got rid of her oranges, and she might just have changed the course of her life.

Chapter Five

Cordy's classes today had taken place in her new music studio. When she'd told her gran about the space, she and Joan had been so impressed. Cordy hadn't burst their bubble by telling them it was little more than a glorified shed with windows. Still, it was a secure place to store the school's meagre supply of instruments. More importantly, it was an independent building where she and her pupils could make as much noise as they liked.

Today, her star pupil, a 14-year-old named Romilly, had come for her lesson and made a whole world of noise, most of it fabulous. Romilly was very serious about her music grade exams and wanted to play the classics. The only trouble was, her playing lacked soul. Romilly was terrific at learning the notes and putting them together in the order they were meant to be in. But she needed to play them with passion. That's what Cordy had been trying to teach her today. It's what her grandfather, Kenneth, had taught her through his love of classical music. It was going to take Romilly time to grasp the concept, but Cordy was determined she'd get there. When she did, Cordy had no doubt Romilly would blow the examiners away. Not to mention the summer concert.

Cordy lugged her grey leather bag across the playground to

the main building. At 4pm, it was already getting dark, but lack of light was no hindrance to the group of boys playing football to her right. She was still pondering how to make Romilly *feel* the music, when a shout of "Miss, look out!" made her look up.

The slap of the football hitting her face stung far more than she expected. Cordy dropped her bag and staggered sideways, clutching her cheek. She had no idea how people played football for a living. Getting slapped in the face with a ball daily would not be her preferred career choice. When she opened her eyes, sheet music was scattered all over the concrete at her feet. Thankfully, the boys were all around her, collecting it as quick as it had escaped. She moved her jaw left to right. Not broken. Eyelid still intact. Eyeball working. It could have been worse.

"I'm so sorry Miss, I didn't mean to hit you." The teenager's face was creased with concern. "Are you okay?" He held out the gathered sheets to her.

"I'll live," Cordy replied. "I thought the goal was that way?" She pointed over the boy's shoulder where jumpers on the ground marked the goal.

He nodded, then looked down at his feet. "Sliced it, Miss."

"He thinks he's Messi, but he's not Miss," said his friend with a laugh.

Cordy took her papers, grabbed her bag and stuffed them in. "Just kick it a bit softer next time I'm crossing the playground."

The boy nodded. "You got it, Miss." He gave her a smile, then led the group away. Not for the first time since taking up teaching in an inner-city comprehensive, she was touched by the care of these pupils. Teenagers got a bad rap, but she had nothing but praise for them. Even when they whacked her in the head.

The staff room wasn't busy when she got there, only a handful of teachers grabbing a breather before the after-school work kicked in. She dumped her bag by a row of three armchairs, and made herself an instant coffee. Nescafé plus Coffee Mate. Creamy deliciousness, rotting her insides daily. Most things that tasted that good normally did. Her flat-share interview wasn't for another hour, so she wasn't in a rush. She needed to check her face was still intact before she went. She didn't want to scare her prospective flatmate on first sight.

Her colleague, Greta, a maths teacher with an impressive shock of dyed blonde hair, filled a mug of coffee beside her. Greta wore a perfume that smelled of floral summer nights. It always made Cordy want to lean in. As did her lilting Irish accent. Greta looked like she should be a TV presenter on one of those home makeover shows, and it was a complete mystery how she ended up teaching maths in London.

"You've got," she said, waving a finger around Cordy's face with a frown. "Some indentations in your face? And it's a bit red."

Cordy nodded towards the window. "Got in a fight with a football. The football won."

"Ouch!" Greta replied. "How was today's battle with children wielding instruments? More tuneful and less painful, I hope?"

"Not too bad. I even recognised some of what they were trying to play, so I can't complain." Cordy shrugged. "What about the world of numbers? Did your lot remember their times tables?"

Greta rolled her eyes as she added three heaped teaspoons of Coffee Mate to her mug. "Absolutely not. The next generation is screwed. Not one of them will be able to add up a single thing without the aid of technology. I fear for our children and their children."

"But they will be able to play 'Clair De Lune' on their recorders. I will make sure of it. All is not lost."

"Thank the lord."

They both walked towards their usual armchairs with a smirk. Outside the main window, the two boys who'd spoken to her scuffled over the football. The smaller boy won and ran off with it. The one who'd kicked the ball at her rugby-tackled him to the floor.

"How's your gran and her new wife? I don't think I'll ever get over their story, or knowing their granddaughter, or the fact that you live with them in a swanky Greenwich pad."

"They're both good, still way more lively than they've got any need to be. I tell them to enjoy their lives at a slower pace. They tell me to speed up and shut up. Youth is wasted on the young, apparently. They might have a point."

Greta leaned in. "It must hurt knowing your gran is getting more action than you."

Cordy stuck her fingers in her ears. "La la laaaaa, I can't hear you." Although there was a grain of truth in Greta's words. "I thought moving to London would mean I'd meet loads of gorgeous women, including the love of my life, obviously."

"Obviously." Greta took a sip of her drink, then put it on the coffee table in front of them. "We could go out after this and see if we can score you one. And me, come to that. I'm off men after Lucas. East London is full of queer women.

They're literally parading down the street. Every day is Pride here."

Lucas was Greta's ex-husband. They'd been separated three months, but Greta had told Cordy she'd mentally left him months ago.

"I would love that, but I'll have to take a raincheck. I have a flat viewing at 5pm today. But how about one weekend soon? We could go to Hackney Wick and hang out, with a sign saying 'queer and in need of a snog'."

Greta gave her a grin. "Deal. Although I was thinking 'queer and in need of a shag', but we've all got to start somewhere."

* * *

The flat was in the leafiest street Cordy had seen in Haggerston. It was in a purpose-built block stacked five storeys high, and it had to work. Cordy had already made the decision in the 25 minutes it had taken her to walk from her school. This was a slam-dunk in terms of area. It was also a huge score on affordability. Now she waited to be told she had to share it with a serial killer. She was desperate enough to consider it.

On the advice of Greta, she had a bottle of red wine and a bar of Cadbury's Dairy Milk in her bag. Greta had secured her first London flat by taking exactly this to an interview and producing it when she got on with the interviewing couple. It had sealed the deal, according to her. "The couple turned out to be a nightmare and, in the end, one of them smashed every plate in the flat in a fit of anger," she'd said. "But the first three months were bliss and got me settled. You need to get your foot on the rental ladder." It was worth a try.

Cordy buzzed the intercom on flat 4 and waited. Her skin

prickled with nerves. She hoped her blemish stick had managed to cover up the redness on her face. She was buzzed up in moments and took the stairs as instructed. She pushed open the heavy fire door and walked down the corridor, giving the door a knock.

Then she arranged her face into what she wanted her prospective flatmate to see. Someone normal, happy, tidy. An absolute joy to live with. She hoped she shoehorned all that into her smile.

However, when the door opened and Cordy clocked the woman on the other side of it, her mouth fell open, neatly dismantling her carefully arranged features. This was not who she expected to see.

Orange Lady. Who hadn't been happy yesterday. From the frown on her face, it looked like today wasn't going much better.

"It's you!" Cordy said, then winced. She had to remember this was an interview. She needed to make a good first impression.

She instantly recalibrated. "How are you? Did you manage to get all your oranges home with no more issues?" Damn, should she have brought it up? She'd done it now.

The woman bit her lip and leaned on the doorframe. Her cleavage was on show again, framed in a navy-blue shirt, her curves punctuating her lean body. A silver necklace glinted against her skin. Cordy kept her gaze firmly on the woman's face. At the moment, she wasn't even sure she'd get invited in.

"I did, thank you. I'm sure I would have lost a few more if it weren't for you." She tilted her head. "What are you doing here? You're not stalking me, are you?"

Cordy smiled. "I'm here for the flat share."

Orange Lady's eyes widened. "You're Cordy?" Her tone was incredulous.

"That's me."

Orange Lady moved aside. "You better come in, then." She put a hand to her chest. "I'm Hannah."

"Nice to meet you again, Hannah."

Cordy was through the door. Strike one.

"Bathroom on your right."

Okay, no formalities, they were getting right down to it. Cordy stuck her head inside. White metro tiles, clean and modern. So far, so good. She was waiting for the catch. Unless that was Hannah. She followed her host down the hallway.

"Kitchen on your right, functional if tiny."

Hannah wasn't joking. The small room could just about fit two people, so long as they were drainpipe skinny. But at least there was a window. Cordy's thoughts flew back to her gran's house, with its sparkling expanses of glass and patio doors from the kitchen-diner that led to their courtyard garden. She'd been spoilt. She knew that. This was the reality of living in London. She followed Hannah into the main room.

When she got there, Cordy allowed herself a smile. Maybe this *could* work. This was far and away the best flat she'd seen in her month of searching. Now she just had to convince Hannah that she was the ideal flatmate. Maybe that's where the wine and chocolate came in.

"This is a lovely room." Dual aspect, spacious (or perhaps a lack of furniture?), gorgeous views out over some greenery to the right, and a balcony through the glass doors on the left. This was London nirvana. A view and outside space in the sky.

Hannah nodded. "It's what sold us in the first place when we first moved in." She frowned at her words. "Not that there's a 'we' now. It's just me. Which is why I'm advertising for a flatmate. The 'we' was my partner." She stole a look at Cordy. "Girlfriend. *Ex-girlfriend*."

Hannah stared, clearly assessing whether or not Cordy was queer-friendly.

Cordy wanted her to know they were on the same team. "Sorry to hear that. I know from experience women can be brutal when it comes to matters of the heart."

Just like that, Hannah's shoulders dropped, like she'd been holding in tension for days. Possibly weeks. Cordy was glad she'd helped her on the tube. Hannah seemed like she'd been through the wringer.

"They are." Hannah's gaze narrowed. Still unsure.

It was Cordy's job to win her over. After seeing this room, she was determined to succeed.

"And this is the bedroom," Hannah continued, showing Cordy through to a light-filled room with a double bed, wardrobe, desk, and a chest of drawers. An airing rack of clothes stood by the window. This was clearly Hannah's room. Why was she showing Cordy her bedroom?

"This would be your room," Hannah added.

Cordy's forehead creased. "Isn't this *your* room?" She couldn't work out what was going on here.

"Right now, yes," Hannah replied. "But that's the catch I was talking about." She held out a hand. "Shall we go through to the lounge and discuss it." Her face twitched as she spoke.

Cordy sat on the beige sofa. It was super-comfortable. Another plus point.

Hannah sat on the mid-century armchair opposite, leaned forward and steepled her fingers. Silver earrings nestled in her lobes, and her hair curled around the top of her ears.

"Here's the deal. Like I said, I was dumped. It was out of the blue. She paid up until the end of the month, but after that, it's just been me, eating through my savings, muddling through. The problem is, this is a one-bedroom flat, and we rented it as a couple."

Cordy tried to connect the dots, but she couldn't quite get there quick enough. "Are you telling me you're advertising for a new girlfriend to share this flat *and* your bed?" Alarm spread through her. "Because if you are, you're very much barking up the wrong tree." All the sympathy she'd felt for Hannah quickly toppled.

She was clearly unhinged.

Cordy hiked her bag on her shoulder and stood.

"No!" Hannah jumped up, too. "Please, sit." She waved her hands in front of her. "That's not what I'm saying at all." She sighed. "Don't go, you seem the most normal and nice of the three people I've seen today."

Cordy wished she could say the same for Hannah, who seemed on edge and had done both times they'd met. But she sat again anyway.

"What I'm suggesting is for you to take the main bedroom, and I'll put a bed over there where the dining table used to be." She gestured to the empty area on the left of the room. "I'll screen my space off, and we can share the rest of the flat together."

Cordy stared at her. This was a crazy suggestion. She couldn't ask this woman to move out of her bedroom, take her bed, and let her sleep in the lounge.

She shook her head. "I can't do that. It would be far too weird. You already live here. It would be like turfing you out of your space."

But Hannah was already shaking her head. "It's the opposite. You'd be doing me a favour." She swept her arm around the room. "Right now, in this world, this flat is the one thing that's going right for me." She made sure she had Cordy's full attention before she carried on. "When Lauren left, the thought of moving filled me with horror. But I worked out I could maybe limp along for a few months while I worked something out. But then, I got laid off from my day job when the owner's son needed a job. I'm now down to my evening side hustle to make money."

Cordy covered her mouth with her palm. "Shit. I'm sorry."

Hannah shook her head. "Don't be. It was a shitty job managing a juice bar in Stratford. But the thing is, without that job, I'm out of options. Which is when I came up with this one. But obviously, with two of us living in a one-bedroom flat, we have to get on." She gestured towards Cordy. "The person I'm sharing with has to be nice. First, because I could use some of that in my life. Second, because if you're not, there's nowhere to hide."

"Certainly not the kitchen," Cordy said.

Hannah painted on a wry smile.

"The oranges were to do with the juice bar?"

The armchair wheezed as Hannah sat down. "Yep. That was my last day. I nicked as many as I could carry. Turns out, oranges are slippery buggers to transport."

"And did you eat them all?"

She shook her head. "I gave them to my neighbours, and one of their mums is making them into marmalade. She's promised me a jar."

Thoughts fizzed around Cordy's brain. Could it work? Hannah needed the money. Cordy needed a cheap place to stay. Maybe she could try it for a month.

She reached into her bag and pulled out the wine and chocolate. "Shall we share these two and chat about the finer details? If we still think this is a good idea after that, then maybe we can give it a trial run. A month, say? Go from there?"

Hannah jumped up. For the first time today, her smile looked genuine. "You're on. And thank you." She ran out of the lounge, then reappeared moments later with two wine glasses and a bag of cheese-and-onion Walkers crisps. "Just in case we need extra sustenance." She sat again. "I should have asked first, though: you've got a full-time job? One that involves you leaving the house? Because two of us in this place all day long might be too much."

Cordy nodded. "I do. I teach music at St John's, which is walkable." She paused. "And I play piano on the side in bars, so I'm out some evenings, too. You said you had an evening side hustle, so you'll be out some evenings?"

Hannah nodded. "I'm a burlesque dancer."

"I was expecting bartender or waitress, not that." Cordy's eyebrows raised as she tried to stop her eyes undressing Hannah, wondering what she'd look like in just a G-string and feathers. She already knew her tits would be incredible. She swallowed hard as heat rose through her body. "I've never seen a burlesque show. I know it involves nipple tassels, but that's about it."

"It does involve nipple tassels, and there's an art to twirling that I have down." Hannah grinned as she spoke. "My ex hated me performing. I prefer doing shows for women only, but I don't mind men, too. The thing is, it's not just men. Loads of couples show up for shows at more mainstream venues, along with hen nights. Burlesque is very big with hen dos, weirdly. I was scaling back because Lauren disproved."

She shrugged. "Now, I want to be a drag king, too. What I've realised over the past year or so is that I love performing." She poured the wine, then fixed Cordy with her arresting gaze. "You should come to a show when you move in. Free tickets. My treat if you say yes to the flat share and do me a favour." She held out the wine to Cordy. "I'll need a couple of weeks to get my bed and storage arranged, so you could move in the second week of February. One month's deposit upfront. What do you say?"

There were so many reasons to say no. But Cordy was desperate. This would get her on the ladder, at least. "I say, let's give it a go." At least her gran and Joan would be pleased. Joan could reinstate her writing room. Plus, they'd been on at her to get out and experience London, just like they had. Now she was moving into Haggerston with a burlesque dancer and drag king. They'd be thrilled. Her prudish dad, less so.

"A toast," Hannah said. "To new flatmates and nipple tassels."

Cordy held up her glass. "I'll drink to that."

Chapter Six

Burlesque had a lot going for it, not least that it kept her fit. Since taking up her sideline, Hannah had become a gym junkie, and her balance and core strength were hugely improved. She needed it for the job. After all, she never wanted to stand on stage, gyrating her nipple tassels, and be unable to sustain the twirl. Unimaginable. But after meeting Theo and completing her two-day drag-king course, maybe there was a different way of performing. A way of tapping into her masculine side, of releasing something else within?

Tonight, the audience whooped as she appeared on stage as Velvet Minnelli, her Liza-inspired Cabaret turn. Her black shorts sparkled as she shimmied one way, then the other, her fitted, low-cut waistcoat leaving little to the imagination. When she'd auditioned, she knew her performance skills helped, but her breasts clinched the deal. Hannah circled her hips as she gripped the back of the chair at the centre of the stage, then eyeballed the audience. Anticipation throbbed in the room as they waited for her act to unfold.

She'd always admired Liza Minnelli's starring role in the movie, which also happened to be her dad's favourite. Hence, when it came to conjuring up a burlesque act, Liza was Hannah's first port of call.

The first minute of her act was taken up with some choreographed feather-dancing. Once the audience was warmed up, she put the feathers on the floor, and lifted her right foot onto the black wooden chair in the centre of the stage, thrusting her hips forward suggestively. Her suspended black stockings pulled on her thigh. When Hannah unclipped the stocking, then rolled it teasingly down and off her leg, the cheers got louder. She repeated the action on the other side, then spun her bowler hat on her right index finger. She turned her back to the crowd, planted her legs wide apart, then bent over and wiggled her bum, staring at the audience upside down.

The cheers turned into whistles and roars.

Hannah grinned, then stood up and turned to the crowd. She tilted her hat, then undid the top button of her shorts, before edging her zip slowly enough for cheers to build. Just like comedy, burlesque was all about the timing.

The couple at the closest table to the stage clapped loudly and stamped their feet. Keen. She circled her hips one way, then the other, then shifted her shorts down millimetre by millimetre, revealing her black sequinned thong.

The crowd went wild, with wolf whistles and cheers, along with more foot stamps. It was always the same when it was late and a lot of alcohol had been consumed.

Hannah walked back around to the chair and straddled it in the famous pose, legs apart. Some had asked if burlesque made her feel less than herself. Her answer was always the opposite. At times like these, when she held the audience in the palm of her hand, she loved the power she held. The absolute knowledge that every pair of eyes in the room was focused solely on her. Hannah could drink it down all night.

She ground into the chair, then undid the buttons on her waistcoat one by one. Heat danced across her skin. When she pulled open one side, the room went wild. Then the other, same reaction.

In the same breath as her waistcoat fell to the floor, she picked up her large feathers to tease a little more, leading up to the big reveal. She turned her back to the audience as Liza sang her heart out, threw her feathers to the ground, then turned, finally letting the audience see her toned stomach and her ample breasts. On cue, the yelling went to the max. She was now naked, bar her skimpy G-string, gold nipple tassels and velvet tie. It was a strong look.

Hannah smiled, took a breath, put her arms above her head and started to bounce. Her sequinned thong glinted in the light as she twirled the tassels clockwise, and the crowd went wild. Someone wolf whistled. Someone shouted "yeah, baby!" Then she stopped, put her hands behind her back and started to bounce again. The tassels went anti-clockwise. More whoops and hollers.

Meanwhile, the woman in the front row sat silent and transfixed. She stared at Hannah's tassels as if they were the opening to a whole new world. Maybe they were. The woman was sitting with a man, perhaps her boyfriend? Maybe she was thinking about how she'd like to twirl her own tassels for her own entertainment? Maybe with him, maybe not. Perhaps she was thinking about being in the same room as Hannah while she twirled hers. This could be her moment of sexual awakening. You just never knew, which is what Hannah loved.

Nobody in the crowd knew she was queer. She loved how she played with stereotype, with sexuality. She loved performing in front of women the most, for their eyes only. It was always who she focused on in her show. Tonight, it was front-row, centre-table woman.

Tassels done, Hannah gave the crowd a wink, shook her booty one more time, then twirled round the stage, soaking up the applause before her final high kicks and jazz-hand ending. The music boomed, Hannah gave her final moves everything she had, then brought it home.

When she walked off-stage, sweaty and out of breath, the compere, Grayson, gave her a high five before striding to the stage. She rushed to get her robe and cover up. Soon, she'd be performing fully clothed, and wouldn't need to apply fake tan badly to her legs. She couldn't wait.

She and Theo had worked out an act, and a stage name: Max Girth.

Embodying him was going to be a whole new adventure.

Chapter Seven

Two weeks after she and Hannah had sealed the arrangement over wine and chocolate, it was finally moving day. It was also Valentine's Day, and Joan's nephew, Vincent, had agreed to help Cordy move. They were going to try their best not to run over any lovers laden down with flowers, chocolates, and fluffy teddy bears en route.

Cordy's possessions amounted to two suitcases, a box, and a keyboard; she travelled light. She arranged them in the back of Vincent's estate car, pulling her navy parka coat closer to her body. She had no idea why the festival of romance was held in one of the coldest months of the year. Surely romance was more suited to summer? Beyond Vincent's broad shoulders, the Thames sat silent and brooding.

"Is that everything?" Vincent, pushed his thick-framed black glasses up his nose, his bald head covered with a fetching lilac beanie. Cordy had got on with him from the moment they met. It wasn't hard, seeing as he was one of the kindest people she'd ever encountered.

Inside the house, they heard a rumble of laughter from his husband, Gary. Vincent rolled his eyes. "I'm not sure if he's coming with us. His idea of a great Saturday is to hang out with Joan and your gran. He's always had a penchant for older women. If I wasn't sure he was gay, I might be worried." But his words were accompanied by a wry smile that accentuated the laugh lines around his eyes. He'd clearly led a very happy life.

"Imagine the scandal if your gay husband ran off with your lesbian aunt."

Vincent let out a strangled laugh. "I think Joan and Eunice have had enough publicity for one lifetime, don't you?" He shook his head. "Mind you, if I'm as happy and sprightly as they are when I'm 80, I'll be delighted."

"Ditto. I hope to meet the love of my life before I turn 80, though." Cordy pouted. "I won't have to wait another 53 years, will I?" Even though she'd spent the night before at the pub telling Greta there were more important things for happiness than relationships, she couldn't help wanting one. It was her default factory setting.

Vincent grinned and crushed his arm around her shoulder. "You're young with the whole world waiting for you. There's no rush. You'll meet a gorgeous woman who'll sweep you off your feet, I have no doubt." He leaned in and kissed her cheek, just as her gran appeared in the doorway, way overdressed for a Saturday lunchtime as usual. What was it about that generation always dressing as if they were about to go to the opera? Her grey-and-white hair was just-so, too, and her navy and lemon outfit was perfectly topped with her trademark clacky beads, which she played with as she spoke.

"All ready?"

Cordy nodded, breathing in the scent of the Thames, mere metres from her grandparents' front door. To the left, the pub which had been there since 1795 stood proud, its lovingly preserved Georgian windows ready to embrace whatever St Valentine blew their way.

"All my worldly goods, easily fitted into a boot. I'm not sure what that says."

"Be thankful!" her gran replied. "It was a right pain having so much stuff when I moved here from Birmingham. Having less stuff is a good thing. Travel light in life."

Two runners wearing the shortest shorts zipped past on the cobbled road, not looking at all out of breath.

"Wise guru Eunice speaks," Gary said.

"Are you sure we can't come too? I want to see where you are and know you're safe."

Cordy walked over and stood beside her gran. "I'd rather move in solo, and invite you round when I'm settled. Plus, I've no idea what state the flat will be in. It's not fair to my future flatmate not to warn her first."

Gran pursed her lips. "Okay. But make sure you invite us round soon."

"I promise." She drew her gran into a hug, feeling the comfort of her gran's arms around her back. Cordy never thought of her gran as frail or old until she hugged her. Then, suddenly, she felt fragile. Every time she hugged her, she never wanted to let her go. She breathed in her familiar musky perfume. "You're the first visitors I'll have, okay?" She drew back and kissed her soft cheek. "Thank you for putting up with me for the past few months. You'll never know what it meant to have a place to stay in London."

Her gran nodded. "You've always got a room with us, doesn't she, Joan?"

Next to her, Joan nodded. "Always. We're going to miss you, even if the bathroom will be cleaner."

Cordy took a breath. She was not going to cry. She was only moving across the river. "I'm going to miss you, too. I promise I'll visit. Plus, I need to come over to use your piano for my private lessons. You'll see me soon for that."

She hugged her gran one more time, then Joan, then jumped in the car with Vincent and Gary. She wanted to leave before she started blubbering. Instead, she blew kisses out the window as the car trundled off on the cobbled streets. This was the start of her new life.

London, take two.

***

When she arrived, Hannah let her in, said hi to Vincent and Gary, then left them "to get settled". The two men carried Cordy's stuff in and stayed for a cuppa, but now, at 2pm, it was just Cordy standing by the front door, stomach churning. Had she done the right thing? She popped her head into the lounge and took in the screened off bed, chest of drawers and metal hanging rail. Guilt overwhelmed her. But then she remembered that Hannah wanted this. She was thankful Cordy had moved in. Plus, Cordy had wanted this, too, and she was paying to be here. She'd made the decision. It was time to own it.

She walked into the small kitchen and filled the kettle, just as she heard the front door open. Fear rose inside. This was like being back at university, waiting to see who was in her halls of residence. Cordy had never flat-shared before. At uni, she'd always lived in halls, and for her post-grad course, she'd moved in with her gran.

She popped her head into the hallway, where Hannah was hanging up her black coat. She wore black jeans, DMs, and a grey polo-neck jumper. Where had she been for the past hour?

She gave Cordy a tight smile as she walked towards her. Maybe she was edgy about the new situation, too.

"Cup of tea?"

Hannah's cheeks flared red from the cold. "Love one." She leaned her shoulder on the kitchen door frame. "This is weird, having someone else make me a drink. It hasn't happened for a while."

"I was just thinking you're my first ever flatmate. If we don't count my gran. Which we shouldn't."

"Let's just agree this might take some adjustment for both of us. But so long as we're both aware, that's half the battle."

The kettle boiled and Cordy stared at cupboards. She turned to Hannah. "Mugs?"

"Above the kettle," she pointed. "Tea bags and sugar in the cannisters on the counter." She paused. "Milk in the fridge."

Cordy raised an eyebrow. "No shit."

They both laughed.

"How do you take it?"

"Strong, dash of milk."

Cordy kept her eyebrow raised. "Same as me. Interesting. Maybe this might work out."

Hannah held her gaze. "I hope so. Otherwise, we're both homeless, right?"

She took a sip of her tea, and they walked to the living room. A bare picture hook caught her eye. Had there been something there previously, or was it a hangover from the last tenant? There was so much Cordy didn't know. She hardly knew this woman at all. She might murder her in her sleep.

Hannah pushed her hair out of her eyes. "I'm going out to a drag-king night at a local bar tonight. You're welcome to come along if you're free?"

Although it was highly doubtful a psycho would invite her out for drinks, wasn't it?

"I'm out with a friend," Cordy replied. "But I can see if she fancies it. I'm sure she might. If so, you're on."

* * *

The first thing Cordy saw when she walked into the bar was a banner that read *Fuck the patriarchy! Fuck Valentine's!* Not a love heart or a rose in sight, which she was thankful for. Valentine's night was always tricky when you were single, but tonight was the start of a new chapter. When she'd talked at school with Greta the day before, Greta similarly told her she wanted no part of Valentine's, declaring it "performative romance shite and a pile of wank."

It had taken a while to reach the bar, after Hannah stopped into Sylvie's Bagels: "dinner" she told Cordy. Hannah and the owner had some verbal sparring back and forth over the counter that showed just how often Hannah came here.

"You need to eat more than bagels, Hannah," Sylvie told her, giving her a warm smile. Cordy guessed she was in her 50s, with sharp cheekbones and an even sharper Eastern European accent. "But I am not your mother. Plus, I need to stay in business, so keep coming." She winked as Hannah paid.

The queer bar they were in, OutRageous, had distressed leather booths on the ground floor, with a low-lit club underneath. Cordy knew without having to confirm her Adidas were going to stick to the scuffed vinyl floor all the way across.

The vibe was very Saturday night: the crowd up, the music loud, the smells a mix of stale beer and perfume. Still, as Cordy bought drinks, she brightened. For the first time since she moved to the Big Smoke, she felt like there might be something here for her apart from work.

Greta turned up five minutes later in too-high heels, a gold-and-white leopard-print jacket, and so much glittery eye shadow, it was a wonder she could open her lids. She squeezed Cordy hello, then shook hands with Hannah, giving her a lingering once over.

Cordy gave her friend a tight smile. Greta wanted to sleep with a woman, but somehow, Cordy didn't want it to be Hannah. She was part of Cordy's new world, and she didn't want Greta barging in on that.

Oblivious, Greta put her lips to Cordy's ear. "Didn't I tell you this area was heaving with queers?"

Cordy glanced around. It was true. She also knew that with her high-waisted jeans, Docs, leather jacket and easy smile, Hannah wouldn't just attract attention from Greta. Which made her stomach tight.

When she turned back, Hannah caught her eye and smiled.

Cordy ignored the blush that crept up her insides.

"Shall we go downstairs so we can get a spot for the drag show. My neighbour, Theo, is hosting. Or rather, their alter ego is, Captain Von Strap."

Cordy snorted. "Captain Von Strap? Now I'm really intrigued."

"They're really good. I just did their drag course."

"Let's get drinks and go see my first drag king," Cordy said.

"Mine, too!" Greta added.

Half an hour later, they'd managed to commandeer a section of ledge by the far wall, a Saturday night triumph. Then the lights dimmed, and Captain Von Strap strutted onto the stage, looking for all the world like he'd just walked off 'The Sound Of Music' set, ready to fight for Austria. His whistle got the crowd laughing, and his rendition of 'My Favourite Things' which included "raindrops on roses and lube spread on dildos," and "girls in white dresses with legs spread akimbo," got them whipped into a frenzy.

"I swear, every fucking night I'm here, the crowd gets more queer. You're looking gay as hell. Are you feeling queer tonight, Dalston?"

A roar from the crowd, as more punters flooded in from upstairs, the Captain's booming voice drawing them in, along with the crowd's volume. He pulled off his peaked cap and raised one hand in the air.

"I said, are you feeling fucking queer?!"

More yelling, as the Captain grinned, replaced his cap, then punched the air.

"Then make some noise for your first drag act of the evening. The first of six in the Kings R Us competition. Someone with swagger. A cut above the rest. Please welcome, Sir Loin of Beef!"

The king appeared on stage in a loin cloth, hair artistically woven on his chest, wielding a large stick in his hand. He then proceeded to do an impressive cabaret set involving comedy and singing. Cordy glanced at Hannah, who was completely focused on the performance. She took in the length of her neck, the way the fine hairs at the bottom of it curled slightly. She had broad shoulders, too. She looked strong, like she could open jars, no problem.

Cordy could also open jars. She was a modern woman, she had a gadget. That was her dad's main worry when she'd come out to him. "But who's going to open your jars?"

When the act finished, the noise was through the roof. Sir Loin bowed, the Captain returned to stoke the crowd, and the next king appeared: Buoy George. This one was dressed as a classic sailor, and did a strip tease to Florence and The Machine's 'Ship To Wreck'. At one point, he also produced a blow-up shark and rode it around the stage. The crowd's reaction when he whipped off his trousers to show off his bulge was off the scale, a level of whistling and cheering normally reserved for someone buying the whole bar a round.

When the Captain introduced the third act, Dem O'Cracy, the crowd in the basement club was even thicker, the air heavy with sweat and excitement. The third king was a political act who performed beat poetry about how he wanted to kill the Tories. It obviously went down a storm. When they finished, the Captain strutted onto the stage, introduced the judges, and declared a half-hour interval amid great applause. Hannah used the break to get more drinks.

Greta gripped Cordy's arm, as the crowd's volume increased. "Why have I not seen a drag king show again? Tell me?" She didn't wait for an answer. "They were all incredible. Especially the Captain. If I saw him in a club, I would literally die. I can't believe Hannah knows him. I might shit my pants if he comes over."

Cordy grinned. Subtlety wasn't Greta's strongest skill.

However, it was about to be tested, because a couple of minutes later, Cordy spied Hannah and the Captain coming their way. When they arrived, Cordy was fascinated with the Captain's facial hair, intricately painted on, including a handlebar moustache. However, his smile was genuine as he handed her a bottle of Brooklyn lager. Having just controlled the crowd for the whole show, it was a little like meeting someone famous.

"This is my neighbour, Theo, or as he is tonight, Captain Von Strap." Hannah glanced at Cordy. "*Our* neighbour." She turned to Theo. "This is my new flatmate, Cordy, and her friend, Greta."

They all shook hands, and Cordy prayed Greta would be cool. Meeting the Captain seemed to have sucked all the words from her, which was as good as Cordy could hope for.

"The Captain is the neighbour I told you about whose mum made marmalade from the oranges," Hannah told Cordy. "He's also my drag parent, holding my hand through the early stages."

"What did you think of the acts?" Captain Von Strap asked, tucking his peaked cap under his arm.

"You were incredible," Greta blurted, fluttering her eyelashes. "It's my first drag-king show, and I'm hooked." She ran a hand through her hair and shook it out. "I know I can't vote for you, but if I could, I would."

The Captain beamed. "That's very kind. I hope it won't be your last drag show."

Greta licked her lips ever so slowly, locking eyes with him. "I hope so, too."

Cordy looked between Greta and the Captain, then back again. Was it her imagination, or was there real-life flirting going on?

"You should come and see Hannah when she performs in a few weeks." The Captain slicked back his hair and leaned in to Greta. She leaned right back. It was like he was a pop star, and Greta was drawn into his rich orbit.

"I would love to." Greta's voice was all weird and wobbly.

Seemingly oblivious, Hannah grimaced. "I know it'll take a while to get up to standard, but hopefully I can get through. But only the top two from each of the rounds progress. No pressure. Sir Loin of Beef was incredible. I don't fancy coming up against him." She gave a sharp smile which didn't reach her eyes. "I'm bricking it, but that's always a good sign."

"You're going to be great," the Captain added. "And Max Girth will finally be unleashed into the world." Then he covered his mouth. "Shit, should I have revealed your name? Have you settled on that yet?"

Hannah nodded. "I think so. What do you think?" She aimed the question at Cordy.

"Max Girth is inspired. And like the Captain said, I think whatever you're called, you'll be great." She'd only known Hannah for a short space of time, but she meant it.

The DJ cranked up the old-school hip-hop tunes, and Greta wiggled her hips. "I love this one. Anybody want to dance?" She asked the group, but the question was aimed at the Captain.

"I would love to," the Captain replied, taking Greta's outstretched hand.

In moments, they found a spot in the corner of the club and were dancing. Was Greta about to break her duck with Captain Von Strap?

"Fast mover, your friend."

"When she wants something, she goes after it. And when she doesn't, she lets go. It's a life skill. She told me never to stay in a relationship just for the sake of it." Cordy gave a soft smile. "Seems to me, people like Greta are constantly in relationships, be they lasting or not." She shook her head. "The same does not apply to me."

"Nor me," Hannah replied. "It's been almost four months since my ex left, and I've slept with nobody." She paused. "You ever get the feeling life is simpler for some people?"

"Constantly," Cordy agreed. "Maybe we can pool our brains to try to make it easier for us, too."

"I like the sound of that," Hannah replied.

Chapter Eight

The pavements outside the bar were busy when Hannah and Cordy left just after 11.30pm. They waved Greta and Captain Von Strap (now back to being Theo) off to "get to know each other over expensive cocktails somewhere bougee", then headed home. To their left, a late bar swayed with noise and heat, while opposite, a kebab shop had a queue out the door, booze-fuelled laughter painting the air.

After four beers, Hannah was the right side of tipsy. Ahead, a straight couple were in a heated argument, the woman holding a love-heart balloon with attached teddy bear as she called him a "shit-for-brains fuckwit". Hannah steered Cordy around them with a protective arm, but when she realised what she was doing, she dropped her arm and hoped Cordy hadn't noticed.

They walked down their tree-lined street, cars parked bumper to bumper on either side. A police siren whirred in the distance. Even though it was close to freezing, the comforting noise of Cordy's footsteps and the gentle sound of her breathing made Hannah warm. It would be nice to have another heartbeat in the flat again. She'd missed it.

They turned into their front path, and almost collided with a bearded delivery rider. He was dressed in thermals, and his thick black gloves didn't make adjusting the strap on his helmet too easy, as he was trying to do now. When he eyeballed Hannah, she realised it was the bike guy from the flat above. Alan. The Tuscan stew his girlfriend Bernice had given Hannah the other night had tasted just as good as it smelt.

"Hi, Alan."

He frowned, then pointed. "It's you, the orange lady!"

"Less of the lady," Hannah replied. "Still working this late?"

"We're swamped, and short-staffed. Everyone wants beer and crisps at nearly midnight on a Saturday. We had a mad rush on boxes of chocolates for those who'd forgotten Valentine's Day earlier, too." He grabbed his bike, which had been leaning against their front wall. "You need a job?"

"Actually, yes." The truest words. "But I don't have a bike."

"Get one, then knock on my door if you're serious."

She blinked. Perhaps her job woes could be cured as easily as that.

Once back at the flat, Hannah persuaded Cordy to leave her coat on and drink wine on the balcony. "It's a circus not worth missing on a weekend. Plus, there's something pretty cool about watching the action from up high."

Cordy grabbed her hat on the way.

Hannah swapped her leather jacket for her black coat that she still needed to sew the buttons back onto. She added two tumblers and a bottle of Rioja to the rickety metal table-top the size of a darts board. The balcony was just about big enough for the table and two chairs, its brick wall coming up to shoulder-height when they sat.

Cordy's chair legs scraped along the ground as she adjusted

her seat, her breath swirling around her face as she pulled her scarf tighter.

"Here's to drinking wine on our first night living together." Hannah raised her glass.

"I'll drink to that." Cordy took a healthy slug, then flicked her gaze to the chalkboard sky. "Shame there are no stars, though."

"Not likely in Hackney. Unless you count that woman from 'Love Island' who was spotted in MacDonald's last weekend."

"I definitely do," Cordy replied.

They shared a smile, and a cocktail of relief and positivity flowed through Hannah. This living together thing might just work.

"Your drag show, then. What's the gist? Do you sing? Play an instrument? Strip? Do beat poetry? The show tonight had a strong start, but the rest were a mixed bag."

"That's how it goes," Hannah replied. "Theo reckons live singing is the way to go, so I'm going to do that. I just need to find the right song, then practice. I've done it before, but not for a while."

"I'm a music teacher. I could help you out."

"Really?" Hannah hadn't even thought about that. "I don't want to take up too much of your time."

Cordy's fiery red hair poked out the front of her woollen hat. It framed her bottle-green eyes perfectly.

"You wouldn't be. Like I told you, I've only been in London for five months. My gran knows more queer women here. Time is the one thing on my side. Plus, live singing would definitely make you stand out. Look at Sir Loin of Beef tonight."

Live singing was daunting, though. Hannah was used to doing burlesque and taking her clothes off. Somehow, singing felt more personal. What would her mum say to either? "You won't make a living on stage. Hardly anybody does. Better to get a good degree and have a good job behind you."

Cordy snapped her fingers. "In fact, you should come to my open mic night at Doyle's next week. Get you used to singing in front of a live audience."

"That sounds positively terrifying. A bit like Theo telling me I should start a TikTok of my journey."

Cordy grinned. "All the best things in life should be scary."

"In the past month, I've met my drag mentor in this building, and moved in with my singing coach. It feels like the universe is trying to tell me something."

"And you were ready to listen." Cordy paused, then narrowed her gaze. "I know it's a bit late, but are you seriously okay with our arrangement? Everyone needs a room of one's own, and I've kicked you out of yours."

"Virginia Woolf never lived in modern-day London, though, did she? Plus, she was born rich."

Cordy smiled. "You read the classics?"

"When I have to. I did a year of an English literature degree at university as a way to differentiate myself from my finance-obsessed family, but then I found I didn't much like it. My parents encouraged me to change course, which meant I somehow ended up with an economics degree."

"That's quite the switch."

Hannah was well aware. "I didn't much like any course at uni, but I stuck with the one that made my family happy. They were paying for it, after all. I got a good job in a big bank when

I left, and I put up with it for a while, but then quit when I couldn't stand it anymore. My parents weren't impressed, but I had to leave. I've drifted from job to job ever since, with the juice bar the latest effort, as I think you remember from the first time we met."

Cordy tapped the side of her head. "Etched in my memory, believe me. You're forever Orange Lady to me."

"And to my neighbours, apparently." Hannah grinned. "But I might apply for that delivery job."

"I've got a bike at my gran's place if you want to borrow it. It's just sitting doing nothing."

"That would be amazing. Just until I can get my own from my parents' place."

"I'll get it next time I'm there." Cordy exhaled, the air fogging up around her. "Your story makes my tale of doing a music degree and then a post-grad a little dull. I always knew what I wanted to do, and my parents supported me fully."

"Even being queer?"

She nodded. "My dad had a wobble, but when my gran – his mum – came out, it made me being queer pale in comparison."

Hannah let out a bark of laughter. "Your gran is gay? That is the best thing ever."

"It really is," Cordy agreed. "She fell for a woman when they were both in their teens, but she didn't see a chance for them back then. But a few years after my granddad died, they met up again, and now they're married."

Hannah blinked hard. "Holding a torch for someone all your life? It's tragic, but also dazzlingly romantic." She paused. "Whereas my last relationship was simply tragic." She took a slug of her wine.

"I spotted a couple of empty picture hooks. Were they photos of your ex?"

Hannah's cheek twitched before she nodded. "I took them down recently. I should have done it when she walked out, but I kept thinking she might come back. Your arrival forced me into action."

"How long were you together?"

"Eighteen months. Although she was away for a lot of that. She worked in finance, and her company was setting up a centre abroad that she was heavily involved in. She said our lives weren't going in the same direction. She was right about that. I was floundering, and she was flying."

"Also, Lauren never thought I was out enough. That I compartmentalised my whole life and was never relaxed." Hannah flexed her calves as her stomach twisted. "I never held her hand when we were out. I never took her home at Christmas. I wouldn't tag her on Instagram. My parents met her once, and it was very stilted, but that was probably my fault, too. Plus, she hated me doing burlesque. She said it buried who I was in real life. She thought I should put more of my queer voice into my performance. She'd approve of me doing drag." Hannah rolled her shoulders. "But maybe that's the point. On stage, I'm someone else. I'm a performer. It's not me." She was a lot freer on stage than she was in real life.

Cordy waited a few moments before she responded. "Did your ex have a point or was she off the mark?"

Hannah cast her gaze to the street. "My family know I'm queer, but I don't let them into my life. They live one life, I live another. There's no crossover. They claim to be accepting of me being queer, but I know the truth." She sighed. "I don't let them in anymore, but do they deserve to be included?"

"That's the hard part," Cordy agreed. "I had to learn to let mine in when my dad didn't deserve it. Especially when my gran was outdoing me, which is never what I expected. But maybe if you open the door a little, they might surprise you."

"But what if it goes the other way and they react as I feared? I could never tell them about doing burlesque or drag, for instance. My sisters are fine, but my mum has trouble saying the word 'girlfriend' when it comes to me."

"You have to be the brave one. You have to push the barriers. Otherwise, nothing changes. It fucking sucks, but it's the truth." Cordy splayed a hand. "As my gran always told me. Don't waste your life on what-ifs. Do the things you want to do. Be with the people you really love." She sniffed, fished in her pocket for a tissue, and blew her nose. "Although if she'd followed through with that, I most probably wouldn't be here, so that one's always tricky."

"It's what Lauren used to tell me all the time. That I push people away rather than giving them a chance. That my internalised shame was a stuck record playing over and over."

Could she really let her family in a little? The thought horrified her. What if she introduced them to someone, and her parents said something homophobic? "Lesbians seem to be everywhere right now. In every book I read, in every show I watch," her mum had once said. "Are they trying to promote it?"

Her sisters said their parents were just clumsy with words. But Hannah thought there was clumsy, and then there was next-level ridiculous. If her parents kept making the same mistake and not adjusting what they said, she had to assume it wasn't a mistake, but actually what they thought.

"Maybe I should take you home. Mum always wants me to bring friends home, and you seem very family-friendly."

"I would be honoured. Although I have to warn you, parents love me, so I'd be setting a high bar."

Hannah could well imagine. Cordy seemed to have it all sorted way earlier than Hannah.

"Have you heard from your ex since she left?"

"Not a peep." The Rioja warmed her as it went down.

"Do you miss her?"

Hannah mulled the question for a few moments. "Sometimes. I was shellshocked when she left. I thought we were doing okay. I knew there were issues, but I didn't realise she was that unhappy that she'd take off virtually overnight. Just take her stuff, plus the dining table and chairs, and leave."

"Must have been amazing furniture."

"Old. Lauren liked vintage stuff."

"And you?"

"I'm still working out what I like." Although perhaps she was starting to find common ground with her new flatmate.

Cordy smiled. "Hopefully, I fall into the like category. And for what it's worth, you're not floundering. You're just taking a little time to double-down on what you want in life. I don't see that as a flaw. It's something to be proud of."

Hannah blinked. "You're quickly falling into my 'like' category with comments like that." She gulped as the moment fizzed through her, then was distracted as a woman below screamed "Sharleeeeeeen! Stop! I didn't mean it!"

The Sharleen in question thudded past them on the pavement below, barely looking over her shoulder. "You should have thought about that before you kissed her, shouldn't you?"

Cordy swivelled to the drama.

"Sharleen!"

"Fuck off, Willow!"

Cordy snorted. "Oh my god, you were right, this is a box seat. We don't need to go out again. Just watch this."

"You just need to get up and dance every now and again to keep the circulation going." Hannah did just that, circling her arms and shaking out her legs. Cordy followed suit, then they both started to throw some shapes, before dissolving into laughter.

Was it mad that Hannah felt like she'd known Cordy for longer than a day? Probably. She was definitely opening up way more than normal. Maybe because she was a relative stranger. Lauren would never believe it.

Cordy shivered, then sat again. "I've got an idea. We're suddenly living in close proximity. We need to speed up the get-to-know-you process." She snapped her fingers. "Tell me three things about you I should know so I don't drive you mad."

"Okay." Hannah tapped her index finger on her lips. "I don't hate many things – apart from myself, according to my ex. Star signs. Can't stand them. Don't tell me my fortune for the week." She paused. "I'm not wild on people eating apples around me." She cleared her throat. "And I'm the baby of my family, I have two siblings, in-laws, nieces, and nephews, and none of them think I'm capable of a single thing in life. Not even the one-year-old toddler." She paused. "I'm not quite sure how I went from apples to family therapy." She drained her wine and grabbed the bottle. "Also, I hate running out of wine."

"We agree on that, and the apples," Cordy said as Hannah topped them up. "For me, I love classical music, which most people my age find weird. Second, I love marmalade, but hate rind in it. Third, I also love country music, even though it's problematic for queers sometimes." She threw up her hands. "What can I say? I love a good story put to music."

"Did you notice how all of yours were things you love, and mine were things I hate?" Hannah wagged a finger in Cordy's direction. "Psychoanalyse me later. But I like this game." She downed a bit more wine.

"Okay, let's keep going. Three jobs you'd love to have. I'll start." Hannah rolled her shoulders. "West End leading lady. Boat Skipper. I think it's something to do with the peaked cap. Pilot. Ditto."

Cordy nodded. "What about playing the role of a pilot in a West End show?"

"Dreams!" Hannah held up her wine glass.

"For me, I'd love to tour playing my piano. If I ever stop doing music, I always thought I'd make a great librarian. Very good with organising stuff. Either that or a chef, but that would involve me actually being able to cook." She raised an eyebrow at Hannah. "My turn to ask. Okay, this might be the booze talking, but we're getting to know each other, right? Three things about your past relationships."

Hannah winced. "What we think about them, or what our exes thought about them?"

"Your choice."

Hannah pursed her lips. "Lauren would tell you I'm stubborn, I've got gallons of internal homophobia, and that I'm too judgemental when it comes to apple eating."

A delicious laugh escaped Cordy's lips. One that made Hannah sit up. "Remind me never to bring apples into this flat.

There are some strong opinions on the subject. Clearly you didn't have them about oranges?"

"I love oranges, although not in biblical proportions."

They smirked at each other.

This was nice. Comfortable. Maybe she hadn't made a huge mistake.

Plus, Cordy was cute. Not Hannah's usual type: she'd never dated a redhead before, dyed or otherwise. But then, her usual type hadn't faired that well so far, had they? Cordy was cute and funny. But that was beside the point.

Very beside the point, Hannah.

The balcony wobbled, and she squinted. Or maybe the balcony didn't wobble. Perhaps it was her? More likely.

"My go," Cordy said. "First, this is probably the most fun Valentine's Day I've had in years. The last one I shared with a partner, they split up with me the day after. Days later, I found out she'd cheated with a mutual friend. That was a Valentine's Day to live long in the memory."

Hannah shook her head. "Women." She paused. "Was it a woman?"

"It was."

"Why are women such cunts?"

Cordy snorted. "No clue."

An easy silence bathed them for a few seconds.

"My exes would say I'm too music-obsessed, which might have been fair. I have course-corrected a little." Cordy grinned. "They would also say that I'm the best lover they've ever had, obviously. And a compulsive liar."

Laughter rattled through Hannah, and it was only then she realised she hadn't laughed like this since... well, since Lauren left. Instead, she'd locked herself away and brooded. That stopped now. She'd missed drinking wine on the balcony and laughing. Cordy was proving quite the tonic.

"We should do more of this from now on. Share titbits of our lives. I like it."

Hannah nodded. "Me, too. Although you've got me wondering about your prowess in the sheets now." She started to undress Cordy in her mind. Then her mind held up a Stop sign.

A blush worked its way onto Cordy's cheeks. "I don't know why I said that. Blame the wine."

"I think, all things considered, this has been a pretty good Valentine's Day for me, too," Hannah said. "You moving in means I don't have to move out." She held Cordy's gaze as she spoke, and a warm glow spread through her. Part-wine, part-new friendship.

Cordy beamed right back, and Hannah's skin prickled under her gaze. She was almost grateful when a car sped along the road below, music blaring, then screeched to a halt right outside their flat block. The pair hung over the balcony to see what was going on. A woman jumped out wearing a cowboy hat, sparkly jacket, and cowboy boots. She threw her arms in the air and screeched into the night air. She'd *definitely* had a good Valentine's.

"Turn it up!" she shouted, and started to dance in the road.

The volume got louder, and Hannah recognised David Bowie's 'Rebel Rebel'. The same song that had swept her mum away that New Year a few years ago. The one she performed with her band. Hannah could still picture her eyes closed, the sway of her hair, and the blissed-out look on her face.

She furrowed her brow. "With that cowboy hat, I was expecting a country song, not this."

The woman below started to twirl and whoop in the street as the bass kicked in. Instinctively, Hannah checked left and right for oncoming cars. She didn't want to witness someone dying tonight. But thankfully, the road was clear.

When she glanced back at Cordy, she was tapping her foot. "You know, this would make a great song to sing for your drag act. Pitch-perfect, I'd say."

Hannah perked an eyebrow. It really would. The lyrics about being non-binary before non-binary was even a thing were spot on. But this was her mum's song. The one that was firmly ensconced in her other life. But maybe if Hannah picked it up again, it would carry on the family tradition. Even though Polly Driver would never know.

Dutch courage pumping through her veins, she leaned back and broke into the chorus. As her vocals slapped the cold night air, they seemed to take on a bold, winning quality. Hannah smiled as she made it through to the end of the chorus. Down below, the cowgirl shouted, "You go, girl!"

Hannah looked over at Cordy, who grinned. "After that, I can't wait for Max Girth to take the capital by storm."

Chapter Nine

"Sorry we're late. The traffic was horrendous. What are they doing with those roadworks around the Blackwall tunnel?"

"No idea, I came on the tube."

Cordy ushered Kate in, followed by her eight-year-old son, Finn. Kate smelt delicious, and she looked even better. When Cordy grew up, she wanted to be Kate.

She turned her attention to her star piano pupil. "How are you, buddy? Ready to knock my socks off as usual?"

Finn gave her a shy smile, then nodded.

Cordy led them through to the open-plan kitchen-diner at the back of the house, where the piano was housed. Joan said she didn't play as much as she used to, and she was thrilled that Cordy was getting some use from it. Her gran and Joan had disappeared to Greenwich market for a browse followed by coffee and cake this morning. Cordy had arrived just in time to give them a kiss goodbye, and smiled as she watched them walk away, arm in arm.

"The congestion is one of the reasons we're moving out. Although I'm not sure the traffic is much better anywhere." Kate stared at Cordy. "How old are you, if you don't mind me asking?"

Cordy shook her head. "I'm 27."

A wistful look invaded Kate's face. "When I was 27, I was working in magazines, hadn't met Meg, and never thought I'd move out of Shoreditch. I've done pretty well staying until now, but the time has come. Two kids who need a garden has pushed us over the edge."

"Are you going far?"

Kate shook her head. "North London, where we're both from. Closer to family and so in-built babysitters. That way, Meg and I can have some nights out just the two of us. We might even have the odd one in Shoreditch. It'll be weird, but times change, don't they?"

"Just ask my gran."

"Ha!" Kate said. "She's the bloody poster girl for change." She shrugged off her lumberjack jacket, then mussed her dyed blonde hair.

Cordy stared, and thought of Hannah shrugging off her leather jacket last week. It had been a look Cordy was here for. Lumber and leather were perennial queer favourites.

"Anyway, I'll go sit in the front room and leave you to it."

"Can I get you a coffee first?"

Kate looked like she wanted to kiss her. "That would be amazing. I didn't have time this morning, what with our daughter having a meltdown, then trying to get everyone out of the flat on time."

Cordy nodded like she understood perfectly. She didn't. She wasn't ready for children yet. She could hardly take care of herself. She wouldn't disclose to Kate she'd had a Bombay Bad Boy Pot Noodle for dinner last night. She walked over to the kitchen, flicked on her gran's coffee machine, and dropped in a capsule.

"How are Meg and Luna?"

"When she stopped having a breakdown about what top to wear, Luna is gorgeous. Meg took her swimming this morning, so all our children are happy." She glanced at her son. "You're excited to play piano with Cordy, aren't you?"

Finn nodded mutely, his shock of blond hair static on his head.

The coffee machine gurgled and spat out its bitter dark liquid. Kate took it gratefully. "I'll leave you to it. Forty-five minutes you reckon?"

Cordy nodded. "Should be perfect, shouldn't it, Finn?"

"I've practiced," he said, holding up a folder which housed his sheet music. "But only at school on their piano. Mum says when we move, I can have my own. Then I'm going to be a pop star."

Cordy glanced at Kate with a wide grin. "We better get on teaching the next big thing then, hadn't we?"

***

Kate came back into the open plan kitchen-diner after Finn dragged her back. He always took a little while to open up, and Cordy had given him some extra time at the end, as she always did. She wasn't in the teaching game for the money. She didn't know many who were. They all sat around the dining table that seated six, eight at a push.

"You were incredible, Finn. I could hear you through the wall, and I thought, 'that kid is going to be the next Elton John'!"

"Rocket man!" Finn shouted, arm in the air, energy boosted after singing and playing.

"My teenage nephew, Luke, thinks I need to update my

reference points, get Finn into grime. But Finn lives with us, and we love Elton, so Finn does, too."

"He's my favourite. And Ed Sheeran," Finn confirmed.

"How's your new place going?" Kate asked. "You're living fairly close to us now, right?"

Cordy nodded. "Up the road in Haggerston. It's going well. My flatmate is lovely, and I'm gradually meeting more people."

With their conflicting schedules, she and Hannah hadn't seen that much of each other since she moved in. But they'd shared one brunch together last weekend and had laughed so much over tea and toast topped with Theo's mum's amazing marmalade, sharing stories of dealing with drunk audience members. Cordy smiled just thinking about her.

Knowing she had Hannah at home had made things that little bit easier. She couldn't really explain it to herself, so she wasn't going to try explaining it to Kate. But eating toast and staring at the sleep crease marks on Hannah's cheek had felt like a moment. Hannah calmed her.

"London was a bit daunting at first, but I'm finding my feet. When I hear Gran and Joan's stories of them dating in the 50s, I feel like I can't moan about how hard it is to meet other women. They risked their lives."

"It's all relative though, isn't it?" Kate shrugged. "You're living this life, not theirs."

"Cordy should come to your big party, Mummy." Finn pointed at Cordy. "She could play the piano. She could play Elton!"

"You're still not coming, even if Cordy does," she told her son.

He rolled his eyes. "I know!"

Kate grinned, then reached into her bag and pulled out a book. "Why don't you go read while I finish up with Cordy?"

Finn dutifully took the book and disappeared into the next room.

"He's the most obedient child I've ever known," Cordy told Kate.

"I know, we got lucky. His sister, on the other hand, is the total opposite." She narrowed her eyes, then wagged a finger in Cordy's direction. "But you should definitely come to our Leaving London party. No obligation to play. Bring your flatmate, too. What's her name?"

Cordy felt her cheeks heat. "Hannah." Happiness flushed through her.

Kate's piercing stare drilled past Cordy's defences. "You might meet some more queer women from the area. Your gran and Eunice are coming, too, obviously."

"Queer royalty, of course they're going to be there." She was glad for the change of emphasis.

Kate went to say something else, then paused.

"In saying that you don't have to play piano, we are looking for some entertainment. What we'd really love is someone to do live karaoke, on a piano would be ideal. Do you do parties, or would you consider it?"

Cordy blinked. She hadn't before. "I play piano bars. You want someone to do a few songs, then play some requests while others sing, and step in when they forget the words?"

"You read my mind. And it would be paid, of course."

That was music to Cordy's ears. "I could definitely do a set."

"Perfect. Our friends are all show-offs, so I don't think we'll have a shortage of singers. We're trying to get Ruby

O'Connell to do a few songs as well, but that one depends on her schedule. She's a friend of a friend. We'd love some other queer performers, too. Make it a proper big night. Do you know anybody who might be interested?"

Hannah's face popped into her mind.

"Actually, my flatmate might do it. Her friend, too. They're both drag kings. Captain Von Strap and Max Girth."

Kate snorted. "If their acts are as good as their names, they'll be perfect."

"I've seen them. They're both really good." At least, the Captain was, and Cordy was sure Max *would* be.

"See what they say, and maybe we can chat. I hadn't even thought of a drag king, but the more I think about it, it seems ideal."

Cordy pictured the scene: her on the piano, Hannah in full costume, crooning for a room full of queers. This was what she'd dreamed would happen when she got to London. Now it was. She better help Hannah out with her singing now, hadn't she? Not that she was going to need much work, just a confidence boost. When Hannah had stood and belted out Bowie on the balcony on Valentine's Day, her voice had soft warmth to it. Like sun-baked earth under bare feet. "I'll mention it next time I see Hannah."

"Fabulous." Kate cocked her head. "Just a flatmate is she, this Hannah? Nothing more?"

Cordy nodded. "Absolutely. She's the reason I was able to move out and leave Gran and Joan in peace. I'd be crazy to sleep with her and fuck that up, wouldn't I?"

Why had she said that out loud? She pressed her hand to her side, lest she use it to smack herself in the face.

Kate smirked. "Unwise? Maybe. Depends how it works

out. But plenty of my friends shagged their flatmates. Most of them would say they never regretted it."

"We're just friends." But the words didn't sound convincing on her tongue.

Kate gave her a knowing nod, and moved the topic on.

Ten minutes later, Cordy waved Finn and Kate off, waited until the front door clicked, and then leaned her back against it. She and her big bloody mouth. Why did she say that about Hannah? Why was she even talking about sleeping with her?

She didn't want to sleep with her. That would be daft. Nothing had happened, nothing was going to happen, so why had she blurted that out to someone she'd met three times before?

Still, she'd scored some work out of it, plus a party invite. What's more, if they were booking Ruby O'Connell, it sounded as if they had money. Which is the one thing both her and Hannah needed.

She got out her phone and called up Hannah's name in WhatsApp. Just the six letters in a row made Cordy smile.

> *Three things that happened this morning. First, a woman on the tube was eating an apple and I didn't tell her to move. I moved instead. Second, my eight-year-old student wants to be Elton John. What is wrong with kids these days? Third, I've got both of us a gig, me playing, Max performing. It's time Max started to flex his vocals. The gig's in June, three months away. Don't panic!*

She pressed send and waited. Max's first round in the drag competition was in a few weeks. Cordy had promised to give him some vocal coaching. Within moments, the message was read, and three dots appeared as Hannah replied.

You've got Max a gig before he's sung a note? Impressive. What's your cut? Second, I borrowed Alan's bike last night to do some deliveries and it got a flat tyre. I'm looking forward to giving yours a flat tyre later. Third, we're out of milk. Can you pick some up on your way home?

A warmth bloomed in Cordy's stomach. It wasn't the first time Hannah had messaged to say they were out of milk, and Cordy liked the ease with which they'd fallen into domestic bliss.

Four. Shall I buy some Jaffa Cakes when I get the milk, too?

Hannah's reply was succinct.

And wine.

Cordy stuck around to have lunch with her Gran and Joan when they returned from the market, giving them both a big kiss before she wheeled her bike from the garden shed and out the front door. She ran through the shopping list in her head as she secured her helmet and waved to her favourite octogenarians. Milk, wine, Jaffa Cakes, crisps.

She'd had a fabulous morning, but she couldn't wait to get home.

Chapter Ten

"And then this woman jumped up, waving a twenty-pound note at me. I think she thought she was in a strip club. The bouncer came and dragged her away, but I got to keep the tip."

Cordy was aghast. "That's terrible!"

"She didn't touch me, and she was cute." Hannah smirked. "Plus, twenty quid."

Cordy couldn't argue with that. "I always have a tip jar on top of my piano, but I can't recall the last time someone dropped a twenty in there. Piano playing tends to bring out the pound-coin brigade."

"You need to get your tits out. Tips go up immediately."

"I'm not sure my tits would get the same tips as yours."

Hannah grinned. But then the thought crept into her mind: had Cordy been checking out her breasts? If the blush creeping up Cordy's cheeks was anything to go by, the answer was yes. Was she happy about that? Also, yes.

"Anyway, shall we sing?" Cordy got up from the sofa and sat behind her keyboard. She wore a long, flowy skirt and a denim shirt, with the first three buttons open. Not for the first time since she moved in, Hannah admired her strong arms, capable hands, and the sliver of skin on show below her neck. What would it be like to kiss it?

She flinched.

Where the hell had that thought come from?

They were here to sing.

"Yes please. I've just finished up my next TikTok, so that part of my day is done." Her voice, unlike her thoughts, sounded normal. "I'm posting regularly and gaining some traction. They seem to like my drag king prep and my cycling videos. I have to get on your bike in two hours, literally. Welcome to the gig economy."

"You and the rest of London. I always thought the term 'portfolio career' sounded so glamorous until I started to live it." Cordy's mouth formed an 'O', then she jumped up. "Hang on, I got you something." She ran out of the room.

What had she got her?

Cordy reappeared moments later with an orange in her hands. But when she gave it to her, Hannah saw she'd drawn a shirt, tie, and jacket onto one half in thick black marker pen. The orange also sported a quiff, big round eyes, button nose, and smiley mouth.

"It's a drag king orange. A motivational orange, if you will." She smiled, then looked away. Was she embarrassed? "I just thought, with oranges being our thing..." She frowned. "It seemed like a good idea at the time." She shook her head as she sat behind her keyboard.

Hannah turned the orange in her hands. Nobody had ever done anything like this for her before. Her own citrus mascot. When she glanced at Cordy, a jolt of attraction stunned her. Cordy was driven, determined, kind. Also, hot. Plus, she had the kind of charisma that might make a nun question her vows.

Hannah steadied herself before she answered. "I absolutely love my motivational orange." She chewed the inside of her cheek as her stomach rolled, then put the orange on the coffee table. "He can observe our first session. See how we do. Let's call him Elvis."

Cordy met her eyes, and gave her a tiny smile.

Another jolt shot through Hannah.

"Elvis it is. Ready?"

Hannah glanced at Elvis, then at Cordy. Was she ready? As she'd ever be. She nodded, then cleared her throat. Hesitation bloomed inside, but she had to get over that. She wanted to take her drag act to the next level. To sing live. To do that, she had to start by singing in her living room.

Cordy took her through a few warm-up exercises to loosen Hannah's vocal cords.

"Breathe from your diaphragm, feel your breath first. Remember, singing is all about using your breath well and connecting with emotion. A little like life."

Hannah smiled. "A philosophy lesson as well as a singing lesson."

"I've always been a multi-tasker." Cordy paused. "It's like I was telling my pupil, Romilly, yesterday. It's all about feeling the music." Cordy put her hand over her chest. "Do it with me."

Hannah's gaze was drawn to the skin exposed beneath Cordy's neck. Particularly where the top three buttons of her shirt were undone, guiding Hannah's eyes towards the dip between her breasts. Cordy tapped that skin now as she demonstrated how to establish musical connection. Hannah's pulse started to thump in her ears as she stared at Cordy's skin.

In response, Cordy raised an eyebrow. "I'm not playing around here. Hand over chest, please."

Hannah blushed, then did as she was told. "You're a bossy teacher."

"It's the only way to be. I'm going to play the Bowie track through once, and I want you to close your eyes, breathe it in, and memorise how it makes you feel."

Cordy started to play the first few notes, and Hannah closed her eyes. She took a long breath, and rested her index and middle fingers on her chest. When Cordy finished, Hannah opened her eyes. She was in a different place than she had been minutes ago. Calmer. In the moment. Focused.

"Ready to give it a first try?"

Hannah gave a nod.

Cordy put a hand over her chest. "You don't have to be perfect first time. Just relax and have fun." She tapped the tips of her fingers on the bare skin of her chest. "Ba-boom. Ba-boom. Ba-boom."

Hannah stared again, as her whole body leaned forward as if she were a sunflower and Cordy was the sun.

"Like *Dirty Dancing*, right?" Cordy added.

"I've never seen it." That admission always got the same response: total incredulity.

Cordy screwed up her face. "You've never seen one of the best movies ever? Where have you been living?" She pointed at the orange. "Even Elvis has seen it."

Hannah shrugged. "My mum and my sisters all love it. I avoided watching it for that reason." She knew it sounded stupid as soon as she said it.

"You need to get over that. We're going to watch it. It's as near-perfect a movie as you could wish for." Cordy shook her head with a look of disdain. "But back to the here and now." She launched into the intro.

At Cordy's nod, Hannah started to sing.

She'd practised when Cordy was out, but this was different. Did Cordy think she was any good? That she had potential? She couldn't be sure, but she *so* wanted her to think so. Cordy was passionate about what she did, and it was rubbing off on Hannah. Plus, after Cordy's pep talk, Hannah truly listened to the words like she never had before. She lived what she was singing.

For the first time, she saw these Bowie lyrics were perfect. Plus, she was sure her mother would be in a whirl if she ever saw her perform this as a man. But yet, her mum had performed the exact same song when she was younger. It still baffled Hannah. Had she listened to the words? Had she ever thought she might be non-binary? Did Hannah think *she* was?

She took a breath and pushed those thoughts aside. She couldn't think about that now. She had to focus on getting the song right, nothing else. No distractions. Like Cordy's tongue, currently sliding along her bottom lip. Hannah flicked her gaze away.

When she got to the chorus, Cordy paused, telling Hannah where to catch her breath so she could make it to the end. They restarted, and Hannah focused on where Cordy had told her to breathe between lines. On her encouraging smile that lit up her face when she played.

At one point, Cordy closed her eyes as she played, and Hannah followed the muscles in her forearm where her shirt was pushed up, her sure fingers on the keyboard. What would those fingers be like trailing down Hannah's back?

She blinked. She *really* needed to work on her focus.

When the song finished, Cordy stopped and leaned back from her keys.

"A great start. Let's do it again. This time, loosen your shoulders, and really focus on singing with your whole body. You're still coming from here," she tapped her fingers on her throat, "and not from here." She tapped her stomach.

Hannah bit her cheek again as thoughts of Cordy's fingers tapping elsewhere on her body invaded her thoughts again. What the hell was going on today?

She nodded as Cordy played the intro again. When they'd sung the song through four times, Cordy finished with a wander up and down the keys, before giving Hannah a warm smile.

"How do you feel?"

Like I want to kiss you.

Hannah flinched. This morning was weird, and she was *not* going to say that. She rolled her shoulders and exhaled to buy a little time. "Like I could actually do this."

"You can more than do it. You just need practice, then to put some moves to the words. Performance in front of other people is what you need. Get you used to it, to using the mic and being aware of your breath. The rest will follow." She got up from behind the keyboard.

Did Cordy's eyes always glimmer like they did today? Hannah blinked more rapidly.

"With that in mind, come to Doyle's open mic this week."

Panic flooded Hannah, washing away all her inappropriate

thoughts. "Like I told you when you brought this up before, I don't know if I'm ready for—"

"—which is the ideal time to strike. Do it before your head says definitely no." She clicked her tongue against the roof of her mouth. "Don't book yourself up for Tuesday. You're coming with me."

Hannah knew better than to argue. Plus, Cordy was helping her, and she had a performance coming up.

"Besides, it's time you moved this along. We've got a booking in three months, and you've got a drag competition to win. You need to get up to speed. Because here's the secret: you'll never be ready." Cordy put a hand on her hip, then pointed at the orange. "What would Elvis do?"

"Eat too many hamburgers?"

Cordy gave her a scowl. "This is *clearly* early Elvis. He'd get on stage and do his thing."

Hannah decided she liked Cordy's teacher vibe a little too much.

"Do you have an idea of what you want to wear?"

"Not sure, but a cool suit? Something gangster, sexy."

"Can you sew?"

"No."

"My gran can. She used to be a fashion designer back in the day. If you need help, she can be our hero. Between us, charity shops, and a needle and thread, we can make this work."

Somehow, Hannah had landed on her feet with Cordy moving in. But she needed to slow her heartbeat down, and stop staring at the skin above her breasts. Stop wondering if the flash in Cordy's green eyes held any kind of want for her, too. Because if there was anything sure to bugger up their dynamic, it was sleeping with her.

That was very much off the table.

Chapter Eleven

"Hello my youngest daughter. How are you?"

Hannah's dad, Greg, leaned across from the driver's seat and pulled her into a hug. His salt-and-pepper bristles grazed Hannah's face as he did, which made her smile. He'd sported a well-groomed beard even before they were fashionable. He'd joked with her that he was a hipster now, which had made all his daughters laugh. With his collection of loud shirts and penchant for wide-brimmed hats, Greg could never be a hipster.

"I'm good, Dad." Hannah clicked her seatbelt into place as her dad pulled away. He'd been picking her up from this train station all on her own for the past five years, ever since she moved to London. She wondered when and if that would ever change. Maybe Cordy would come back with her one day? She'd already said she didn't hate the idea.

"Nice to see you. Christmas was nearly three months ago. It's been a long time."

Guilt stirred in her stomach, but she ignored it. She liked her family well enough, but they lived very different lives to her. She didn't enjoy explaining over and over why she wasn't working in a well-paid corporate role, so she came back when needed. Christmas. Birthdays. Event days. Like today.

"Your sisters will be pleased to see you, too. As they keep

reminding me as we shoo your mum out of the kitchen, they're mothers too, so they also deserve a rest on Mother's Day. Apparently, you and I should be preparing Sunday lunch."

"They just love to moan. Try and kick them out of the kitchen, and they'd soon moan even more."

When they arrived at her parents' detached house, the smell of roasted meat and delicious desserts hung in the air. She might not come home as often as her family would like, but when she did, the food was a big draw. Food was serious business in her family. Not for the first time, Hannah thought she should have paid attention at home. Maybe then she'd be able to do more than scramble a few eggs and butter some toast.

"Have you lightened your hair?" Eldest sister Amy held some of Hannah's locks in her hand and studied them. Nobody else in her life manhandled her like family.

"She's just naturally light because of the stress-free life she leads," middle sister Betty told her. "No kids, no stressful job, living her best life in London. I swear, in a decade, Hannah will look younger than she does now."

Hannah held her tongue. Her family had no idea about the stresses of her life. Mainly because she didn't tell them.

Her mum, Polly, gave her a tight smile, then tapped her on the shoulder, like she was feeling for a plug socket in the dark. She tilted her head as she assessed her youngest daughter. "Are you eating okay? You look thinner." She pinched her waist, and Hannah recoiled. "And where are the buttons on this coat?" Her mum held up the spaces where buttons should be. "I asked you that at Christmas, and you said you were going to sew them on. Do you want me to do it?"

Her mum was always practical, if not tactile. Hannah shook her head. "Can I get through the door without you all poking and prodding me?" She handed her mum a gift bag containing a bottle of her favourite New Zealand Sauvignon Blanc, along with a Terry's Chocolate Orange. "Happy Mother's Day."

"Aren't you freezing with no buttons?" Amy asked, taking her coat and hanging it up.

"Shut up, Grandma," Hannah replied.

Her mum peered in the bag and smiled. She knew what it was, Hannah got her the same thing every year. "Thank you, love."

Hannah walked through to the kitchen, glancing into the lounge as she walked by. No sign of her brother-in-laws or her nieces. "Have you given your husbands and children back to the shop? Faulty goods? I thought the warranty would have run out by now."

Amy and Steve had been together forever and had two daughters, Chloe and Harper. Betty had only married Ben two years ago, and had yet to spawn any kids, although they were trying. "Don't mention it at the weekend, whatever you do," her mum had texted. "It's a sore subject."

Hannah made a mental note.

"They've taken Chloe and Harper down the pub. They love the play area there. You should have seen how quickly Steve and Ben agreed."

For now, then, it was just the five of them. The original quintet. There were ten years between her and her sisters, Hannah the youngest. However, apart from her, none of her family had ever moved out of Surrey, or done anything they shouldn't with their lives. Her parents met at college and married in their early 20s, and both her sisters had done the same. They were all solidly middle-class, shopped in malls, ate at chain restaurants, and routinely watched the latest blockbuster movie whenever it came to the local cineplex.

Even though she knew her family loved her, Hannah also knew she confused them with her life choices. Hence, they held each other at arm's length, never getting too close. It was a vicious circle she'd like to break. But that time was probably not today.

"What can I do to help all you mothers, then?" Hannah pushed up the sleeves of her black top in a show of willing.

Amy rounded the kitchen island and shooed her to the other side. "It's done already."

"She can set the table," her mum countered.

Next to Hannah, Betty sighed. "You already made me do that."

Mum put a hand to her chin. "Did I? Going senile in my old age." She paused. "Get yourself a drink, then. You can stack the dishwasher later."

Hannah already knew that, too, would never happen. Her dad was territorial about his dishwasher. She perched on a stool at the kitchen island, trying and failing to relax.

Betty opened the fridge and held up a beer.

Hannah nodded, and her sister flipped the lid and passed it to her.

"What news then, little sis?" Amy grabbed some honey from the cupboard above the bread bin, then turned to Hannah. "Any new women in the pipeline?"

"No. But I do have a new flatmate since we last all saw

each other. She's called Cordy, she's a music teacher, and she's lovely. I think you'd all like her."

Hannah's pulse raced a little faster, reminding her that she definitely did.

Her mum picked up the gravy granules from the counter, then furrowed her brow. "Is that the new term for it these days? Flatmate? I thought everything was out in the open now?"

Hannah shook her head. "I'm not seeing her; she's actually my flatmate."

"But you live in a one-bedroom flat."

Hannah could understand the confusion. She took a swig of her beer before she replied. "She's got the bedroom, and I'm sleeping in the lounge. We've cordoned off an area with screens, so I've got a proper bed, and we've still got a lounge." She held up a hand. "And before you all start going on at me, this is what people do these days. London isn't cheap. If I wanted to keep the flat after Lauren left, I had to get creative. Or sell my body. I chose the former."

Her mum put the granules down and gave Hannah a hard stare. "If you need money, you come to us. You know that. We could have loaned you some."

Every hair on her body bristled. "I can look after myself, and I'm doing just that."

But the disappointment on her mum's face was evident. "But you had a good job where you could afford the rent solo. It's not too late to admit you made a mistake and go back to the bank. I'm sure they'd take you back. You were doing so well there—"

"—and I was miserable. I know you don't remember that part so much, but I really was."

"Are you that much happier now? Working in a juice bar is not what you got a degree in economics for."

"I don't work there anymore. Plus, I never wanted to do that degree. I was eyeing up the performance arts course, you know that."

"We never forced you." Her mum sighed. "You did English first. That was your shot at the arts and you didn't like it. You were the one who switched to economics when that didn't work. Plus, you did star in the uni productions, so you got your creative fix. You know that stage work and performing aren't the steady job we wanted for you. We were just thinking of you and your future."

"And I was thinking of you, too. Maybe that was the problem." Hannah frowned.

Her mum shook her head. "The only thing we want in the world is for you to be happy."

They always said that, but did they really mean it?

Her mum walked over and stood next to her. She tapped the top of Hannah's hand.

Hannah bit back tears. She wished she could come home and not feel like a fuck-up.

Eventually, she lifted her head. She'd managed not to cry, but she was sure her face told a story of vulnerability. "I haven't got a significant other, and I did a useless degree. I'm not like everyone in this room, who had it all worked out from a young age." She bit her lip. "Not everyone's life is as easy as all of yours."

Her mum let out a strange sound. Was it a snort? Her sisters did the same.

"Nobody knows what they want to do in life, we're all just winging it," Amy told her.

Hannah frowned. "But you've got the job, the house, the husband, the life."

Amy shrugged. "Doesn't mean I don't admire you. What you did, giving up your job, takes courage. Because once you're used to the money and you need it to support your lifestyle, then you're locked in. Whereas you're trying to forge a different path, and that takes guts." She reached over the island and put her hand on top of Hannah's. "Don't be dozy, we all support you. You'll work out what you want to do eventually. Better to take time than get it wrong. Just ask my husband. He hates his job, but won't retrain now."

This was information that had never been shared before. Maybe everyone else's life wasn't quite as rosy as she once thought.

"I should have taken that performance degree, because it's what I want to do." Hannah froze as the sentence escaped her lips before she'd truly had a chance to think it through. She did not intend to rock up here today and tell her family her deepest desires.

"What kind of performer?" Her mum's words were icy.

"I think you'd be an amazing singer or actor. You were great in that play you were in at uni." Betty's features perked up. Hannah had always got on best with her. But she could never tell her family she was doing burlesque or drag. That was a step too far. Letting them into her life a little too much. It wasn't who Hannah was. She needed to say something to throw them off the performer vibe.

"I haven't quite narrowed it down yet, but I'm leaning into that side of my life."

"What side of life are you leaning into?" Her dad wandered

into the kitchen, then stopped and frowned. "Have I missed something? Why is everyone staring at Hannah?"

Hannah took a breath. "Let me catch you up, Dad. I've jacked in my juice job. I want to be a performer. I've got a new flatmate which means I'm now sleeping in my lounge." She paused. "And one more thing that might tip Mum over the edge: I've got a new job as a cycle courier to pay the bills."

Her mum slapped her forehead with her palm. "Bikes in London? Have you got a helmet? Hi-vis clothing?" She shook her head. "You know what, everything else I can live with. Perform as a stripper, if you want. Women fought hard for the right to do that."

Hannah kept her mouth shut very tight lest anything else slip out.

"But cycling in London is so dangerous."

"And you're sleeping in your lounge?" her dad added. "We can lend you some money. Even give you some. Both your sisters have had their wedding money. You're owed that. We can give it to you up front?"

"What if I want to get married down the line?" Did he not think she was the marrying kind? She bristled at that news. Then she thought of Cordy telling her to breathe through it. To relax. Her singing lessons related to life, too.

"We can work something out."

Her mum held her head in her hands and exhaled. "You know what, you lot were far simpler when you were kids. Now I have to worry about Hannah getting killed on the road or starving trying to make it, Amy getting over her issues with Steve, and Betty getting pregnant."

"Mum!" shouted Amy and Betty at the same time.

Her mum held up her hands. "What? I never know what I can and can't say. We're all family here, we should all talk like normal people."

Hannah's ears prickled as she slowly cast her gaze around the kitchen. Perhaps she didn't know her family, but how much did they know of each other, either?

***

After a surprisingly relaxed lunch – Chloe and Harper could chat under wet cement – and after Amy, Steve, and the kids left to get home in time for the football, Betty dragged Hannah into the kitchen under the pretence of clearing up. Hannah knew it was really an interrogation. When Betty cornered her against the counter, it only confirmed it.

"Come on then. There's more to this than you're letting on. Spill." Betty's coffee breath reminded Hannah of her favourite teacher at school, Mrs Brady.

"What do you want to know?"

"All of it! Are you sleeping with your flatmate?"

"No!" She thought back to their chat on the balcony. The fact that Cordy had messaged her a link to some good breathing exercises to warm up her voice. The way she looked forward to Cordy's presence when she walked into the flat now. Even if she wasn't there, her tea mug on the draining board or her cardigan on the armchair warmed Hannah. She hadn't realised how lonely she'd been until Cordy moved in.

"Quick answer." Betty tilted her head and moved her face closer to Hannah in a way only family or lovers did. "Are you telling the truth?"

"If I sleep with her, you'll be the first to know."

"If or when?"

Hannah rolled her eyes and pushed Betty away.

Betty laughed, then started to stack the dishwasher with the plates.

"Don't do that. You know what Dad's like."

Her sister ignored her. "He'll get over it." She dropped a knife and fork into the cutlery block, but the fork bounced off and landed in the bottom of the dishwasher. Betty swore, and fished it out. She got gravy up her forearm in the process.

Hannah bit her lip not to laugh.

"Say I believe you're not sleeping with this woman. My next question: is she cute?"

This time, Hannah couldn't help the blush that worked its way onto her cheeks.

Betty grinned as she sponged her arm with the dishcloth. "When, then." She gave Hannah a triumphant smile. "And performing? What does that mean?"

Hannah shook her head. She wasn't ready to divulge that. She was only telling her family the truth when she had something real and tangible to point to. "It's a work in progress. I'll tell you when I'm sure."

Her sister threw up her hands. "Your life is so mysterious. But I'll wait until you're ready. Twenty quid says you'll sleep with your flatmate before I see you next." She paused. "Seriously, I think it's great you've got a flatmate. Whether you're sharing a bed or not. I know Lauren broke your heart. I'm glad you're moving on."

"Thanks, sis."

Betty's arms encircled her, and Hannah had to admit, even if her mum was prickly, her sister more than made up for it.

***

Hannah pulled out her phone as the train unzipped the surrounding countryside. Beside her, her bike was firmly wedged into the six-seat space she occupied. Luckily, it wasn't a busy train.

You home tonight? She messaged Cordy.

She got a thumbs up moments later, followed by, *but you can have the lounge. I'm lesson prepping in my room and having an early night. Hope your lunch went well.*

> *It was one of my more interesting family days.*

> *Sounds intriguing,* Cordy texted. *Top three family dinners? It's a toss-up between when my brother told Dad he'd got a tattoo. I thought my dad would storm out. Which is what he did when Gran told him she was gay and had lived a lie all her life. My third most favourite was the day we first went to McDonald's as a kid and Mum bought me and Elliott Happy Meals. Nothing will ever top that.*

Hannah grinned stupidly at her phone. She loved getting these little insights into Cordy's life. She often re-read them.

> *Top three family dinners? The best was the Christmas my eldest niece Chloe pulled the tablecloth, and the stuffing and gravy jug fell onto the carpet. Carnage ensued. Closely followed by today when my mum told me she'd rather I be*

a stripper than a cycle courier. Words I never expected to come out of her mouth. Then there was the time my dearly departed gran told me, in a really loud voice, that she regained her love of reading when she discovered sexy books. She waited until a good lull in conversation to ask me if I read sexy books, too.

She received a line of laughing emojis back from Cordy, followed by, *What's your ETA?*

8.30. Stopping for a bagel en route and to say hi to Sylvie. She's excited about the drag king competition. Says she used to know some in Ukraine. That woman has hidden depths. Shall I pick you up a bagel?

Yes please! I'll have the kettle on. Elvis would like a bagel in the form of a burger.

Chapter Twelve

Cordy pulled in her piano stool and flicked out the back of her tailcoat. She liked to dress the part for nights like these. With her sparkly gold shoes, ruffled white shirt and top hat sitting on the piano, she hoped she succeeded. Maybe there was a bit of a drag king inside her, too, and she'd just never named it. That thought made her smile.

Beyond that, Doyle's Cocktail Bar was a regular, local gig that paid well, and she wanted to do everything in her power to keep it. Plus, she got to perform a little herself, which was always a treat. She didn't get to strut her stuff in the spotlight often, and she was thrilled that Gran and Joan were here to see her, along with Hannah, Greta, and Theo. She was well aware that Theo being here made Hannah sweat, but as Cordy had told her, wasn't it better to try out her act somewhere other than on the night it mattered most? Plus, they'd practised together. She was ready.

Cordy launched into her first number: a slowed down, piano version of Shania Twain's 'Man, I Feel Like A Woman!' Her foot caressed the pedal, and her fingers did the same to the keys. Her voice was a little rusty at first, but when she got to the first chorus, the rust fell away and she hit her stride. This was a number she hadn't done too much before, and when she glanced up, Hannah's eyes focused on her, her mouth quirked one way. What was she thinking? Was she nervous about her upcoming performance? Impressed with Cordy? She hoped so. Cordy's family had seen her perform before, but this was Hannah's first time. She hoped, that unlike Shania's other big hit, she impressed her much.

The crowd applauded politely when she finished, a clear sign it was the first song. Cordy didn't mind, that was her job. She was the warm-up act, the fluffer. So long as the crowd applauded the public who got up to sing, her night was winning. She waited for the applause to die down before she continued.

"Thank you so much. I've got one more, before I invite my grandparent, Joan, up to join me for a song. This is not nepotism, it's purely because nobody else has put a request in. If you'd like to sing a song, please put your requests in to the lovely Khadeja who is circulating with an iPad. By the magic of technology, it'll then pop up on my screen and if I can play it, you can sing it. If I don't know it, you'll have to sing louder."

The audience laughed, and Cordy grinned. The vibe was good. The crowd would dare to put up requests soon – Khadeja was already being flagged down as she walked the room. Cordy launched into her second number, a gorgeous version of Kate Bush's 'Running Up That Hill'. She imagined her hand over her heart as she played, and felt the music pulsing through her veins as she sang. Ba-boom. Ba-boom. Ba-boom. She wasn't joking when she told her students to do this. When she'd told Hannah and Romilly to do it, they'd really improved.

True to her word, for the next song, Joan joined her at the piano. She'd worked in theatre production all her life, but she was also quite the singer. It had taken some prodding to get Joan to agree to do this, but now she stood at the mic, her grey hair short and pristine, her navy-blue suit made to measure. She could just imagine her in the 50s. She'd seen the photos. Her gran had good taste. Cordy would have fallen for her back then, too.

Cordy leaned into the mic. "Everyone, this is Joan, my gran's wife. She used to sing this song back in the 1950s in the factory where she and my gran met, and in the underground gay bars on the scene. Joan even sang it at the historic Gateways club. Joan is a queer icon." She never got tired of saying stuff like that.

The crowd cheered this information, and the crew at the table beside Cordy sat up a little straighter. She glanced at Joan, eyes glistening, a wistful smile on her face. Cordy gave her a nod, then launched into the opening bars of 'You Belong To Me.'

Joan's voice was smooth from the start, and tonight, she sang only to her wife. Cordy couldn't look at her gran if she wanted to make it to the end. When she and Joan got there, the applause was rapturous, with many of the bar on their feet. Joan walked back and kissed the top of her gran's hand. Cordy swallowed the lump in her throat. Her grandparents' love for each other always left her breathless.

"Give it up for the superstar that is Joan, and my wonderful gran, Eunice!" More whistles and applause from the crowd. "Next up to follow that we have Davina, Rex, and Yves, followed by Japhet, Christina, Stefan, and then Hannah. Come on up, Davina!"

A woman in her 40s with a slick black bob and perfect lipstick sidled up to the piano, with a swagger that told Cordy this was not her first rodeo. Cordy checked she knew the words to this Carpenters' classic, then launched into the intro. Davina nailed it, and took her bow. Rex and Yves roared out a couple of crowd-pleasers. Japhet sported a smooth trilby, and matched its vibe with an equally smooth cover of Boyz II Men. Christina was the Susan Boyle of the evening, hitting a note-perfect cover of 'I Know Him So Well.' Meanwhile, builder Stefan was a piano-karaoke virgin, but nailed The Killers' 'Mr Brightside' with aplomb.

"Last up before I go for my first break, we have my flatmate, Hannah. It's also her first time singing live with a piano, so please crack out your warmest applause as we welcome her to the stage for a spot of Bowie."

Cordy's gaze followed Hannah from her seat to the piano. She wore a pair of black trousers and a black denim shirt, both of which fitted her perfectly. She'd also managed to sculpt her hair into a new style, one more befitting of a drag king. Hannah might not know it, but she was already moving towards Max. It was a look that made Cordy's heart pump that little bit harder, her thighs flex beneath her keys. Hannah was giving off a different vibe tonight. More confident. It made Cordy want to lean in and touch her.

Hannah clutched the mic, took a deep breath and gave Cordy a panicked stare. Cordy didn't start to play right away. She simply held Hannah's gaze, put a hand over her heart and tapped, while mouthing: "Ba-doom, ba-doom, ba-doom."

Something flared behind Hannah's eyes. Something that told Cordy she understood. That she might be able to do this. Even though her opening lines wobbled slightly, when Hannah hit the first chorus, muscle memory took over, and she flew.

Then, encouraged by whooping from Greta and Theo, she started to engage the audience. To sing *to* them. To perform. And when she did, she lit up. So did Cordy. Seeing Hannah do this, and knowing she had a part in it was what she loved about teaching. It was freeing. The audience reaction should tell her she was good. Now she just had to believe it and sell it. As she hit the final note and raised her fist in the air, she did just that.

"Thank you, Hannah, and to all my first-act performers. See you in 20 minutes for more of the same. If you haven't put up a number, there's still time. We're only one act down, two to go!"

Cordy jumped up from her stool, walked to the table and embraced Hannah. She swore she could almost feel the thump of her heart through her clothes. When she let go and their gazes latched, her equilibrium shifted, and she had to take an extra breath.

"You were amazing! You remembered everything we talked about, and you sold it."

"She totally sold it!" Theo agreed, giving Hannah a slap on the back as Cordy sat on the vacant stool beside her. "First Joan, then Hannah. We have a talented table!"

Joan blushed bright red. "You know what, it was marvellous. I haven't sung in public in forever. It really took me back."

"You weren't the only one," Gran chimed in.

"I enjoyed it, too," Hannah said. "But it just confirmed that I need all the practice I can get."

Theo smiled broadly. "You were great. Plus, by the time you come to perform, you'll be even more fluid. You won't know where Hannah stops and Max starts." They leaned forward. "Once you've got your makeup and costume on, it's going to be perfect. Just imagine doing it to a room full of queers, all of them wanting to sleep with you."

Hannah blinked. "All of them?"

Theo grinned. "All the women."

"Blimey." Hannah looked like she couldn't quite compute that. "It was good having you all here, though. More pressure on me, which is what I need to get used to." She pointed a finger between Joan and Cordy. "Although I can't ever imagine performing with my family in the audience."

"You need to invite them first," Cordy said.

Hannah shuddered. "Not likely. It's not really their scene."

"You never know until you try. I speak from experience," Gran added. "Maybe they'd love to come to your drag show."

"They're far too strait-laced."

"Or maybe you are."

Cordy blinked. Gran was sharing some tough love.

Hannah studied the floor.

Cordy embraced the awkward pause with a spread of her arms. "Whereas I like to mix up all my groups, and I'm living proof it can work."

Khadeja delivered a glass of red wine to Cordy. She thanked her, took a sip, then pointed to Theo. "Are you up for opening round two?"

Theo nodded. "Of course. Gotta show Hannah how it's done, haven't I?"

* * *

Hannah's second song, a slowed-down rendition of Bruno Mars' 'Uptown Funk', had gone down a treat, too. When she'd arrived back at the table, Cordy's family and friends swallowed her up in a blur of hugs, which had given Cordy goosebumps. Ever since she'd moved in, Hannah had slowly taken on more importance in Cordy's life, and she wanted her gran and Joan to like her, too. Tonight had been a good start.

Now everyone else had disappeared, and Hannah was currently a few steps ahead of Cordy, holding open the gate to a kid's playground near their flat. At nearly 11pm, it was empty.

"What's this gate doing open?" The sign on the wire fence beside it told Cordy the playground closed at 7pm.

"I guess whoever normally locks up took the night off." Hannah inclined her head. "Fancy a go on the seesaw?"

They walked in together, and Cordy waited for Hannah to straddle the seesaw, before doing the same herself. "Ready?" she asked.

Hannah nodded, and without any warning, pushed off.

As the seesaw sailed into the air, Cordy's arse almost wobbled off its wooden perch, but she managed to grasp the metal handle at the last to save herself.

"Fuck me!" she shouted as the seesaw went down, then up again. But this time, Cordy was ready. Just about. "I nearly crashed to my death there. Good job I've got strong fingers from all my piano playing." Did that sound as dorky as it sounded coming out of her mouth?

"Is that what you say to all the girls?"

Cordy stuck out her tongue in a very mature response. Then tried not to think of whether or not Hannah's fingers were strong, too.

"Anyway, enough about my fingers." What the hell was wrong with her mouth? "Let's talk about how you fucking killed it tonight."

Hannah also might *actually* kill her if she kept pushing off as if she was aiming for space. Cordy hung on as if her life depended on it. Which it did. She could imagine the headlines if she fell off and hit her head: *Tipsy pianist hits head and dies. Claims Darwin award.*

"It went okay, didn't it?" But Hannah's smile, lit by moonlight, told her she thought she'd killed it, too.

"More than okay. Think how good you'll be when you play Kate and Meg's leaving party." Up above, the night sky was a patchwork quilt of stars.

Hannah cast her gaze there before replying. "That's the plan. But didn't you say Ruby O'Connell might be playing it, too? I've only done two songs. I'm not sure I'm ready to be on stage with a worldwide superstar."

Cordy was finally getting used to the ebb and flow of the seesaw. The whoosh of air on her face as she sailed upwards. How did kids do this so effortlessly? They were more talented than she gave them credit for.

"It hasn't been confirmed yet, but if she does, what an opportunity. Apparently she's lovely, and it's a chance for us to impress her. You never know, she might want some drag kings on her next tour. If nothing else, it's a room full of affluent queer women who might want to book both of us again."

"She might hire you as her piano player."

"Stranger things have happened," Cordy replied, the final part of the last word swallowed up as Hannah's push-energy got the better of her, and she nearly fell off again. "Okay, hold up." When she reached the ground again, she didn't push off. "Can we go on the swing, please? Something I'm in control of?"

She dismounted gingerly, fully expecting the seesaw to slam up and hit her in the face, but she managed to escape with no injury. Hannah joined her on the swings in a matter of seconds. They both got their momentum going, looking to their left through the fence where a bunch of teenagers sat on a bench, laughing. Luckily, nobody had joined them in the playground yet. The wind whistled through Cordy's hair as she swung forwards, then back. Being on any playground ride was a little like life: get some momentum, hold on tight, then hope you can keep it going and hang on.

"Thanks for tonight, by the way. It was good to do that in front of an audience before the big drag night next week."

"No problem." Cordy paused. "When I see Kate again, I can tell her you're definitely on for performing at her party?"

Hannah gulped in a big breath of air, then nodded as she swung. "Sure, it will give me something to aim for post-competition." She shook her head. "Look at me, aiming for things." She glanced at Cordy.

Cordy's heart stuttered, then melted.

They both slowed to a gentle swing.

"You've given me the push I needed. I was brought up to believe that performing was something other people did. Spreadsheets are what my family do. That, and not rocking the boat. I share a lot of my family values, but you're helping me to uncover my own."

"I think you were doing fine on your own doing burlesque, which is hardly conforming." The swing's metal chains were cold under Cordy's fingertips. It was in stark contrast to her heartbeat, which thudded in her veins.

"I get that, but this path feels more like me. Burlesque was my rebellion. But singing live is pushing me more. It feels more daring than shaking nipple tassels."

"Don't do yourself down." Cordy slowed to an almost stop as she traded gazes with Hannah. Something was on the tip of her tongue, but she couldn't quite work out what it was.

Hannah's rich gaze didn't falter for a moment. It flowed through Cordy before Hannah spoke again. "One other thing. Seeing you and your family together tonight made me think that I should try more with mine. Try to remedy things a little. But them seeing me in drag might be a step too far. Maybe they could meet you first? The woman who's pushing me out of my comfort zone. Would you come home with me one Sunday? My mum would be thrilled. As would I."

"I already told you I'll come." The answer was crystal clear.

"You don't need to check your diary?"

She shook her head. "If I have something, I can rearrange it. This is important to you, so it's important to me, too."

"Thank you." Hannah glanced shyly at the ground, then brought her swing to a stop.

Cordy followed suit. When she put her foot on the ground and drew up alongside Hannah, their eyes locked again. Something inside Cordy roared. Something she hadn't felt in a very long time. Something she wasn't sure she was ready for. Heat and desire thumped through her.

"I wasn't sure how our flat arrangement was going to go, but it's turning out to be fantastic. You've helped me so much, and if there's anything I can do in return, just let me know." Hannah's golden eyes flickered in the fresh moonlight, then her gaze dropped to Cordy's lips.

Cordy's breath hitched as the situation suddenly became very real. Had she thought about kissing Hannah before? Maybe, but they'd always been vague images in her mind that she couldn't define. Now, the colours were rich, the pictures of what could happen fully formed. She could lean in right now and kiss Hannah. And damn it, she really wanted to. She'd been pushing the attraction away, but it wasn't going anywhere. Instead, it appeared to be growing. Could Hannah see her conflicted emotions in the dark?

Hannah's gaze dropped to Cordy's lips once more. "Anything you want. You deserve good things because you're a good person." Her lashes lowered with her gaze. The thick sweep of them was delicious. What would they feel like on Cordy's skin? On the back of her neck if Hannah kissed her there? She wanted to find out.

Cordy leaned in. As she did, the heat inside roared again. If Hannah was the fire, Cordy knew she risked getting burned. She didn't care.

"You're a good person, too," she replied.

Their lips were within inches of each other.

Cordy's heart rate accelerated.

Hannah's gaze roamed her face. Was she thinking the same thing? Searching for confirmation?

A buzz of excitement ran through Cordy. Should she go for it? Was she reading the signals right?

"Blake, there's two lezzers on the swings and they're gonna kiss!" The holler rang out into the night sky.

Cordy swung her head, to see two of the teenagers heading into the playground.

She and Hannah jumped apart and both stood up, brushing themselves down.

If anything was going to happen, it wasn't going to be here.

Chapter Thirteen

"Max, look sharp." Captain Von Strap snapped his fingers to demand attention.

Hannah's heart pumped her blood at rapid pace. No. Not her heart: Max's heart. Max tapped his moustache one final time to check it was still there. It was. Max's dance moves, patter, singing, and timing? That part, Hannah was less sure of. She'd practised in the flat, and in front of Theo to get some pointers. She was as ready as she could be after a month of living and breathing Max Girth. As Theo pointed out, "Just get out there and put your all into it. Nobody's expecting you to be Beyonce." Thank god, because Beyonce would look terrible with Max's five o'clock shadow and his slick, 1950s-style hair.

The Captain had just come off stage to rapturous applause. He was a fabulous singer who crooned exactly like a man. People didn't believe the Captain wasn't miming because his voice went so low, but he was the real deal.

Unlike Hannah, Theo was a professionally trained actor and singer. They'd worked in the West End, and now ran a silent disco company, as well as performing drag. Theo was the ultimate portfolio performer, never able to sit still, always wanting to juggle more. When Hannah asked if they could actually juggle, too, they'd rolled their eyes and nodded. "Of course I fucking can."

"Listen. Five minutes until you go on. The audience are lovely. Remember, you have the power, you know this shit. Just go out there and slay like the fucking king you are. Don't be a drag, just be a king, okay?"

Hannah nodded. She was a drag king. Fuck, she wished she had her nipple tassels. But right now, she had to become Max. Walk tall in his suit jacket, tight trousers and shiny black brogues. Feel the itch of his painted-on stubble.

Before he knew it, the Captain was back on stage, and Max's name was announced. Max filled his chest with air, then strode onto the small black stage just as he'd rehearsed with Theo. Wide stance. Swagger. Hips forward. Chin up. Adrenaline swirled around his body. The lights were brighter than he'd imagined. Max gripped the mic.

A flash of his mum singing the Bowie song ripped through his mind. That was Max's closer, song two. He'd love his mum to see him perform. He pushed that thought aside. Max had two songs to sing. A competition to win.

"Hello, fuckers!" Hannah's voice was naturally low. She didn't need to change a thing for Max. "My name is Max Girth, and I'm here because you deserve the best goddamn things in life, and I am one of them. Gold fucking standard. You ready?"

The audience hollered their approval.

Good start.

"I'm gonna do two songs for you before I have to rush off and see to some mobster business. Because life never stops, you know? People always need to be reminded they owe me money in the nicest possible way." He gripped the mic with his right hand and drew his shoulders back. "One song now, one song after the break. This first one goes out to all the ladies in the house. Music, maestro, please."

Max eyeballed the crowd and ran his left hand over his slick hair. The opening chords to Bruno Mars' 'Uptown Funk' waltzed through the bar, and the crowd went wild. He brushed who was in the audience from his mind: Theo, Cordy, Greta. Instead, Max focused on a woman he didn't know in the front row, and on what he had to do for the next three minutes. Act like a man, and sing like this was his last performance on earth.

However, as the first line approached, his mind went blank. There was nothing there. Max's shoulders tightened, his mouth a rictus grin.

He had to nail this.

It *had* to go well.

The intro ended and the first line of music sailed in. Max did not fill in the blanks. Shit, he was going to bomb. His whole drag king career over before it had even begun. Maybe Mum was right. The stage was where dreams went to die.

Dance. That was all he could do. He had to hope that the audience didn't notice he hadn't sung the first line, and now the second. Or that they were too drunk to care. He searched his mind, but it was a barren wasteland. He'd practised and practised. But perhaps he hadn't practised quite enough.

Suddenly, out of the corner of his eye, he spotted Cordy. Mouthing the next line.

Of course!

As soon as she filled in the space in Max's mind, all the

other lyrics dropped into place. It was as if his mind had pressed a button in a Vegas casino, and all the best fruits had dropped in a line. The song was now fully present in his mind. All thanks to Cordy. What would he do without her?

Adrenaline pumped through his veins as he hit the next line like it had never been an issue for a moment. When he started to sing and work the stage, the audience hollered and swayed along, their faces stretching into smiles when he hit the chorus and they joined in, just like Max had hoped. He held the microphone up as the crowd got louder.

Max cupped his ear. "I can't hear you!" He might have fucked up the opening verse, but he could still pull this back. He thrust his crotch for good measure, and as the audience screamed back at him, Max puffed out his chest.

At the front, three women had their hands in the air, unable to take their eyes off him. Plus, their eyes kept zipping from his face to his crotch. Were they trying to see if he was packing? That thought sent a buzz to Max's brain.

This was so different to burlesque, and yet, the performance dynamic was the same. You held the power. The audience wanted to be you, or fuck you. Max could live with either. But there was only one person he wanted to impress, and she was in the audience tonight.

Max had no time to process that as he slid into the second verse, then the chorus. The crowd were on his side. For the first time since that butt-clenching opening, he semi-relaxed. When the music stopped, the volume quadrupled, and he took a bow.

From the panic at the start, he could barely believe it was over. What started with a bunch of forgotten words and exposed nerves, ended with Max grinning from ear to ear. To his right, two women wolf-whistled. Straight ahead, a woman with a skull tattooed on her forearm eyed him hungrily. As the applause and cheers subsided, he allowed himself a shift in his eyeline, to the left, where Cordy grinned and gave him the thumbs-up.

"Thank you so much, I'm Max Girth. If you owe me money, I'll see you soon. Everyone else, I'll see you after the break!"

It wasn't until he got backstage that Max allowed himself a full breath. Every fibre of his being buzzed with endorphins. Moments later, the Captain was in the room, hugging him, telling him how well he did.

Max bounced on his toes, then shook his head. "I can't believe I forgot the words. Plus, I missed a few moves—"

"—only you noticed that. You were great, especially for your first go." Theo gave a who-cares shrug. "You've got the swagger, I'm telling ya! That performance was lit!"

Max certainly felt it. As did Hannah.

"Don't worry about the fuck-up. You recovered, that's what counts. If I were you, I'd get out there, go and meet your public. It's the interval now. If they see you, they're more likely to cheer. You're the last song on after the break. More of a chance to stick in their memory."

Max stared in the mirror: he liked what he saw, although he'd love to tweak his look for his next performance. Hopefully in this competition if he got through. Cordy's gran had said she could help.

But more than that, dressing like this, as a man? Hannah had always dressed in what her mum would call a 'boyish' way, but she naturally toned it down, because that's what society told her to do. But this look? With the exaggerated makeup, socks down the pants to create a bulge, and her breasts strapped down? She couldn't quite articulate how much she loved it. It made her walk taller, made every cell of her body applaud. She didn't want to be a man, but she loved impersonating one. That was becoming clear even after her first performance.

When Max walked into the bar, the noise and chatter seemed louder. Maybe everyone had got a little more drunk in the half hour since he went on stage. He scanned the bar, and clocked Cordy's red hair, then her wave. Max went to walk towards her, but his route was blocked by two women who stared like they wanted to devour him.

"We just wanted to say," said the woman on the left, "we thought you were incredible."

"And hot," said the woman on the right. Then she covered her mouth. "Shit, I can't believe that came out of my mouth, sorry."

Max brimmed with laughter. "I've had people tell me worse things, so thank you. Compliments always welcome." He navigated around them, but didn't make it to his destination without a man telling him he was amazing. Another thank you went his way. When Max arrived at Cordy's side, she flung her arms around him and squeezed tight.

From dodging heated gazes and wandering hands all the way here, this was a hug both Max and Hannah actually wanted.

When Cordy stepped back, she couldn't meet Max's eye. "You were incredible, and the crowd loved you. Your singing was on point." Cordy's gaze finally met Max's.

What Max saw there was unmistakable. Cordy looked at him just like the other women had. With desire. But was that just because she wanted Max? Or did she want Hannah, too? Were the two interchangeable? Even Hannah hadn't worked it out yet.

Was this the same look Cordy had given her on the swing the other night, when they'd almost kissed? Max couldn't be sure, but he'd swear it was close.

"Fuck me, Max," Greta said, shaking her head. "If I wasn't already having incredible sex with the Captain, I would spend all night trying to jump your bones after that. If anybody in this entire room doesn't want to fuck you, they must be dead."

Max spluttered. "Thanks, I think?"

Was it true what Greta just said? But even if it was only half true, that meant his ability to get laid might have exponentially increased. Nearly five months after Lauren, was he ready? He'd never know until he tried. It was the power of Max. People wanted Max. Maybe including Cordy, whose gaze still burned his skin.

Cordy put a hand on Max's arm, and he flinched. His skin flared hot under his shirt. Max's skin. His breath caught in his throat. Something had changed in the past hour and he didn't know what.

"Can I get you a drink?"

"Red wine," Max replied, suddenly in desperate need.

When Cordy returned moments later with drinks, Max was on his own.

"Where have the Captain and Greta gone?" Cordy asked, not quite meeting Max's gaze.

He nodded towards the stage. "The Captain's on again in a minute. I'm the final act, so I can stay for a little while. The backstage area isn't very big."

Cordy's gaze crawled back to him, but when she connected with Max, she looked to the floor.

Max did the same. Could Cordy feel the current humming between their bodies, too?

"I got your performance all recorded so you can upload to TikTok later. You were amazing, just as Greta said." Cordy gulped, and didn't meet his eye. "You ready for your final song?"

When they were at home, their conversation was easy. But tonight, something had shifted. He nodded. "As I'll ever be. I'm more confident now I've got the first one out of the way." He paused. "Thanks for saving me when I forgot the first line."

When Cordy smiled at him, her eyes crinkled adorably. "I've always got your back. But you'd have remembered it in the end. Because you're Max Girth." She gulped. "And for the record, I agree with what Greta said. You're fucking hot as Max, too."

Max gulped his drink. "Just as Max?"

Cordy thought for a moment, then shook her head. "I like all your flavours."

Chapter Fourteen

The following morning, Cordy was still discombobulated when she woke. She'd had a dream she couldn't remember, but all she knew was that she'd woken up hot. She stripped off her T-shirt, threw back her duvet and breathed out hard. In the next room, she heard movement. How had Hannah slept? Had she woken up thinking about last night, and more importantly, thinking about Cordy? Because beneath all the heat and fever dreams, Cordy was well aware of the root of the issue. Her growing attraction to Hannah. Not Max, who'd captivated everyone else last night. It wasn't the face paint or the performance that had lured Cordy. That was just the cherry on top. She wanted to get to know the person beneath more. She wanted to get to know Hannah. Or rather, to touch her after weeks of getting to know her and liking what she found.

She swung her legs out of bed and got up, rubbing her eye with the pad of her index finger. She peered through the curtains and eyed the pavements. They were wet. Just like she'd been watching Max perform last night.

As a performer herself, Cordy knew there was nothing as affirming as putting all your hard work into practice and seeing it pay off. As a performer and a teacher, it hit her sweet spot. Max had hit her sweet spot. Hannah had hit it again and again over the past few weeks. Now Cordy knew she wanted her to hit it in a new way. Her tangled dreams told her that. The surge between her legs confirmed it.

But there was one problem. She couldn't possibly tell Hannah that. They were living in a one-bedroom flat, in close quarters. If they had sex and she ultimately fucked this up, there would be no place to hide. And she couldn't turf Joan out of her writing room, that she'd already reclaimed. Plus, was Hannah even over her ex yet?

Max's gaze when he came off stage had been questioning. On the swing the other night, Hannah's lips had been close. So close, Cordy could smell the red wine on her breath, see the promise in her eyes. If she'd gone with her feelings and kissed Max last night, would Max have lifted a hand to Cordy's neck, trailed a thumb down her cheek, pressed his lips to her and kissed her right back? The thrill of getting off stage after you'd nailed your performance was a high that few people experienced. She hoped the thrill of kissing her might have topped it.

However, matters of the heart were never that straightforward. Even if she had kissed Max, Hannah might have stumbled back. They both needed this flat share. Against all the odds, it was currently working, and working well. Neither one of them wanted to be the reason that stopped.

Plus, if Hannah wasn't having the same thoughts, it would be a disaster. Cordy would have to live in this room forever. Only be in the flat when Hannah was at work. That was reason enough to be thankful she hadn't acted. Hopefully, she could keep her attraction under wraps. Pretend it wasn't really there. Go back to being Hannah's biggest cheerleader. She was good at that. Being a nurturer came naturally to Cordy. Being an assertive woman who knew what she wanted and went after it no matter what? She was still working on that part of her personality.

She shrugged on her dressing gown and eased open the bedroom door. When she stepped into the lounge, she was pretty sure she heard a sound from behind Hannah's partition. She was out of the shower. Which was good, because Cordy desperately needed a wee. She sprinted across the lounge without looking back just in case Hannah was half-naked, then opened the bathroom door, ready for the morning steam.

Only, morning steam wasn't all she got. No, when Cordy stepped into the bathroom, Hannah was still in there. And when the steam cleared and Cordy's eyes adjusted, beyond the steam, she saw skin. A whole lot of it.

Hannah had one leg up on the bath, still towelling off after her shower. Why hadn't she locked the door?

More than that, now all Cordy could think of was how it might feel to embrace Hannah's naked body with her own, part Hannah's legs, and press into her hot skin in every way possible. When she dragged her eyes up from Hannah's shapely legs, they landed on her impossibly taut stomach, and then onto her shapely breasts. Breasts that made Cordy involuntarily lick her lips.

Hannah, frankly, had cracking tits. Ones that were not at all suited to being a drag king. But ones that made Cordy's clit wake up with a start. She recalled Max trying to reign them in for his performance. But then, how Cordy had also been aware of them trying to break free as Max strutted and thrust his hips. When he found her in the crowd, she'd grown breathless.

It wasn't a patch on how she was feeling now.

However, that's clearly not what Hannah was thinking as she let out a shriek before hopping onto both legs, nearly tumbling into the sink, but righting herself at the final moment. When she realised she was fully naked and that Cordy was definitely looking, Hannah hoisted her towel in front of herself, before yelping "what the fuck?" at Cordy. "Did you ever hear of knocking?"

Even through the fog of steam, Cordy could make out her tomato-red blush.

"I'm sorry!" Cordy replied, backing out of the bathroom as she spoke. "I thought I heard you in the lounge so I assumed the bathroom was free."

"You didn't, and it wasn't."

Cordy was well aware. "I know that now." She pulled the door closed, then pressed her back up against the wall, and clutched her chest. She'd seen Hannah naked. She wanted to see it again. Her mind scrambled, and her bladder was insistent.

She turned back towards the door. "Also, can you hurry up. I'm dying for a pee!"

"Fuck off!"

Hannah definitely liked her, too.

* * *

This morning had raised more questions than answers, despite her resolve when she woke up. Seeing Hannah in her birthday suit only made Cordy want to break the rules that little bit more. She'd never been one for playing by them in the first place. Being queer in itself was a rule break of sorts, even though she had no control over who she found attractive. But if there was one thing she'd learned from her gran's life, it was that playing by the rules wasn't always the right thing to do. But was she brave or foolish enough to cross that line?

Luckily, work provided enough distraction for now, with her regular music students along with the school summer concert preparations in full flow. Greta, despite teaching maths, was helping her out. She wasn't sure if she did it for the love of the kids and the school, or just the general amusement of seeing 13-year-olds sing pop songs that weren't really suited to their age.

"I'm telling you, the Head is going to go a different shade of purple when he finally gets to hear this on the night." Her bright pink top made her resemble a tub of Vanish.

Cordy frowned as she packed her bag, waving goodbye to the final students. "He's going to love it. I've already told him it's a pop-themed concert. Plus, the pupils should sing what they want to, not prescribed old stuff that was made up by some bloke years ago. That way, they really put their heart into it."

"What about Romilly, doing her piano solo with Barry Manilow's 'Mandy'?"

Cordy laughed hard at that. "Her parents are big into Barry, and they persuaded her to 'try something modern'."

"Are they time-travellers from the past?"

"It wouldn't do for us all to be the same, now would it?" But even Cordy couldn't contain her smirk. She'd thought she might lose the kids doing Take That, but they all seemed to know it. When Romilly had rocked up with the sheet music to 'Mandy', she'd been gobsmacked.

"Indeed not."

Cordy lowered the lid on her piano and wrinkled her nose. The school auditorium always had an air of dust about it, even though it was cleaned regularly. She could also still smell the cottage pie and chicken supreme that had been on the menu for lunch today from the school canteen next door.

"Fancy a drink before you go home?" Greta asked.

"Yes, please." Hannah had a burlesque gig later, and Cordy didn't want to face her today. She needed a bit of distance from the situation after the bathroom incident this morning. Distance would remind her that she needed this flat more than she needed to jump Hannah. She just hoped that Hannah was having the same thoughts.

Or perhaps she hoped she wasn't.

Greta snapped her fingers in front of her eyes. "Hello? Earth to Cordy?"

Cordy shook her head. "Sorry, miles away."

"I could tell." Greta paused. "Anything you want to share?"

Cordy bit her lip. She'd love to, but if she did, it would make it more real. She didn't need that at all. Right now, she and Hannah as anything other than friends only existed in her head. She shook her head.

"No, just a lot on my mind with the concert and getting everything right." It sounded plausible enough.

They walked across the hall, turned out the lights, and exited into the school grounds. To their right, the main teaching building stood in darkness, just the head teacher's office light still on. Cordy nipped into the staffroom to get her coat, and then they walked to the nearby pub, the Dog & Duck.

It being a Thursday, the place was heaving with an after-work crowd. They ordered two pints of lager and some crisps, and found a table in the corner under the dart board. So long as it wasn't in use, they'd be fine.

Cordy took a sip of her drink. "How are things with you and Theo? They were on fire again the other night." She leaned in. "Tell me, are they Theo or Captain Von Strap when you get home?"

A wide grin took up residence on Greta's face. "A little bit of both, lucky me." She linked an arm through Cordy's. "I owe you for introducing us in the first place. If I hadn't come to that first drag king night, we'd never have met, and I wouldn't be having the best sex of my goddamn life."

"You're welcome."

Greta grinned. "What about Hannah? Does she strut around as Max at home all the time?"

Cordy chewed on the inside of her cheek to stop herself saying anything. "A little, especially in the buildup. But not in the same way as you two, clearly. We're not together."

Greta tapped her arm and raised an eyebrow. "But might you be? I picked up on something between you the other night. I'm not just imagining it, am I?"

But Cordy was quick to shake her head and shut down Greta's line of questioning. "We're getting on, and you've seen the size of the flat. Neither of us can afford to fuck up what we've got with a mindless shag."

"Does it have to be mindless?"

"It couldn't work in the long run, could it? I need this

flat, so does Hannah. Friends is where we are and where we'll stay."

Greta held her gaze, then picked up her drink. "If you say so."

"I do," Cordy replied.

An awkward pause sat between them. Luckily, Greta jumped in to save it. "I meant to say, Theo's putting on a drag brunch in a few weeks. Third Sunday in April. Fancy coming along? If I stay at theirs the night before, we could walk together. I know Hannah can't make it because Theo already asked her."

Cordy pulled out her phone and looked up the date. A blush crawled onto her cheek because she knew how her reply was going to sound after what she'd just told Greta.

"I can't make that. For the same reason that Hannah can't make it."

Greta raised an eyebrow. "What are you doing together on a Sunday?"

Cordy pursed her lips before she replied. "Going to Hannah's family for Sunday lunch. As a *friend*." But even she knew that sounded like anything but a friend.

"Let me get this straight. Or not. Your flatmate, Hannah, is taking you to meet her entire family for Sunday lunch?"

"That is correct."

She tilted her head. "Are you sure you haven't slept together?"

Cordy couldn't help but laugh. "We haven't. It's just..." She didn't want to share too much. But then again, she had to share something or she'd go mad. "Hannah keeps her life and her family separate. They want to be let in. She asked me to come with her so her family can meet me as they're curious. It's a big step for her, opening herself up to them." Cordy put a hand to her chest. "I'm just happy I can help."

Greta made a sound somewhere between a grunt and a laugh. "That's very noble of you."

"It's very friendly of me. Because we're friends. Nothing more." She was now very sure her cheeks were on fire. "Now let's change the subject before I dump this pint in your lap, shall we?"

Chapter Fifteen

"Please come in here and try on the stuff." Cordy put a hand on her hip, fingers splayed. "I have a big mirror and great light to do your makeup."

Hannah sucked on her cheek. She didn't want to make things muddled. This was Cordy's room now, not hers. But she knew the light was the best in there.

"It makes more sense, and I won't take no for an answer. I'll even wait in the lounge while you change." She raised an eyebrow. "Although I have seen it all before."

"Touché." She wasn't going to give up on this, was she? "Okay. And thank you." Hannah grabbed her makeup bag and walked through to the room.

She'd only glimpsed it since she moved out, hadn't truly been in the space and breathed it in. It smelled different, of Cordy: sweet and warm. Cordy had also strung some coloured lights above the bed, and had a couple of prints on the wall, too. In the short time she'd been there, she'd managed something that had eluded Hannah. To truly settle into her space, and make the flat her home. Hannah hadn't done it with Lauren, and she certainly hadn't done it since her ex left. Maybe she'd never done it in her life. That was a sobering thought.

"It feels good in here. Homely. Relaxing." But perhaps it wasn't about the space. Perhaps it was more about the person occupying it.

Cordy caught her eye and gave her a smile. "Thanks." She paused. "How many outfits are we trying today?"

"A few different ties and shirts. Trousers and jacket are already decided, after your gran worked her magic. Did she get the chocolates I sent?"

"She did, and she loved them."

"I love her," Hannah grinned. "Anyway, that, plus makeup. Do I go full beard or five o'clock shadow? Do I keep the moustache? All these choices men have to make on a daily basis."

"Poor them. It's incredible how they get through the day." Cordy raised a sarcastic eyebrow. "Is Max based on anyone you know?"

Hannah shook her head. "I met some kings at the drag workshop who were basing their characters on their dads or brothers. But my dad is not a macho guy. Also, he was never a mob boss."

"That you know of." Cordy tapped her index finger on her nose.

Hannah grinned. "I watched some movie clips of the 1950s mob bosses, and based Max on them." She flexed her jaw and pulled back her shoulders. "I thought about making myself a boat skipper or pilot, just for the peaked cap obvs, but everyone at the workshop seemed to be going that way. Plus, I didn't want to tread on Theo's toes. Instead, I figured I'd just be as macho as possible and ham it up. Truly get into character. Be a lady-killer."

"Maybe you need to practice that in real life. Like on those dating shows where they make participants approach people and ask for their phone numbers."

Hannah shuddered. "That sounds like my worst nightmare."

"You need to work out who your character is, really feel him. Max is a part of you, so let's work it out while you're applying your facial hair." Cordy pulled out the stool tucked inside her dressing table. "Take a seat, please," she said, with an arm flourish.

Hannah frowned. "Why do I feel like you should have been running that drag workshop? You sound like Theo." She sat.

Cordy grinned. "We're performers, we know what it takes." She paused. "How does Hannah chat up women?"

"She doesn't. I thought we already established that. No sex for months, remember?" Hannah grabbed a brown pencil, leaned into the mirror and began dotting on some stubble. The mere mention of the word 'sex' in Cordy's bedroom made her pulse tick that little bit faster. She avoided eye contact and cleared her throat.

"How did you and Lauren get together?"

Hannah stopped her application. "We bumped into each other at a bar, drank too much sambuca, ended up in bed. The usual."

"How would Max have chatted her up?"

She thought for a moment. "He'd have been far more intentional. He'd have watched her, bought her a drink, chatted her up, made her feel special. He's an old-fashioned gentleman under the bluff and facade."

"Would Hannah like to be more like Max?"

Heat rose in Hannah's cheeks. Her clit hardened under Cordy's intense gaze. She cleared her throat before she answered. "Of course, but it only works when I'm in character. When I do burlesque, I'm Velvet Minnelli, the sexiest woman on the planet. When I do drag, I want to be the most irresistible and charismatic man in the room. But Hannah can never hope to get to those levels."

"Why not?" Cordy stepped in front of her, wielding a darker coloured pencil. "Do you mind if I add in some flecks on this, too? Under the lights, this is going to stand out more. Something I noticed from the kings at the other show we went to."

At Hannah's nod, Cordy leaned into her space and shaded in Hannah's cheekbones.

Hannah breathed her in. She tried not to stare into Cordy's cleavage, which winked at her from close range. Cordy's breath tickled Hannah's face and her fingers were centimetres from her skin as she worked. Hannah admired their dexterity. And perhaps their strength. She wondered what they might feel like elsewhere.

"Have you done this before?"

The tips of Cordy's fingers grazed her skin as she smudged the make-up across Hannah's cheekbone. A tiny tremor ran through Hannah. It had been a while since anybody had touched her like this. A while since she'd allowed it. The closeness sent a tingle through her body. She'd missed it.

"I'm a musician from a creative family. I've had to step in at the last minute backstage on many occasions to touch up makeup. You don't have to worry."

"I wasn't worried."

Cordy narrowed her eyes. "Good." She flexed her arm, then brought the pencil back to Hannah's cheek.

She didn't know how Cordy had landed in her life, but Hannah was very glad she had. She was a positive influence. Someone who somehow understood where she was coming from and where she wanted to be. Cordy didn't hold back. A little like Theo. Also, a little like her ex, Lauren, whose parting shot at Hannah echoed in her head.

"You're never going to be who you really are until you accept yourself and start living your life for you. That means doing a job that allows you to be free, holding your girlfriend's hand in public, and telling your family about your life."

Maybe Hannah had finally found her calling, but letting her family in was still some way off. Her life and theirs couldn't co-exist. They'd probably never even heard of drag kings. They rarely even came to London.

All of that played into keeping her real life under wraps, and not believing in herself. She knew that. But she'd lived that way for so long, she wasn't really sure how to change it. It wasn't as easy as flicking a switch.

Cordy stood back, assessing her handiwork, then pointed at her mirror. "What do you think?"

Staring back at Hannah was someone with a very prominent five o'clock shadow. It suited her. Something stirred deep inside. Was this who she was meant to be all along? She stood up and touched her cheek. She circled her hips and stood taller.

"I love it." She turned to the left, then the right. "I feel stronger, taller. I almost want to grab my crotch, which Theo encouraged in the drag workshop."

Cordy pinned Hannah with her vibrant green gaze. "Why don't you do it, then?"

Hannah stared at her, this woman who supported her dreams, rather than questioning them. A thrill ran through her. Before she could second-guess herself, she put her hand between her legs, clutched, and thrust her hips forward.

A slow smile spread on Cordy's lips, and her eyes narrowed. "Do it again." Her voice was dark molasses. "This is how you get to know who your character is. You're up against Sir Loin of Beef in the next round. You need to bring your A game."

Heat rippled through Hannah. This was how she did it? By touching herself up in front of other people? But it did unlock something inside her. A certain masculine energy. Hannah thrust once more, not breaking their connection, but this time it felt even more powerful. Like she was unlocking something in their relationship, too. Cordy was here to share the moment when Hannah truly stepped into her new identity. It was as if she knew how important this was, too.

She removed her hand, but sexual energy fizzed through her. She'd felt the same thing when she did the drag workshop, but this was in her own space. The intensity of the feelings took her by surprise. She had no doubt it had something to do with Cordy. Hannah looked away and cleared her throat.

"I'm not sure I know Max any better, but I do know that grabbing your crotch in public is a really weird thing to do."

"You're not doing it in public, you're doing it in front of me." Cordy touched Hannah's arm. *Max's* arm. Her voice was still rich, syrupy. "Big difference. This is a safe space. Remember that."

With Cordy standing in front of her, cleavage still winking, her red hair wild, her piercing green eyes trained on Hannah, she was pretty sure this was anything *but* a safe space.

Cordy put a hand to her chin. "I think you need to go bigger on the eyebrows, then I like this makeup." She gulped, then stepped closer. "You look rough and ready, but also chiselled enough to have women lean in."

Cordy did just that.

Hannah's clit hardened that little bit more. "That's my goal."

Their gazes connected, and a wave of want crept up her back like a whisper in the dark. Was this working on Cordy, too? Hannah shook her head and stepped back.

"I need to equal or better Sir Loin of Beef." She paused. "Do you like these trousers?" Good distraction. She turned around. "Are they okay on my arse?"

Cordy laughed. "Max wouldn't ask that. Neither would Sir Loin."

"Yes, but Hannah would." She pointed, and Cordy assessed.

"They look good. Your arse looks good." She cleared her throat. "You've got a good arse." Cordy mumbled the last part.

Hannah turned, then blinked. The tips of her ears warmed. That wasn't a sentence she'd expected to hear tonight. "Thank you."

Cordy blushed. "You're welcome." She dropped Hannah's gaze.

Was it Hannah's imagination, or did the heat in the room just go up a notch?

"Where are these tie and shirt choices?" Cordy made herself busy, tinkering with the many pencils at her disposal.

Hannah grabbed the hanger from the door handle, laden with three ties and two more shirts. The first shirt had a black and white zig-zag pattern. The second was blood red. She held up the first shirt. "This one with this tie and then the black jacket on top?" She held the tie to her neck.

Cordy nodded. "I think so. But try it on to be sure. Do you want me to step outside?"

Did she? When Hannah had first walked into Cordy's room, she'd felt a little shy. But since grabbing her crotch, the energy in the room had changed. Hannah was feeling powerful, invincible. Cordy's stare told her she knew it, too. Hannah didn't want her to leave.

She shook her head. "You can stay. Like you said, it's nothing new." Just thinking about that made her whole body warm. Before she could think about taking off her clothes with Cordy in the same room, she tugged off her tie, then started to unbutton her shirt. Her heartbeat started to race. Cordy's thick gaze was on her. Hannah was surprised to learn she wanted it just where it was. In the space of half an hour, she'd gone from being shy, to wanting Cordy to look at her. This was what Max did to her. Or was this what Cordy did to her?

Perhaps a little bit of both.

Her fingers shook as she undid a second button, then a third. When she glanced up, Cordy flinched, then looked away.

"Sorry," she muttered.

Hannah raced through the final three buttons, shed the shirt, then hastily did up the replacement, before threading her tie and tightening it at the knot. She pulled back her shoulders, then shrugged on her jacket, looking in the mirror. She tugged down her shirt sleeves inside the arms of her jacket, then turned to Cordy.

"What do you think?"

Cordy stepped forward. She gave her a slow nod, her eyes dark. Hannah had a sudden urge to step forward, pull Cordy close and kiss her lips. Her mouth went dry as Cordy's long, slim fingers reached up and straightened her tie, her tongue skating across her bottom lip as she focused on her task.

"I think," she said, "this look is the winner. The one you wore at the first show was a little too polished. This one's got a bit more edge. The clothing and the makeup. Max Girth 2.0." She pressed her index finger to Hannah's knot. "This one is going to get you noticed."

Heat flared in Hannah's core, as Cordy's gaze raked her face, and stopped somewhere near her mouth. When it returned to Hannah's eyes, the sexual dial in the room cranked up another notch. Hannah's heartbeat thumped in her eardrums. Damn it, she wanted to kiss Cordy.

Air. She needed air.

"Shall we get a drink?"

***

Hannah had spent the past half an hour walking around the flat with some socks stuffed down her trousers, trying to walk like a man. She hadn't expected to feel quite so vulnerable doing it.

Cordy was trying and failing to contain her smile. "You really got it on that third go. You were walking more normally and less like you'd just got off a horse."

Hannah grinned, rearranged her socks, then grabbed her crotch for good measure.

Cordy pointed. "An hour ago that would have made you blush. Now you're rearranging your crotch like a pro."

That was true. "You know, I think this is going to open me up in ways I hadn't even considered." Hannah sat on the sofa. The socks put pressure on her clit. She wriggled her arse and tried not to portray the sensations currently flooding her system.

"I think, to get comfortable, you need to be Max around the flat. At least, pack all the time you're here to get used to it. That way, I'll get to see him being formed, too. I'm still bummed I can't come to your second-round show. Damn my dad and his birthday party." She pointed at Hannah's crotch. "Does it feel weird?"

Hannah was giving nothing away. Her heat levels were off the charts, with the socks pressing into her, and Cordy's gaze undressing her. "You could try it yourself. You don't have to be a drag king to put some socks down your pants."

Cordy frowned. "I guess you don't." She jumped up, went to her bedroom, then reappeared moments later, rearranging her crotch. "Oh my god. You didn't tell me it feels so fucking daring. And more than a little sexy."

Hannah ground her teeth together. She hadn't mentioned that, had she? "I didn't want you to feel weird."

"It explains why you might have needed more space than the bedroom." Cordy walked around the sofa circling her hips, then did it again, legs apart. "I feel like I could conquer the world with a pair of socks in my pants. Who the fuck knew?"

"Not me."

Cordy stopped near Hannah, flicked her hips out to the side, and suddenly, Hannah could tell what she was feeling. Horny. Powerful. Like if they didn't move right at this second, something might happen that neither one of them could take back.

Hannah flinched, then nodded to the kitchen. "That drink?" They still hadn't had it.

She moved first, making her way across the lounge, trying not to think about whether or not Cordy was checking out her arse. Hadn't Cordy just told her she had a good arse? That thought made a smile flicker on Hannah's face. She shut it down. Now was not the time for smiles that could be taken the wrong way. Now was the time for concentration on not fucking everything up.

Even though she *really* wanted to fuck everything up just for one night. Then they could go back to whatever they had been since Cordy moved in.

Friends. A friend who made a difference to her life. Made her feel more like herself again than she had in a long time. A friend who she more than occasionally wanted to kiss.

However, once she was in the kitchen, Hannah realised her mistake. It seemed even tinier than normal. Had it shrunk in the wash like her favourite sweatshirt when Lauren put it on the wrong setting? Hannah still wasn't over that.

"Hi, Elvis." The orange sat on the counter, but didn't reply. She opened the door of the fridge and stood behind it, peering around what was inside.

"Two cans of IPA that I still have no idea how they got there, and a bottle of Echo Falls finest."

"Or some soy milk," Cordy added, standing in the doorway.

Hannah pulled out the wine, then shut the fridge door. She grabbed two glasses and avoided looking at Cordy.

"Remember when I first moved in, and we stood awkwardly in this tiny kitchen?" Cordy's voice was soft, like her gaze.

Hannah shifted. So did the balled-up socks stuffed down her pants. She tried to ignore them. "I do." She glanced up.

"Who would have guessed that six weeks later, we'd be stood here packing."

"Not me." Hannah allowed herself a small smile.

"I like how it feels, though. Maybe we could perform together one day. Me behind the piano in drag, you all dressed up, singing. We already know that we work well together. We could be the ideal double act, like back in the day of the Victorian music halls."

Hannah blinked. "That's not a bad idea at all." She took a step towards Cordy, then leaned against the small kitchen counter.

Cordy took a step towards her, too, and stopped when the outsides of their wrists touched.

A shot of adrenaline coursed through Hannah, making her shudder.

They both stared.

"I think we could work really well together on so many fronts."

Hannah's brain flared hot. She tried and failed to unscramble Cordy's words. They were fudged together in her brain like a ball of goo. Instead, she snapped her gaze back up from Cordy's wrist, and it landed on Cordy's nose. Then crept up to her eyes. When that proved too much, she switched it to the cabinet by the side of her head. Which needed a wipe.

She took a breath, then dared to look back to Cordy. What

was she saying? "You do?" Hannah only trusted herself to utter two words.

Cordy nodded, then moved towards her. "I do." Her tongue darted out from behind her perfectly straight teeth to her bottom lip, then stayed there.

Hannah was transfixed, as her blood rushed south. When she moved her hips, the socks in her pants pressed against her.

Before she could think about what might happen next, Cordy put a hand up to Hannah's face, but stopped short of touching it. She gave a shy smile. "I don't want to ruin your makeup."

"I don't care about my makeup."

Hannah took a deep breath, taking in all of Cordy. Her smooth, pale skin. Her petite nose. The way her green eyes crackled with anticipation. Even if she still wasn't quite sure what Cordy was saying through her words, she could see it in her eyes. She wanted Hannah. Or Max. Hannah wasn't sure. But right at this moment, she didn't care. Because she and Cordy had come close to kissing on the swings, and ever since then, she hadn't been able to get Cordy's pink, full lips out of her mind. Now, they were inches from her own, she wasn't going to shy away from where this might go. Even though it was possibly the worst idea in the whole world.

Then again, most adventures never started with a good idea, did they?

"Are we on the same page here?" Hannah couldn't do this without asking first.

"The same really-bad-idea page?" Cordy replied, her cheeks flushing red.

Excitement and fear tumbled through Hannah. She didn't say another word. Rather, she leaned forward, steadied herself on the kitchen counter, and pressed her lips to Cordy's. She didn't want to let this moment go. Whatever happened next, she'd deal with the consequences.

But as their lips melded, her whole world changed.

The kitchen counter she leaned on turned into a velvety surface, the most comfortable in the world. The lights in the kitchen dimmed. Inside, someone stoked the furnace of her heart, and it roared anew. Just this first touch of their lips was something different. Something Hannah had never experienced before.

Did Cordy think the same? Hannah wasn't going to break away and ask. But in response to the kiss, Cordy reached out, grabbed Hannah's tie – *fuck me, that was a sexy move* – and pulled her closer.

The first thing to mesh together was their breasts. Swiftly followed by their packed socks. Which also sent a flame of desire romping through Hannah, ending right between her legs. Her eyes sprung open with the intensity of it.

Cordy's did so right at the same time.

They stared again, but this time, the quality of the stare had marched up a few notches. This time, they knew exactly what it would feel like to kiss the other. And there was no doubt in Hannah's mind that it was going to happen again.

"That tie pull, by the way?" Hannah gasped. "Sexy as fuck."

Cordy's mouth went upwards at the edges. "That's because you fit the same bill."

When she pressed her lips back to Hannah's the second time, she did so with skilled precision. When her tongue slid into Hannah's willing mouth, Hannah thought she might collapse, but the soft kitchen counter was there to catch her and keep her attached to Cordy's silky lips.

Hannah had been worried about how this would go down, but she shouldn't have been. Pressing close to Cordy felt like she'd landed exactly where she was supposed to be. Like this was the place Hannah had been searching for all her life. Somewhere that lifted her up and bedded her down. That's how good Cordy's lips felt on hers.

Cordy's fingers let go of her tie and clung to Hannah's waist, drawing her closer still.

A spark ignited in her stomach. She hadn't realised there were this many pleasure points on her body. That she could have this much fun fully clothed.

When Cordy withdrew her lips, Hannah gasped. But then Cordy trailed her tongue up Hannah's neck, leaving a line of electric sparks in her wake. Hannah's mind flashed forward to what the same move might feel like on her inner thigh. Lying naked in Cordy's bed. With the full warmth of Cordy's naked body on top of her.

But then what? The same insecurities and shit would surface as before? Cordy would get fed up of her and her inability to commit, to be out, to be open and honest about who she was? Then she'd move out and Hannah would have to as well, and she'd end up in a bedsit in Tottenham. A mouldy one at that. All because she couldn't control herself when it came to kissing her flatmate. She let her heart rule over her head. Or rather, her clit ruled, currently being pressed deliciously.

Just imagine what it might feel like if it was Cordy doing the pressing, rather than a pair of socks...

Her mind trailed off as Cordy brought her lips back to Hannah's. Fastened them together as if she'd been doing this all her life. Swept her tongue over Hannah's top and bottom lip, then kissed her with a force that left Hannah breathless. Leaving her no option but to kick all her negative thoughts in the throat and leave them for dead. She couldn't let her past-self ruin this moment. Even though she knew her past-self was simply biding its time, waiting to pounce.

Hannah pushed her thoughts off a cliff and grasped the back of Cordy's neck.

They were both on fire, because this kiss was off-the-scale hot. It was going into Hannah's all-time kiss collection. She was going to frame it and put it on her mental mantlepiece. She wasn't going to forget the elation that sparked inside her right now. A Cordy-fuelled explosion of want and lust.

It couldn't last forever, but it could last until they had to come up for air.

Which happened moments later.

Hannah panted at Cordy.

She panted back. "Fuck."

Hannah winced. "Is that a good fuck or a bad fuck?"

She pressed her lips back to Hannah's as if that was going to answer her question. "Fucking amazing?" She winced. "Also fucking complicated?"

Hannah's libido screamed. Cordy was having doubts, too.

She wanted to bang her fist on the counter in frustration. "But you have to admit..." Hannah shook her head. "That was an incredible kiss." She searched Cordy's face for signs she wanted to take this further. She couldn't read her.

"But we should leave it here for now?" Hannah hated herself

for saying the words. "What with us having to live together in a confined space." Why were the words even coming out of her mouth? Surely that was the reason they *should* take it further?

Cordy blinked. Then blinked again. The colour drained from her cheeks. Sadness sliced across her face before she rearranged her features. "Oh."

That was a fatal "oh."

But Cordy recovered quickly. "Right. Of course."

What did that mean? But Hannah ploughed on with what she thought she *should* say. Just like always. "Best not to... muddle things." Even though they were already fucking muddled.

Cordy didn't reply. But her eyes got glassy, then she bit her lip and looked away. When she looked back, Hannah could see she was gathering herself as if she was going into battle.

"Gotcha," she replied. "Heat of the moment. We can pretend it never happened. Despite the fact it was incredible."

"You're incredible." Fuck. That just came out, straight from the heart. That was not in Hannah's original script.

Cordy stared, then licked her pink lips. "We wouldn't want to muddle anything, would we?"

Chapter Sixteen

"You are getting so good at this song, I might start calling you my rocket man." Cordy wasn't kidding, either. The size of his fingers wasn't going to stop Finn playing the Elton John classic to the best of his ability. Plus, Finn was that rare breed among most of her pupils: someone who practised. She'd only been teaching full-time for less than a year, but she already knew practice was the enemy of most, but particularly most teenagers. According to her head of music, she was lucky she had a handful that did.

"Can we play it one more time? Please, Cordy?"

Right at that moment, the doorbell went. That was probably Kate come to pick up her son; she'd nipped out to do some shopping while he had his lesson.

"Do you want to play it for your mum?"

He frowned, then shook his head. "She's probably sick of hearing me practice and getting it wrong."

Now it was Cordy's turn to furrow her brow. "But you've been hitting every note like a champ. If only everyone I taught was as talented and enthusiastic as you!"

Finn sighed. "It works when I'm here. Playing in front of my mums makes me nervous. Plus, Luna always comes up and whacks the keyboard and ruins everything."

"I'm going to be here, though." Would he follow her train of thought?

But Finn had already made his mind up. He was going to quit while he was ahead. He stood up and reached for the sheet music.

Cordy kicked her small suitcase out of the way, opened the front door and was greeted by Gran and Joan, along with Kate and her wife Meg, plus their piano-bashing daughter, Luna, who was even blonder than Finn if that was possible.

"Hello, gorgeous boy!" Meg walked over and gave Finn a hug, while he squirmed as most young boys do. "How was the lesson?"

Finn nodded. "Okay."

Cordy couldn't leave it there. "He was very impressive, he's clearly been practising very hard."

"Playing that stupid song!" Luna chimed in.

Kate pulled Luna towards her. "What have we told you? You love football, your brother loves piano. He's allowed. Let him enjoy it."

Luna pouted her answer, and Cordy had to hold in a smile. There was clearly little love lost between the siblings. She thought back to her own childhood with her brother, Elliott. They used to sabotage each other all the time until they grew out of it. By her reckoning, Kate and Meg still had at least 15 years of this to put up with. "Cup of tea or coffee before you all head off?" Gran asked.

"I could murder a coffee, Eunice," Meg replied.

"I'll put the kettle on and fill the coffee machine." Cordy turned, and they all followed her into the kitchen-diner. As she leaned on her gran's kitchen counter, her mind wandered back to her own kitchen counter. One that had been witness to her first, jaw-dropping kiss with Hannah. Cordy was almost glad she'd had two lessons at her Gran's on Saturday morning. It meant she didn't have to stick around and be awkward with Hannah today. Cordy was staying here tonight and leaving early for her dad's birthday in Birmingham tomorrow, then working at Doyle's Monday and Tuesday. If she played it right, she might be able to avoid Hannah all week.

But that wasn't what Cordy wanted, was it? Really, she wanted to check Hannah was okay, and ready for her second round tomorrow night. Hadn't Hannah told Cordy that she was a motivating factor in her new career? Cordy didn't want a kiss to wreck it all. And, it hadn't ruined anything. *Not* kissing her again would be criminal.

Cordy wanted to do that more than anything. Pop the buttons on her shirt. Slide her fingers into Hannah's trousers. Into her.

These were not appropriate thoughts to be having while stood in her gran's kitchen.

"How are the new digs going?" Meg materialised next to her.

Cordy ran a hand through her hair for something to do, sure Meg could read her thoughts.

From the slight grin on her face, maybe she could. She leaned in and whispered, "And how's it going with the new flatmate? Your gran tells me it's only one bedroom. How's that working out?"

Cordy's brain exploded. Was her living situation the talk of the 40-something lesbian circuit? She glanced up at the prime suspect of the rumour-spreading.

Her gran held up her hands. "What? It just slipped out. Blame my brain. It just happens when you're old."

Cordy didn't believe that one bit, but if she berated her gran, she was sure the whole kitchen would give her knowing looks. Even when nothing had really happened.

At least, not much.

Yet.

She busied herself getting mugs from the cupboard like the question meant nothing to her at all.

"It's going great, thanks. Hannah is lovely, and we're all geared up to play at your big farewell to London party." She paused, putting teabags in the bone-china pot. "You did mean that, right? I've told Hannah and her friend Theo that it's a real, paid gig."

"Absolutely! We can't wait. Our friends are going to think we're so cool, having a couple of drag kings *and* Ruby O'Connell." Kate flashed Cordy her magnetic grin, then ushered the kids through to the lounge with their juice and Jaffa Cakes.

Cordy got on with making Meg's coffee, then brought all the drinks into the lounge. She took the floor, letting Luna stay in the armchair that used to be Cordy's when she lived here. She didn't mind, and she didn't want to disturb the volatile four-year-old, who everyone appeared to handle like a bomb about to detonate.

"We should go to a drag-king show beforehand." Kate held up a hand. "Not to check up on you, but just to see one. It's been forever since I have, and there are far more about now than ten years ago, aren't there?"

"Drag is big business these days. I was helping Hannah with her look the other day, and even I had a go." She knew as soon as it came out of her mouth that it was a mistake, and that her cheeks had likely flushed aubergine.

"Are you going to drag up for the party, too?" Meg sat up. "Maybe we all should. Oodles of lesbians in drag sounds like a fun night to me."

"I'm not sure about that," Kate replied. "But we could definitely get a sitter and go to a drag show before our leaving do, while we still live here. Like we're young and not middle-aged." She turned to Gran and Joan. "What about you? Could we tempt you?"

"Absolutely not." Joan laughed. "We'll see them at your do. From what Cordy's told me, drag king nights are generally held in dingy basements or clubs, which are the province of the young. Or at least, the under 60s. But we've met Cordy's flatmate and can confirm she can sing. Is she performing again soon?"

The question caught Cordy off-guard. She sipped her tea and didn't meet Joan's eye.

"She's through to the second round of her drag competition tomorrow night, but I can't go because I'm here and we'll be in Birmingham tomorrow for Dad's birthday." *She's also through to the second round of kissing me.* However, Cordy kept that thought to herself. "I'm going to her parents' for Sunday lunch next weekend."

Why the hell did she say that? Because she was still high from that kiss. But now, all four of them turned their bodies and stared.

"Meeting the parents? Is there something you haven't told us, my dearest, darling granddaughter? You did seem very close when we met her the other week, but I thought you were just being a good mentor." Gran glanced at her wife. "Joan, on the other hand..."

Joan tilted her head to show what she thought.

Cordy shook her head. Far too quickly if the narrowing of her gran's eyes were anything to go by.

"Nope! Nothing like that. Just good friends."

"In a one-bedroom flat," Meg added, her voice syrupy.

"The plot thickens," Gran added, one eyebrow raised. "Have I told you that Joan and I used to be just good friends back in the late 50s?"

At that, the whole room dissolved into giggles.

"We'll get it out of her on the drive up to Birmingham tomorrow. We've got a whole two hours in the car where she can't escape."

***

Cordy was still kicking herself for opening her mouth, but so far, she'd resisted telling Gran and Joan that she and Hannah *had* kissed. For now, that news was just for her. The pair had let it lie eventually over a delicious dinner of stuff they'd bought from the French deli in Greenwich market, but Gran reminded her about their pact. That if something was worthwhile, she shouldn't hold back. Cordy could never forget that, but in real life, it was somehow far harder to put into practice.

Cordy lay on the pull-out sofabed in what was now back to Joan's writing room, the place she'd called home for her first few months in London. She scrolled on her phone to Hannah's TikTok page, where she'd been uploading a constant stream of her performances, her thoughts, and her getting ready to be

Max Girth. Her views were off the scale, her followers climbing every day. Hannah had told her she'd had plenty of boob shots in her DMs. It didn't happen to pianists, and Cordy could barely imagine.

On a whim, she messaged her, minus a boob shot. Even though she was tempted. They had kissed, after all.

You working tonight?

She knew the answer. She just wanted to speak to her. That kiss had left its watermark on her heart. Invisible to the naked eye, but Cordy knew it was there.

Hannah saw it straight away and messaged right back.

Yes. Want to come? Playing in Soho. Doing back-to-back shows, but I can come and say hi in between. Come see my first one. Compare and contrast my Velvet Minelli with Max Girth.

Was that an invitation she should accept? Hannah stripping off down to her G-string and nipple tassels? Before she could talk herself out of going, Cordy hit reply and told her she'd love to come. She wanted to see the whole of Hannah. She'd seen the drag king. Now for the burlesque. They were leaving for Birmingham at 8am tomorrow, but she could survive on a couple of hours less sleep. For Hannah, it would be worth it.

I'll leave a ticket at the door under your name. Come to the Soho Variety Club 10pm.

***

Cordy sat with her glass of red wine. Anticipation swirled in her veins. The room was full of out-of-towners, looking for a special moment to take back to their suburban lives. What did everyone think when they saw her, alone? That she had a husband at home, looking after the dogs, waiting for her return? Whatever it was, she was sure they would never work out the real reason she was here. That this was the closest she was going to get to seeing her flatmate naked.

Unless she burst into the shower again.

However, when Hannah came out, dressed in a black corset, suspenders, fishnets, heels, hair slicked back, Cordy was not prepared.

Not one little bit.

Because Hannah was the definition of hot.

Cordy's insides sluiced with something wet and warm.

Pleasurable.

Real.

The lights on the stage dimmed.

The noise in the club increased, but all Cordy could hear was a dull whirring sound in her ears. When she focused, she realised it was an alarm. Blaring in her head. A warning sign.

She already knew it was too late for that. She'd kissed Hannah. Slid her tongue into her mouth, felt the contours of her bottom lip. She'd also seen her wet and naked. Felt her breast through her shirt. Wanted to be the sock in Hannah's underwear.

But that was then. Tonight was a whole different vibe. One that made Cordy move aside her red wine, sit up and pay close attention. Because she knew she was attracted to Hannah. She knew she was attracted to Hannah as Max. But this? Hannah in a corset, fishnets and heels? This was not Cordy's usual jam. Having lived with Hannah for the past couple of months, she knew it wasn't hers, either. It was an act, a persona. Hannah had told her that. She'd accepted it. But seeing it live and in the flesh?

Hannah was a fucking sex goddess as this character. Her curves, which Cordy had noticed on day one on the tube, were accentuated beyond anything Cordy had ever dreamt. Did she like curves? She liked Hannah's curves. Encased in small, thin straps of leather and PVC. Tiny strands of cotton. All of which were soon likely to come off.

That thought made Cordy's breathing slow, until it was a burning crawl up her spine.

The music kicked in to the Cabaret tempo, a familiar refrain to everyone all over the world. Hannah, supremely comfortable in this act in a way she wasn't quite yet with Max, grabbed the wooden chair, planted it in front of her, spread her legs and sat down.

Cordy released the slowest breath of her life. Then, as Hannah slowly kicked up a leg, Cordy inhaled again. Perspiration prickled the top of her forehead. She didn't know what she'd expected from this evening, but she had not expected to be this... *turned on*. She wasn't unhappy about it, but it felt like she was a voyeur to a show she hadn't paid for. This was her flatmate. Who she'd longed to see naked with no steam, no obstructions. Now she was going to do so with a whole room full of other people at exactly the same time.

She shook her head. This was Hannah's job. She wasn't doing this for her or for any of the other people in the audience.

But in Cordy's heart, this *was* for her.

Hannah's eyes searched the audience as she bent forward, expertly undoing her fishnets from her suspenders.

Was she looking for her? If it was the other way around, Cordy knew *she* would be. Damn it, she should have sat closer. But then again, she hadn't wanted to do that. Because somewhere inside, she hadn't wanted to see Hannah too close. That was far too personal to do in a room full of strangers. If she was really going to see Hannah naked where her flatmate didn't run for cover, she didn't want to do it in public. Call her old-fashioned.

When Hannah peeled off her fishnets and heels, Cordy gasped, as her heart thumped against her sternum.

When she snapped open her corset, Cordy's cheeks flushed and she took a gulp of her wine. It only made her hotter.

When she tipped her hat forward, did some crazy-skilled chair play and stripped down to her G-string, Cordy wondered if she should look away. Also, that there was *no way on earth* she would. This was Hannah stripped, yet Cordy knew the truth. That Hannah wasn't stripped by this. Nor by Max. She was stripped by real life. Cordy had to help her realise that if she could play the part of herself as well as she could Velvet Minelli and Max Girth, her life would be so much simpler.

Cordy blinked at the realisation. She made a mental note to tell Hannah when they were home.

But not right now. Because at that moment, Hannah turned, prized her hands from her nipples, put her arms in the air and began to shimmy. As she did, her nipple tassels twirled, and a big grin broke out on Cordy's face.

Hannah was good at this. She was also good at twirling tassels with a sexy, moody look on her face.

Cordy decided then and there she wanted to see Hannah's nipple tassels for herself. Up close and personal. Not in a room full of people. She didn't care of the consequences anymore.

Tonight had only affirmed to her: she wanted Hannah, and she was going to make it happen.

Chapter Seventeen

Just before he went on-stage for his second-round performance, Max re-read Cordy's message. It had arrived this morning.

> *Three things that will happen after tonight's show:*
> *1 – You'll feel fucking amazing because you are amazing.*
> *2 – Sir Loin of Beef will be quaking in his boots.*
> *3 – Have a beer. You deserve it. You sex god.*
> *Ps – tell Velvet she's not so bad, either. Cx*

It put a massive grin on Max's face, just as it had every time he'd read it. She'd also left a tiny sticker over Elvis's slightly mouldy and shrivelled mouth before she left. It read: *Go, Max!*

He wished Cordy was here tonight. What if he forgot the first line again? Impossible. Max had practised way more since then. Cordy had supervised. He was a well-oiled machine. Plus, Theo was a great back-up, and Greta had told him he looked like "a fucking prince", so he had to believe they weren't all lying.

When he was ready, he'd snapped a photo and sent it to

Cordy, but she hadn't seen it yet. Max knew she was out for dinner with her whole family. What would that be like, out and proud in who she was and what she did?

Hannah couldn't even begin to imagine, but maybe Max could. He thought of Cordy's words the other night, just before they kissed. "How would Max chat up a woman?" Perhaps the same thing should be asked about this. "How would Max deal with his family?"

The answer, of course, was that Max would be unapologetic about who he was. He would be loving and caring, but his family would have to accept him on his own terms. Hannah was Max. Max was Hannah. Would they ever meet and shake hands?

Max pulled back his shoulders as the Captain gave him a nod from the stage. He put his phone on the ledge in the wings, then took a deep breath.

"Please welcome to the stage, the one, the only, Max Girth!"

Max tugged on his lapels, cleared his throat, then strode out onto the stage like he owned it.

* * *

Max punched the air. He could still hear the screams and cheers through the wall, along with Captain Von Strap bigging him up. The crowd did one final cheer, then the Captain was by his side, drawing him into a hug.

"You, my friend, were fucking sensational out there tonight. If you don't get through, it's a bigger travesty than Brexit."

Max snorted. "Let's not take it too far." But the crowd were wild tonight. Was it because of his ever-growing social media presence? Max was sure it didn't hurt.

The Captain held him at arm's length. "I mean it, man. You had the audience in the palm of your hand. Your confidence was way above your first time, your singing was next-level, and you just performed, you know?"

Max did know. He could feel it strumming through his bones. Like this is who he was meant to be all along. Burlesque was an act. Drag kingdom felt like a calling.

Two sides of the same coin, but if Hannah had to flip, she knew which side she'd be wishing for. But where did Hannah fit on the coin, if one side was Velvet, and the other was Max? She pushed that thought aside. She wasn't going down some existential side road tonight. This was a moment to enjoy the performance.

And she would. *Max would.*

The Captain and Max strode to the bar, and Max immediately recalled Cordy's three-point message. He did feel fucking amazing. He was going to have a beer to celebrate. And as they waited at the bar, three women looked at Max like they wanted to eat him. Or better still, be eaten by him. Max was a sex god. Cordy had been correct in her prophecy.

She'd missed one thing, though. The fact that even though Max could probably have any woman in the bar tonight, he didn't want any of them.

Because none of them were Cordy.

***

"Hey Sylvie." The warming, familiar smell of freshly baked bagels filled Max's nostrils. Sometimes, Sylvie's felt more like home than anywhere else in the world. It also helped it was open 24 hours a day. Max hadn't been sure Sylvie would be here tonight, but he'd got lucky.

Behind the counter, she narrowed her eyes, until realisation dawned. "Hannah?"

"Max Girth, actually." Max had turned up at Sylvie's dressed as Max minus the makeup before the show, and he'd promised to stop by after so Sylvie could see the whole get-up. From the look on Sylvie's face, he was glad he had. He'd also had some double-takes on the short walk here.

She clapped a hand over her mouth, then released it. "Oh my goodness, you look really good! Like a man! Sort of like a Ukrainian man I used to know."

Max laughed. "If he's your long-lost high-school sweetheart, don't go getting any ideas."

Sylvie let out a snort. "You're thinking like a man, too." She tapped her forehead. "Stupid." She walked out to appraise Max fully. "Tonight was the next round?"

Max nodded.

"How did it go?"

"It went well." Max did a spin, arms in the air. "I'm through to the quarter-final."

Sylvie, not one for smiles or hugs normally, broke both her rules. "I knew you'd do well. I'm so happy! After Lauren, you were so sad. Now you have Cordy, and you have Max. Both put a smile on your face."

Sylvie had noticed both?

"You and your bagels do that, too," Max added.

Sylvie beamed right back. "I had some people in the other day because they'd seen the shop on your TikTok. I thought maybe I should sponsor you." She raised a cheeky eyebrow at Max. "I'm so proud of my bambino. From a woman to a man. A bagel on the house to celebrate your win. The usual?"

***

When she let herself into the flat, the space felt quiet. Hannah was used to Cordy telling her how to walk, asking if she wanted a cuppa, or watching her reality TV shows. She missed her.

She took off her makeup, got changed into joggers and a T-shirt, and breathed a sigh of relief. She didn't bind her breasts as tight as some, but it was still a relief when they were free. Hannah's phone chirruped, and she slumped on the sofa, pulling it out of her bag. It was from her mum. It was late for her to be messaging.

> *Just checking to see if you're still coming this weekend, and are you bringing a friend? You were non-committal when we spoke last time, but I need to know how many will be at the table. Let me know when you get a chance, love.*

Hannah messaged her back, then pressed her head into the back of the sofa. Her mum was reaching out and asking to be let in, but Hannah still wasn't sure she'd want to know the real story. Then again, seeing Cordy so connected to her family made Hannah think she should try harder. She forgave and moved on. Could Hannah do the same?

If it was just one thing, maybe. But with her mum, it was everything. The tiptoeing around her sexuality. The silences about what she was doing with her life. Even worse, the condemnation. "The stage is where dreams go to die. Better to keep your dreams manageable."

That kind of statement had never mattered to her sisters, but it had to Hannah, who'd always had stars in her eyes. Those few bricks laid by her mum were enough to build a wall between her and her family. One that first, Lauren, and now Cordy had tried to dismantle. But they couldn't do it without Hannah's help.

She stood up, walked to Cordy's room, then pushed open her door. Cordy's smell rushed into her senses. If a room could smell of sunshine, this one did. It never had when Hannah lived here. Maybe Cordy was what this flat needed all along. She walked over to Cordy's desk, her monitor's green light a spike of illumination in the darkness. She touched Cordy's deserted coffee mug. Her pen holder in the shape of a pineapple. Her alarm clock. Who the hell had an alarm clock these days? Cordy did.

Cordy was due back tomorrow. She should leave her a three-things note. Not interrupt her again this weekend.

Hannah looked around, and saw the note pad on Cordy's desk. But she couldn't use that, because then Cordy would know she'd been in here.

Instead, she walked to the kitchen and grabbed the spiral-bound notepad they used to note down stuff that needed restocking. On the top page, Cordy had written *ketchup*, *loo roll* and *smoked garlic* in the swoopy handwriting that was so her. Hannah ripped a page from underneath, put it back on top of the pad so she had a bolstered surface to write on, then stuck the top of the pen in her mouth.

Three things that told Cordy she was an idiot, she liked her, and she wanted to kiss her again. All, of course, without telling her any of that.

Three things I realised when you're not here:
1 – I miss making you tea.
2 – You were right, Max was pretty awesome, and he's through to the quarter-finals.
3 – I'm looking forward to you getting home.

She picked up the note, went to screw it up, then admonished herself. She put it next to the pad so Cordy could find it when she got home, then stepped into the lounge. Her phone buzzed in her pocket. She pulled it out. Her sister, Betty.

"Hello?" Betty didn't normally call, especially at nearly 11pm.

"What's wrong?" Her stomach dropped, and she braced for bad news.

"Mum tells me you're coming at the weekend with your new flatmate."

Hannah hadn't quite been aware that the family grapevine would work within half an hour. Then again, her mum and Betty were close and called each other all the time. Hannah sometimes envied their relationship. Her mum had always kept Hannah at arm's length.

"You've never brought anyone home without months of pressure. We only met Lauren when you moved in together, and she was your *girlfriend*." A pause. "I just want to know, honestly, before she walks in: are you together and you just don't want everyone else to know?"

Hannah sighed. "No. We're not." She was aware this was a white lie and not the family honesty pledge she'd recently signed up to, but they weren't together. They'd kissed, then retreated. Right now, it was an intense, heated friendship. With packing.

In response, her sister sighed. "You know this dance is really exhausting, right? You dangle a little part of your life on a fishing rod, reel us in, then pull away at the final moment. You have to at least let us bite. Give us something to hold on to."

"I am!" Hannah replied. "I'm bringing a friend home. Isn't that what you and Mum wanted?"

"It has to be what *you* want, too. Otherwise, you'll just sit through dinner like someone has a gun to your head and not say a word. As you did when you brought Lauren."

It was true. She couldn't deny that.

"The thing is, Hannah, you came out to us. But then you shut us out, so you might as well have kept it a secret. Mum and Dad might say stupid things occasionally, but they support you. They've always supported their children."

"No, they've always supported you and Amy. Their straight children who did what they wanted. Never got on stage."

"They've supported you, too! They want you to be happy, but they've no idea how they can help. They want to, though." Another pause. "And as your sister, I want to be in your life more, too."

Hannah thought of all the messages her sister had sent that she simply never replied to. The invitations to their house she'd rejected. She thought she had nothing to bring to the party when she'd been dumped. Before that, she didn't want to introduce

Lauren because she didn't want to overstep. Now, her sister was begging her to overstep. Or perhaps it wasn't overstepping at all. It was just a sideways shuffle. One she should have done a while ago.

"I'm sorry. I'm bringing Cordy on Sunday as my friend. There's honestly nothing more to it at the moment."

"At the moment." Her sister's voice audibly brightened. All she needed was one piece of bait to snack on. "I like the sound of that."

"I'm sorry I've shut you out. I'm going to try to be better. I promise."

Betty sighed again. "That's all we want to hear. See you at the weekend."

Chapter Eighteen

Cordy had been trying to decipher the note Hannah left her since she got home on Monday. She missed making Cordy tea. What did that mean? She was beyond thrilled that Max had made it through to the quarter-final, but she wasn't surprised. It was the final point that had struck a chord. She missed her. That was easier to work out.

As she walked home from school, she readied herself for her first meeting with Hannah since the burlesque show. Since the kiss. Since her whole life turned on its head. Since they'd unofficially started to avoid each other.

When she walked in, Hannah was in the kitchen, bottle of Peroni in one hand, bottle opener in the other. She was wearing jogging pants and a T-shirt, but somehow pulled it off with aplomb.

When she saw Cordy, she held up the bottle with a tilt of her head.

Cordy nodded right away. "Yes please. You wouldn't believe the day I had."

"You wouldn't believe mine," Hannah replied.

Was it just the light, or had Hannah's cheekbones got more contoured since she saw her last?

"I got knocked off my bike—"

"—Fuck, are you okay?" Cordy's heart lurched.

Hannah waved a hand. "It's not the first time. Just please don't tell my mum this weekend. It's literally her worst nightmare. Her friend works in A&E and tells her horrific stories about cyclists being maimed."

"Was it a white van driver?"

"No. Would you believe a little kid leaned out a car window and pushed my delivery sack when I wasn't expecting it, which meant the bike and I went down rather theatrically. It would have been funny if it hadn't been at a main junction just as the lights changed."

"Fucking hell."

"But then a kind woman saw what happened, and gave me a chocolate bar. There is still good in the world. But after surviving another day on London's mean streets, I decided it called for a beer." She paused. "What happened to you?"

"Just budget cuts to the arts. Nothing new, or nearly as dramatic as you."

Hannah got her a beer, uncapped it and held it out to Cordy. When she took it, their fingers touched. Cordy jerked as a spark of desire lit inside her. Yes, she was still thinking about the kiss and where it might take them. When she looked up and caught Hannah's gaze, she was pretty sure Hannah had been thinking about it, too. It had happened right here in this tiny kitchen. Who knew this 6x8ft room would leave such a mark on their lives?

"You were right, you know. With your note. Max was great, and women threw themselves at him. I was bought drinks. Slipped numbers. It was something else."

This was news. "Did you call anyone?"

Hannah shook her head. "I didn't want to. The only person I wanted by my side wasn't there."

"Alan from upstairs?"

Hannah gave her a soft smile. "How did you guess?" She reached out her fingers and caught Cordy's with her own. "The person isn't standing so far from me right now."

Hannah's touch sent electricity skittering up Cordy's skin. Okay, they were going there. Her insides corkscrewed left, then right. She hadn't expected honesty from the start. This wasn't the Hannah she'd got to know. But it was certainly a Hannah she was here for.

"I wished I could be there, too, but I guarantee I'll be at the next round." She flicked her gaze to Hannah's lips, then higher. "I want to see Max strut his stuff. I was there when he was born. Now I want to see him fly."

Hannah wanted that more than she cared to admit. "Talking of dates, you're still on for this weekend? Meeting my family?"

Cordy nodded. "Can't wait." She moved closer to Hannah. Could see the glint of beer on her lip. "I assume you're going as Hannah, not Max."

Hannah's mouth quirked at the edges. "I don't want to tip them over the edge before we've even started. If I turn up packing, hair slicked back and full makeup, my mum might keel over."

"If you did that, it wouldn't just be your mum I'd be concerned about. I might be in danger of keeling over, too." She stepped forward into Hannah's space. Cordy could feel the warmth of her body now. She was intoxicated. "I'm glad you're back and we're finally in the flat together again."

"It's been a while," Hannah agreed, her gaze holding Cordy's. "Since that kiss."

Thunder rumbled through her. She couldn't stop it if she tried. Plus, she didn't want to. "I know. I haven't thought of much else since it happened. Especially when I saw you at the club the other night. You certainly put on a show with Velvet Minnelli." Cordy ignored the frisson that ran through her just thinking about it.

A smile crept across Hannah's face. "Sorry I didn't get to see you that night after you came especially." She paused. "But did you like it? It's a little different to Max."

Understatement of the year. "It was. But I didn't like it."

Hannah's face dropped.

"I loved it." Cordy grinned teasingly. "Especially when you took off all your clothes. That was my favourite part."

Hannah's hand slid around Cordy's waist and pulled her closer still. They hadn't talked about what may or may not happen, but it was as if they'd silently agreed. The kiss had set them on a singular path. Hannah inviting Cordy to her burlesque show had been a kind of foreplay. They'd spent too much time together and knew too much about each other to row back now. Especially when they were in this kitchen.

This kitchen was their kryptonite.

"Do you prefer me with a beard, or with nipple tassels?" Hannah edged closer until their breasts touched.

Cordy eyed Hannah's breasts, looking delectable under her T-shirt. Then her gaze found Hannah's lips. She already knew they fitted perfectly over hers. Would they fit just as well all over her body?

"I prefer you here, close to me. If you're packing or wearing nipple tassels under your clothes, that's a bonus." Her gaze drifted up to Hannah's conker-brown eyes, now glittering with gold. Her blood fizzed, like someone had dropped an Alka Seltzer in her veins. Tiny pops and explosions pulsed all over her skin while she waited for Hannah to continue.

"Funny you should say that," Hannah replied, taking Cordy's hand and leading it to her crotch.

Cordy's fingers connected with something firm but soft. Socks. Hannah's package. *Max's package.* Her tongue snaked out across her lips as heat swept through her. She'd never experienced anything like this before. This want. This need. This overwhelming urge to press whatever Hannah was packing. So she did. And when she did, they both flinched, then held their breaths.

Cordy shook her head. "I don't know what this is between us, but it feels… different." She wanted to say so much more, but her brain was having trouble forming the words. All she could think of was slipping her hand inside Hannah's trousers and doing unspeakable things to her. Or perhaps she would speak them. Shout them out loud. Because that's how she felt right now.

Wild. Untamed. Did Hannah feel it, too?

Hannah nodded, her pupils blown dark, her head coming closer to Cordy. "You want to try being on the receiving end." Then she closed the distance between them, gripped the back of Cordy's neck with her palm, and pressed her lips to Cordy in the surest way possible.

Pleasure pulsed inside as Cordy twisted Hannah around and pressed her against the kitchen counter. This time, she knew Hannah wouldn't stop her. They'd tried saying no, but they were only human. What had her gran always told her? To live in the moment. Cordy was taking her advice and seizing it with both hands.

Rather, she was seizing Hannah with both hands. One hand pressing on the bulge at her crotch. The other clawing at her T-shirt.

Only then did Hannah break off, her eyes blazing, her mouth red. "I've wanted you again ever since we kissed." She claimed Cordy's mouth with hers again.

She didn't need to tell Cordy. She could feel it. In the cadence of Hannah's words, in the desperate crack in her tone. In the grip of her fingers around the back of her neck. Hannah wanted Cordy just as much as Cordy wanted Hannah. Cordy trembled under her touch.

She anchored herself to Hannah's mouth, revelling in its wetness, its warmth. Hannah pulled back and teased Cordy's lips with her tongue, a sensual smile on her face. Cordy wanted to be that smile. That thought made her blink. She was going from zero to 100 in the blink of an eye. It felt appropriate for the moment. It felt *right*.

Hannah whipped off her T-shirt, while Cordy shrugged off her top. They stood in their bras, panting in the kitchen.

Cordy slipped a finger under the strap of Hannah's plain black number and pushed it from her shoulder, following the strap's descent with a line of kisses on Hannah's warm skin. When she reached Hannah's hand, she licked the inside of her wrist, pressing a wet kiss to her pulse.

Hannah shivered, a wide grin on her face when Cordy glanced up. "Damn, girl, you've got skills."

Cordy cracked a smile. "I saw it on a medical show. Apparently, your pulse is an erogenous zone."

"My whole body is when you're around."

Cordy licked her way back up to Hannah's mouth, and placed a gentle kiss there. "Smooth talker, I like it." She reached around and unclipped Hannah's bra, then pushed it off. When Hannah's breasts were presented to her, she growled. "You are exquisite, you know that?"

Cordy took both breasts in her hands and slid the pads of her thumbs over Hannah's dark pink nipples. They were beyond perfect, and they were hers. For how long, who knew? But for tonight, she should revel in them. With that thought in her mind, she took one of Hannah's nipples in her mouth, and ran her tongue all around it. She'd wanted to do that ever since they met.

The deep noise from Hannah's throat shook Cordy's foundations.

"That a sensitive zone, too?"

She kissed Hannah's lips again, her chest heavy and hot. With every press of their lips, every swipe of her tongue, Cordy could feel the pressure building inside. In truth, it was a pressure that had been escalating since the moment she moved in. At first, in small increments, but lately, in seismic strides. Until now, where Cordy wanted to rip the rest of Hannah's clothes off and fuck her senseless. Maybe she should do just that. From the blissed-out look on Hannah's face, she was pretty sure she wouldn't get any pushback. But maybe they should take this elsewhere first.

"I love your lips on mine," Hannah gasped. "And your hand on me."

Or maybe Hannah was just as desperate.

Should she? When Cordy glanced right, she saw Amy

Winehouse. Elvis's replacement orange when he'd gone mouldy. Amy sported a beehive, held a glass of wine and had a fag dangling from her mouth, smoke drawn in fine wisps. She reached out and turned her to face the wall.

Hannah followed Cordy's actions, gave a dazed grin, then pulled her in for a bruising kiss. "You're too much." They locked eyes again. "But also, too little. I want you to touch me."

Cordy was done questioning. She got rid of everything Hannah had below the waist – joggers, underwear, socks (on her feet and down her pants) – until she was naked.

Then she cupped her. Pinpricks of pleasure rushed up Cordy's body and lodged deep inside her brain. "I've got you in the palm of my hand."

"I'm well aware."

And then before Hannah could speak again, Cordy slid two fingers over her clit which made Hannah groan, before slipping them inside.

They both gasped.

"You're so fucking wet."

"You make me so fucking wet."

Hannah grabbed Cordy's backside and ground herself down.

Cordy groaned again.

"Fuck me."

Cordy's heartbeat was loud in her ears. "Here?"

"Right now." It was an instruction. Hannah's tone made that very plain.

Cordy wanted to give Hannah whatever she wanted. She eased in and out with a steady, building rhythm.

Hannah shuffled a little left. Cordy went with her. She

rested her foot on the footstool they used to reach the higher cupboards. Cordy's access was now that much wider. She grabbed Hannah's waist, and thrust a little harder, testing her. Fuck, she felt glorious. "That okay?"

"You can't hurt me. I want all you've got."

Challenge accepted.

Cordy added another finger, changed her angle, and gave Hannah just what she wanted. As her fingers played her, Cordy licked up the inside of Hannah's neck, and she dropped her head back to allow it. Cordy had wondered if Hannah would want to be in control when it came to sex. It was, in fact, the opposite. The more out of control she was, the bigger the smile on her face.

What a fucking time to be alive.

Moments later, Hannah's hips bucked, her arm wound around Cordy's neck and she shouted obscenities into the air as she came standing up, her face red, her eyes alive. After a few moments, she kissed Cordy hard.

"Bedroom?" Cordy asked, her fingers still curled inside Hannah.

"Somewhere I can sit before I fall."

* * *

Cordy let Hannah drag her into the lounge, then around the divider to her room, and onto her bed. Hannah had a just-been-fucked flush of red on her chest, and wore a determined smile.

"You can take a moment, we've got all night."

But Hannah shook her head. "I want all the moments with you now. We can take it slow later."

Hannah stripped the rest of Cordy's clothes, pushed her onto her bed, then settled her naked body on top of Cordy.

A long, slow groan escaped Cordy's lips. Hannah kissed her lightly, eyes open, then ran her fingertips up and down her side. She slipped a thigh between Cordy's legs, and Cordy ground up into her. The friction was delicious. Touching Hannah had been such a long time coming, and this almost felt decadent. Just the slightest of touches from her made Cordy drown in pleasure, like she never wanted to surface. Hannah hadn't even touched her anywhere else yet.

"If it's okay, I'd love to taste you." Hannah lifted her head, still within kissing distance. "I want to feel you in my mouth."

Cordy's eyes went wide. "I wasn't expecting you to say that." Hannah in the sheets was way different to Hannah on the streets. Or perhaps this was Max's influence. Whatever or whoever it was, Cordy was here for it.

She reached her hand around the back of Hannah's neck and pulled her down for a fierce, powerful kiss. Was she a crazy person asking that? "It's more than okay."

Hannah's eyes were dark and brooding. *Sexy.*

"I love it," Cordy added. "Do your worst."

She was ready for whatever Hannah wanted to give. Ready to spread her legs. Ready to come whatever way Hannah wanted.

Hannah kissed her way down Cordy's body, peppering her skin with a feather-light touch.

Cordy's breath knotted in her throat as heat swirled through her. Then Hannah pushed Cordy's legs apart, and licked up their insides until her hot breath hovered over her centre.

Cordy's hips jerked and she squirmed under Hannah's touch. Now she'd spelled out what was going to happen, Cordy's patience was shot.

Hannah paused, and eyed her with a lazy smile. "You're pretty irresistible." Then she placed a hot, wet kiss right next to Cordy's pussy, and Cordy's brain misfired. The anticipation was killing her. She clung to Hannah's white sheets as her heart slammed against her chest. "Is it Max or Hannah between my legs?" Her voice cracked as she spoke.

"They're both here." Then without further ado, Hannah lowered her head and swiped her tongue through Cordy's wet centre. A long, slow lick.

Cordy dropped her head back with a groan. Hannah's tongue wiped Cordy's brain clean.

She'd literally dreamed about this moment, but it was far better in the flesh. She and Hannah were not your obvious pairing. They moved in together in odd circumstances. But despite all of that, they'd connected.

Right at this second, as Hannah slid two fingers into her and sucked Cordy's clit into her mouth, their connection was off the charts. Yes, they hadn't spoken about what this meant, but she didn't care. This moment was what was important. Just the two of them, with her pulse racing, getting swept along to the boom of her heart and Hannah's tongue.

Hannah gripped the sides of Cordy's thigh with her left hand, as her right did the more important work. With every second that passed, the heat inside Cordy rose, and the steady white noise in her brain increased, until it became impossible to ignore. Hannah's tongue stopped, circled, then pirouetted, until Cordy didn't know which way was up and which was down.

"Don't stop," she managed to get out, just before she couldn't stop, and her orgasm shrieked through her, shredding everything in its path. Cordy moved her legs as wide as they could go and thrust her hips upwards, slowing gradually as she rode out the heady sensation. Warmth smothered her like honey as she looked down, to see Hannah grinning up at her.

"I should have known the first time with you would be memorable."

"I aim to please," Hannah replied, before putting her mouth right back on Cordy.

Who died on the spot.

Chapter Nineteen

Now they'd started to have sex, they couldn't seem to stop. Every second they were in the flat together, they were pushing each other against walls, down on to the nearest bed, or simply coming together on the sofa or the floor. Nowhere was off limits, and there appeared to be no boundaries to jump. Hannah had slept with a grand total of five people before, but never like this.

Their sex was wild. Surprising. Fabulous. When she'd told Cordy those things, Cordy had simply nodded and agreed. Neither of them had talked that much about the future, though. They didn't want to break whatever this spell was. It was too early. For now, Hannah was revelling in Cordy, and she hoped, vice versa. It was enough.

But today was going to be their biggest test yet. Today was meet-the-parents day. When she'd originally suggested Cordy come home with her, they'd just been friends, and Hannah had no idea their connection would escalate. However, now it had, there was no getting away from the fact it complicated the day somewhat. Okay, *a lot.*

Hannah's fingers were still inside Cordy as she thought this. Then she felt guilty for thinking about anything else than pleasing Cordy. Her mind had been completely in the moment throughout, and Cordy had a blissed-out look to prove that. But now, as she moved on top of her and kissed her pink lips, she wondered if her family were going to guess. How obvious they'd be. Nobody else knew yet, because nobody else had seen them together since things changed. Greta was none the wiser, nor Theo. Cordy hadn't seen her gran and Joan, or any of the wise London lesbians. They'd been in a bubble of their own.

Today, it was about to be popped, and they had to talk about it first.

"You feel and look fucking amazing." Hannah placed another kiss on Cordy's lips, then withdrew her fingers.

Cordy's eyelids fluttered shut, then opened again, her pupils dark with want. "And you are a sex goddess. Maybe you should put that on your TikTok."

Those are words that should have made Hannah rejoice. But she was already in family mode. On the defensive. Her natural state when it came to going home.

"Can you keep that to yourself this afternoon?"

Cordy snorted. "At your family's house?" She kissed Hannah's lips again. "I had been planning to go in and tell them what a whiz you are at eating pussy while your dad was carving the roast beef. But if you'd rather I saved it until dessert, just let me know." She grinned, but after a moment where Hannah didn't reply, she frowned. "That was a joke, by the way. You remember humour, right? You had it last time I checked."

Hannah eyed her, then rolled onto her back, covering her eyes with her hand. "Sorry. I've just come over a little funny about today. My family are meeting you for the first time, and we've spent the last five days shagging each other senseless. I don't know what this is and I'm not ready to tell them anything until I do and..."

Cordy rolled into Hannah, climbed on top of her and pinned her arms above her head. Then she lowered herself and kissed her lips.

Hannah shut up.

"I didn't expect this," Cordy said. "Neither did you. I don't know what this is, and I don't want to speed it up or ruin it, whatever it is. If you want us to just be friends today, I can do that." She looked directly into Hannah's dark gaze. "To be clear, if this develops into something more and we decide we are a couple, that will need to change. But I don't want to go to your family's home telling them we're something we're not." Another pause. "Unless you want to discuss it now?"

Fear screamed through Hannah so hard, it was all she could do not to jump off the bed. Which would have been hard with Cordy on top of her. Instead, she shook her head. "For today, we're just friends. Which we kind of are. Friends with benefits."

The skin around the edges of Cordy's eyes wrinkled. Something crossed over her face. She took a deep breath, then rearranged her shoulders. "Right. Friends with benefits."

But her tone told Hannah she didn't like it.

Hannah winced. "I'm not saying that's what we are *necessarily*. It was a just a phrase that popped into my head. Plus, it's only been five days." She paused. None of this was coming out right. "We have to leave to get the train home soon, so there's not much time to discuss it."

Cordy swung a leg and got off her. "You don't have to

worry. We're friends with hidden benefits today, and I will act accordingly."

But the mood in the bedroom had changed significantly.

Shit.

Hannah grabbed Cordy's arm as she went to get out of the bed. "I didn't mean anything by it. It just slipped out. If it helps, you're a friend who's taken over my brain entirely."

"Even though it short-circuits on occasion and says dumb things?"

Hannah deserved that. "Even then." She knelt up and kissed Cordy. "Sorry. Are we good to go?"

Cordy pursed her lips, then nodded. "I'm a very good actor when needed."

"So am I. We should get together."

Cordy rolled her eyes, then gave her the middle finger.

Chapter Twenty

"Do you play classical or all types of music, Cordelia?"

"Call me Cordy," she told Hannah's mum as she reached for the gravy. "The only people who call me Cordelia are my parents when they're disappointed with me."

"Cordy it is," Polly replied.

"And the answer is, everything. I teach, I play in bars and clubs, and I do everything I can to make a living with my art in one of the most expensive cities in the world. Hence, when I found this flat-share with Hannah, it was a godsend. Cheap rent in London is hard to achieve."

"Such a good job you get on living in such close quarters," Hannah's dad added. "When Hannah first told us about her plan, we all thought she'd lost the plot. But I'm glad it seems like it's working out for everyone."

Cordy nodded, her mouth full of a home-made roast potato that tasted so good, it made her want to weep. Pub roast potatoes never quite tasted the same as ones made at home. Whoever did these clearly put a whole lot of love into them. Which didn't surprise her, as there was a whole lot of love around this table. Including Hannah's parents, two sisters, their husbands, and her two nieces. When Hannah had described her relationship with her family and how she was the black sheep because she didn't follow the family blueprint, Cordy had assumed they'd be strait-laced and she'd have nothing in common with them.

On the contrary, Hannah's family appeared pretty normal, with a sense of humour and a huge love for their youngest child. Cordy was well aware she'd only just parachuted into this picture, but although she'd expected the day to be like walking on eggshells, she was even enjoying it a little. Although, that could also be down to the delicious roasties, and the wine which Hannah's sister, Betty, was freely pouring.

"It's more than working out," Cordy replied, glancing at Hannah and pressing her thigh into hers.

In response, Hannah froze and gave Cordy a death stare.

Cordy was pretty sure friends had their own language as well as lovers, but she smiled to gloss over it. She wanted to tell the family what a fantastic performer Hannah was. How well she was doing in the drag king competition. But Hannah hadn't told them any of that. To them, Hannah was keeping herself afloat with her courier gig.

"I think it's wonderful that you're earning a living as a teacher, and also playing the piano in public, getting paid. Doing so with a job that doesn't risk your life daily."

"Mum." Hannah's voice came out as a warning growl.

Polly put down her cutlery and looked Hannah in the eye. It made Cordy wonder if she'd practised in the mirror. If performing was in the genes.

"What?" Polly said. "I've told you what I think about that. I'd rather you didn't end up as another statistic on London's roads. Tell me you're wearing a helmet and whatever else you need?" Her mum didn't wait for an answer. "Perhaps you can use some of Cordy's rent so you don't have to ride as much?" She wasn't done. "You were talking about performing too, which I don't approve of, either. But you're less likely to get killed. Any more on that?" The pained disappointment on her face was so vivid, it shattered the surrounding air.

Hannah sighed and moved her carrots around her plate.

Cordy jumped in. "These potatoes and roast veg are incredible. Are you responsible, Polly?"

Polly duly blushed. "I am, thank you."

"And is it honey on the carrots?"

"It is, and you just par-boil them first. Same with the potatoes."

An awkward silence ensued as Hannah picked up a carrot, ate it, then put down her cutlery.

"I'm not just doing delivery, if you must know. I'm doing a couple of other things, too, that could lead somewhere."

Now it was Cordy's turn to pause, mid-chew. She hadn't expected that.

Neither, it seemed, had anyone else.

"Like what?" Her mum's voice rose. "You're not on one of those terrible websites where you show off your body to strangers for money, are you? What's it called? Lonely fans?"

Cordy bit the inside of her cheek and held her breath. Now would not be a good time to laugh.

Hannah whipped her head up to look at her mum, a frown creasing her forehead. "I tell you I have other things I'm doing, and you immediately think I'm getting my tits out online? Thanks for the vote of confidence, Mum."

"You do have the best tits of the three of us," Betty chimed in.

Cordy bit harder and sat on her hands to stop herself agreeing. She still remembered them in her mouth this morning.

"You said it yourself, London is expensive," Polly countered.

"Which is why Cordy moved in!"

If Cordy had thought the silence earlier was awkward, she hadn't bargained for this one. The whole family stared at Hannah, then at her mum, waiting for who was going to play their next move.

"It's not anything illegal, is it?"

Hannah dropped her head backwards and exhaled. "I tell you I've got a couple of side gigs in the age of the gig economy, and you think I'm drug dealing or working online as a stripper."

"Nobody said anything about drug dealing—"

"—It was implied." Hannah paused. "I'm not stripping or drug dealing, just to be clear. But I am performing. And getting paid for doing so. First, as a burlesque dancer."

Beside Cordy, Amy spluttered and covered her mouth with her hands. "Isn't that a form of stripping?"

"It's an art form and it pays well," Hannah countered, glaring at her sister.

Amy looked suitably contrite as she mouthed "Sorry!"

"And I'm also working my way up to performing on the cabaret circuit. A routine with singing in it."

There was that silence again. Cordy wanted to jump in and help. Friends did that, right?

"I'm helping her out, playing piano, helping her to practice her songs. She came along to one of my piano open-mic nights and brought the house down. Her versions of 'Uptown Funk' and 'Rebel Rebel' are set to be legendary. You should come and see her, she's absolutely incredible."

The whole family sucked in a breath at that final revelation, and beside her, Hannah went rigid.

Cordy had said too much, hadn't she?

"You're using my song?" Polly asked Hannah in a stage whisper. "My song for your act?"

Hannah's face flushed purple. "It's David Bowie's song, strictly speaking. It fits my act perfectly."

"And you're performing it on stage? To other people?"

Hannah nodded again. "I am."

Cordy reached under the table and squeezed Hannah's thigh.

Hannah's muscle flexed under her touch, and she gave her the tiniest glimmer of a smile in return.

"This is a lot to take in, but it sounds like your life is one exciting whirlwind of action, unlike ours," Hannah's dad said. "Dancing, singing, living the dream. Good for you. Isn't that right, Polly?"

Her mum gave Hannah a weak smile. A little like the one her daughter had just given Cordy.

"You know my thoughts on performing. That it's a route to disappointment. The only way Hannah can afford to live in London is to move into her lounge. It's hardly ideal. Taking her clothes off, singing and dancing. Especially for someone with a degree in economics."

"I tried going that way, you know that." Hannah stared at her mum. "This is why I don't tell you what I'm doing because I don't think you want to know."

"That's not fair, I do want to know, and I'll support you."

"That's not what it sounds like."

"I just worry. It's what mothers do. I worry someone will take advantage of you, that you'll get hurt, that performing won't be the golden ticket you think it could be."

Hannah balled her fist by her plate before she spoke. "Mum, I'm performing on the cabaret circuit in London. Nobody thinks the streets are paved with gold anymore. I like performing, you know that. I've found what I like to do, and I hoped you might be happy for me." She glanced at Cordy. "Cordy has been instrumental in helping me see that performing can be my job."

Her mum stared, gripping her cutlery tight. "And you get paid? People come to see you?"

Hannah nodded. "They do."

Her mum took that in. "I'll admit, that's positive. Well done." She wrinkled her nose. "If you can get people to come and see you, it's a good start. It means you've got something."

The whole family held their breath at this breakthrough. Even Hannah's niece, Chloe, who'd been banging her spoon on the wooden table ever since she sat down. This was a mother-daughter moment they hadn't seen coming. Cordy was new here, but she was pretty sure it didn't happen every time Hannah came home. From what she'd told her, her mum was the tougher nut to crack. A congratulations from her mum was akin to her blessing.

"Hannah tells me you once sang in a band. If you want to rekindle your performance days, I run my open-mic night every week," Cordy told Polly, trying to smooth the waters as the silence stretched. She was no good with silences. Hannah knew this. "You're very welcome to come along. The two of you could do a Bowie duet."

When Cordy turned her head to Hannah, her face spelt foreboding.

She'd said too much again, hadn't she?

* * *

"I nearly died laughing when she invited Mum to her open-mic night." Betty did almost die laughing at that moment while she retold the story to Hannah. "Not because I think it's a bad thing – on the contrary, I'm all for it – but nobody in this family would dare say that to Mum."

Hannah was well aware of that. At the time, she'd wanted to reach over and put a hand over Cordy's mouth. But now, she was glad she'd said it. Glad that Cordy made her mum see that singing just for the sake of it was not a bad thing. In the end, her mum had mumbled that maybe she would. The whole family had been stunned. "Maybe she needs a newcomer to challenge her. Shake her out of her 'performing is terrible' rut."

"I agree. But she's been comfortable in that rut for years, and she knows it well. It might take a few tries for her to leave. But well done to Cordy."

Who was currently drinking coffee with the rest of the family in the dining room. What more might she be saying?

"One last thing. How long have you been sleeping together?" Betty put her hand on her hip and fixed Hannah with her stare. "And don't try to tell me it's not like that, because *please*." Her sister splayed her hands and waited, eyebrow raised.

Hannah bit the inside of her cheek. She knew she'd been rumbled. She flexed her hands for a few moments before she replied. "It's very new, like five days old, so please don't say anything. It's the reason I'm not saying anything. I still don't know what it is."

Her sister's face lit up and she pulled Hannah into a hug.

Hannah let her, smiling over her shoulder. She was pleased about it, too. Despite her stupid 'friends with benefits' comment. If she could take that back and stuff it under the rug, she would.

"I am so thrilled! She seems so lovely, and she's helping you with your cabaret, which is brilliant. Are you going to tell me anymore about exactly what that involves? I'm intrigued as you 'fessed up to being a burlesque dancer, so what could be more risqué than that?"

Hannah's cheeks burned. She'd love to tell her sister, but it was better kept a secret for now. Especially with her quarter-final coming up next weekend. Get through that, and Max was only two shows away from winning the five-grand first prize and a regular booking. Wouldn't that be a better option to present her family with? "I'll tell you when I've got my act together. Literally."

High off one victory, Betty didn't press her further. "Back to Cordy. It might only be new, but I think this could be good. You seem happier. More relaxed. Which is not a word I normally use about you around family. Even when Mum was being peak Mum."

It was all true. "She's made me come out of my shell, live my life. Be who I really am."

Betty gave her an impressed grin. "It's about time you lived your life for you and nobody else. Mum will get used to whatever you do. She loves you, remember that. Now, shall we go and rescue Cordy from our parents' clutches?"

Chapter Twenty-One

They practically ran home from Max's quarter-final, wishing goodnight to Theo and Greta with such a fake feigning of tiredness that Hannah had to hold in a laugh. Theo had caught them snogging after the show, so the cat was very much out of the bag. When they shut the front door and stared at each other, Hannah tried not to be overwhelmed with lust. But then she decided to give all of those feelings to Cordy. Lust, after all, was a dish best shared.

She led her to the bedroom and let Cordy grab the wet wipes, then straddle her lap, before taking the makeup off Max's face with careful precision. Minutes later, her face bare, she was back to Hannah. However, nothing had changed inside. She was still awash with the same energy when it came to Cordy and what she wanted to do to her. From the look in Cordy's eyes, the feeling was reciprocated.

"You were so good tonight." Cordy shook her head as she stared down.

But Hannah shook her head. "Apart from when I forgot the words again. If this is my USP, I'm not sure I like it."

But Cordy just shook her head. "You remembered them eventually, but tonight was about your performance. You *owned* the stage. I wish your mum had been there. It might change her mind if she could see you were born to do it." She kissed her lips, smoothing Hannah's cheek as she did.

A rush of desire streaked with contentment swooshed through her. Sure, they might be just fuck buddies, but Hannah wouldn't want to be a fuck buddy to anyone else.

"Plus, it didn't matter that you forgot the words as the audience loved you and you're through to the semi-final. Who would have thought that when we first met?"

Hannah shook her head. "Not me. But you clearly saw something. So did Theo. I couldn't have done any of this without you, and I'm grateful. More than you know."

"It's been an honour watching you flourish." Cordy bent her head and placed a delicate kiss on Hannah's lips.

This time, when she pulled back and smiled, it was like an earthquake. It came out of nowhere, and was instant and devastating. Hannah focused on steadying her breath.

Cordy sat back, and slowly undid the knot of Max's tie and pulled it off.

Hannah felt it *everywhere*.

Cordy threw the tie over her shoulder, then got off Hannah, leaning down to unbutton her shirt. With every button she popped, she applied a slow kiss to Hannah's face, ending with the final button and kissing her lips. Hannah shrugged off her shirt, while Cordy carefully unwound her binding. When she was finally naked, Cordy sat back on her lap.

Hannah wriggled her shoulders and breasts, glad to be free. Especially under Cordy's heated gaze. Hannah's breath staggered around like it was drunk. She didn't care. It was what Cordy did to her.

"You know what I want? What I was thinking about when

you were strutting around on stage tonight, being all cool as fuck?"

She could still taste the 'fuck' as Cordy's tongue slipped into her mouth, and her arm wrapped around her waist, holding her in place.

"Tell me."

"I want you in nipple tassels tonight." Cordy reached down and pressed between Hannah's legs. "Plus, I'd love it if this soft pack was something harder that could go inside me."

Hannah gulped. She didn't need to touch herself to know she was wet. Should she say what just flew through her mind? "I…" she began, then shook her head.

"What?" Cordy tilted her head, her gaze soft. "Tell me."

Hannah bit her lip, then bit the bullet. "It's just… I bought a new toy this week. With that in mind. If you want to try." She reached out her hand and skimmed her thumb along Cordy's pale cheekbone. Her green gaze burned bright under the bedroom light as she moved in for a kiss. A kiss so hot, so in the zone, Hannah wished she'd brought up the toy earlier. When they broke apart, she was dazed.

"You're going to make my dreams come true?" Cordy got off her lap and held out a hand.

Hannah gave her a sly smile. "That's the plan." Then she shed her trousers, underwear and packing, and stood naked. Cordy let her eyes roam Hannah's body, and Hannah instinctively covered her breasts with her arms. "You're making me feel weird."

Cordy stepped into her space and gathered her up. "You don't need to be. I just want you to know that I'm an admirer of both Max and Hannah. Of their bodies and their minds.

Of who they are. I know being Max has made you question some things. If you decide you're non-binary, I'll totally support that. If you decide you just want to be both, I can get behind that, too. In fact, whatever you want to do, just know, I'm beside you."

Something rushed through Hannah, something that got caught in her throat, and threatened to leak from her eyeballs. She hugged Cordy tight, and wondered, not for the first time, what she'd done to deserve her.

"Thank you," she managed, before catching Cordy's mouth in a fierce kiss. "You're the best. You're also fucking sexy. And you've got far too many clothes on."

Cordy grinned, then got naked.

"Now lie on the bed and close your eyes."

Cordy did as Hannah told her.

Hannah ran back to her bedroom and pulled her new toy from her chest of drawers, along with her silver nipple tassels. She attached the latter, then walked back into Cordy's room. "Keep your eyes closed." She hadn't anticipated getting this toy out so soon, but she guessed they could learn to use it together. She couldn't wait for Cordy to clap her eyes on it.

She lay beside Cordy, put a palm on her arse, and pulled her onto her side. "Okay, open your eyes."

Cordy did, looked down at the tassels, and grinned. She reached over and twirled one between her thumb and forefinger. The sensation rattled through Hannah. Tonight was going to be next-level, she already knew.

"I've got this, as well." She took Cordy's hand and brought it down to the jet-black toy.

Her eyes widened. "Two ends, you really did think of

everything." She sat up, turning it in her hands, one end longer than the other, one with a wicked curve that made Cordy gulp. "I have a confession to make. I've never used one of these, with one end or two. But you make me want to do things I've never done before."

Hannah sat up, too, and kissed her. Damn, her lips were somewhere she could live forever. "We can take it slow. Let's just see what happens."

But Cordy shook her head. "I want to try. What's the best position?"

"I think with you on top." A smile spread across Hannah's face. "Which suits me."

Cordy looked at her like she held all the answers. "Let's try that, then." She licked her lips. "Maybe we should ease into it first. So to speak."

"You're on top, you can take the lead."

"In that case, I want you flat on your back, and ready for me."

Hannah didn't need to be told twice.

In moments, Cordy straddled her neck, then moved herself up until her pussy hovered over Hannah's mouth.

She blinked. When Cordy said she wanted to use a toy, Hannah hadn't expected to *be* the toy. Then again, Cordy was not what she'd expected. She should have guessed.

"I want you to lick me, then fuck me."

Hannah was glad she was lying down, because if she'd been standing, her entire skeleton would have crumbled to dust. Heat spiralled through her, and she did as she was told. As her tongue got to work, above her, Cordy moved her hips and hissed her approval. Hannah rolled her tongue, feeling the undeniable wetness between her own legs. She couldn't wait to use her new toy. The anticipation tasted deliciously sweet, just like Cordy.

"I've been wanting this all night long," Cordy whispered, reaching around and playing with Hannah's tassels.

Hannah couldn't reply. Instead, she swept her tongue with expert strokes, until Cordy came with a buck of her hips and a satisfied scream. Eventually, she slid down Hannah's body until their faces were level. Hannah swore she could feel Cordy's elevated heartbeat thumping beside her own.

As Hannah stared at Cordy, at everything she was, raw emotion rolled around her chest. Because there was something else there, too. Something that told her she didn't want to lose Cordy. That this could be *something*. Something that had never happened before.

Cordy stared at her, too, but they said nothing. Silence wrapped tight around them, holding them close, until all Hannah was aware of was Cordy's emerald gaze, and the boom of electricity zapping between them.

Then, Cordy was between Hannah's legs, toy in hand.

"We can stop at any time," Hannah said "There's no right way or wrong way." If Cordy was involved, it could only be right.

Cordy exhaled, then nodded. "I'm ready. Are you?"

Hannah reached over and gave Cordy the lube. "Make sure it's slick. Although I don't think you'll need it."

Cordy reached a finger down and eased it into Hannah.

A guttural groan escaped Hannah's throat.

Cordy leaned forward and kissed her. "Better safe than sorry."

Doing this together was another first in their relationship.

Another building block of trust. Of whatever this was between them.

Cordy brought Hannah's hand down and together, they edged the toy inside.

As it slid in, Hannah closed her eyes and gasped. She was already in the zone, and this was taking her higher. She let go and watched as Cordy took over, until it touched her G-spot. When it did, the breath she sucked in was deeper than the Grand Canyon. Another groan.

"Kiss me," she told Cordy.

Cordy held the toy in place, then slid up Hannah's side. The kiss she pressed to Hannah's lips told her how turned on she was. It was languid, deep, dirty, with sharp sounds that transmitted her needs.

"I need you," she gasped when she broke the kiss. Cordy's pupils were blown wide with want.

"Then take me," Hannah replied.

Moments later, more lube applied, Cordy knelt between Hannah's legs and guided the toy between her own legs.

Hannah was already at breaking point, full to the brim, but watching Cordy ease herself down, focused but with her face contorted, she realised just what the rush was. That earlier feeling she'd had. The L word. But it was too early, surely? A trick of her brain while she was having sex. Lust talking as every pleasure point on her body was pressed.

She pushed that thought aside. She couldn't think about that right now. Not with Cordy starting to ride her, looking like a flame-haired goddess above her. When Hannah glanced up, Cordy's mouth was open, one hand behind gripping Hannah's thigh to steady herself.

"You okay?" With the dildo pressing into her, it was a struggle to form words.

Cordy didn't reply, just nodded, getting used to the toy, groaning as she did. Moments later, more confident with where she was at, she slowly tested a hip grind.

The movement was all encompassing. A swell of desire surged through Hannah and she raised her hips, then gasped as Cordy responded.

Their gazes locked. They were inside each other, feeling the same thing at the same time. Even the slightest movement caused a pleasure riot. It was almost too intense. Too much for Hannah's brain to handle. But at the same time, it was exactly what she wanted. This connection. This answered need. Simply, Cordy.

The L word flashed again in Hannah's brain, like a flickering neon light. She shut her eyes, but then reopened them, because she didn't want to miss a thing. Her mind was playing tricks on her. She was having the best sex of her life.

The difference was Cordy. She was a force to be reckoned with, an avalanche of feel-good. No more so than right at this moment.

As her orgasm built, and Cordy's finger found her clit, Hannah cried out and thrust.

Above her, Cordy panted hard.

Every movement was more heightened than the last: new, glorious, a spiral of pleasure. Hannah tried to anchor herself by sifting through all the golden moments they'd had over the past couple of months. But none of them had been as perfect as this. With Cordy on top. Hannah so close. With Max nearing perfection, and her family ship turning itself around. What had been the catalyst for all of this magic happening? Cordy, with her can-do attitude and her relentless positivity that had somehow rubbed off on Hannah.

She'd never lived like this before. She'd never had sex like this before. As her orgasm ripped through her like lightning, and on top, Cordy threw her head back and gasped, Hannah knew she never wanted to live like this with anyone else.

Chapter Twenty-Two

Hannah fiddled with her helmet strap, and kicked off the pavement, setting sail once again into the murky waters of London traffic. But this morning, she'd been woken up with Cordy's head between her legs, so she was feeling pretty invincible. Like the largest lorry in the world could try to take her out, but it wouldn't succeed. Because Hannah Driver was in a different world altogether, floating on a cloud.

She swung the bike into the next road, kicked the stand, then jumped off and opened the box on the back of her bike. Three still-pretty-hot pizzas for the people behind the canary-yellow front door. What was going on that they were ordering pizza at 11am? Then again, was there a bad time for pizza? She wished them a good day, and the guy with the straggly beard and sleep creases still on his cheek stared at her like she was speaking a foreign language. She got back on her bike. Two more deliveries to do, and then she was done.

When she got home, she dragged her bike up the stairs, then balanced it against the hallway wall on her floor. With all the riding, lugging deliveries and her bike, along with performing, she hadn't needed to go to the gym of late. She'd never moved more, and she was in good shape. She made herself a coffee and took it to the balcony. Or what she now considered, 'their balcony'. Just the thought of Cordy made her heart beat that little bit faster. She pushed the feeling away, like she had ever since it crept up on her at the weekend.

They were just friends with benefits. They hadn't talked about anything else. Hannah didn't want to. Whenever she'd progressed her relationships from casual to firmer ground, they'd always gone tits-up. She couldn't cope if this one did the same. Hence, she was happy keeping it just where it was. Nameless. In a love bubble. Or a fuck bubble, as Cordy had told her with a smirk this morning, wiping her lips.

She put her coffee on the table, leaned over the railing and got out her phone. Her TikTok had blown up so much lately, she'd had to turn off notifications. What's more, the TikTok adulation for all the performers had contributed to a boost in ticket sales. So much so, they'd moved the semi-finals and the final to a new, bigger venue in Shoreditch. Also, because of that, they'd changed the date of the final. It now clashed with Cordy's school concert.

When Hannah had got the email this morning, her heart sank. Yes, this was great news for *their* show, but she'd promised to help Cordy with the concert makeup. Cordy was teaching today, and she had rehearsals after school. Hannah hadn't allowed herself to panic about the clash just yet. She wasn't through to the final of the competition, so there might not even be a clash. She was trying not to think that far ahead. One show at a time. Whatever happened, she had to help Cordy, because she'd done nothing but help her.

A message in her WhatsApp blinked at the top of the screen. The top line of the message appeared on her home screen.

Hey stranger. How are you?

Hannah froze. It was from Lauren. Her ex. Should she click on the message? She hesitated for a few moments. Then realised she had to click, whatever the message contained. She gulped as she pressed her forearms against the balcony wall, staring at her phone like it was a bomb.

A breeze tickled her face. What did Lauren want? Lauren, who'd told her to get her shit together so she didn't treat her next girlfriend the same way she'd treated her. Lauren had been right on all counts. It still didn't mean that Hannah was in a space where she wanted to speak to her. Especially not *now*.

> *Hey stranger. How are you? I'm back in London, and wondered if you fancied meeting up? I've realised a lot of things, and it would be good to chat after I left so abruptly. Let me know. I hope you're good.*

Hannah's hand shook as she held her phone, staring at the words. Lauren wanted to meet her? She'd realised things? What the fuck did that mean? Did she want her back? Did she want to move back into the flat?

Her mind filled with an image of Cordy's face looking up at her this morning. Hannah had moved on, Lauren had given her no choice. She was with Cordy now. She was a different person. Did she want to meet up with Lauren and have her past-self thrown back in her face? The answer was a resounding no.

She took a deep breath.

What should she do? Then it hit her. She was going to ignore it. Bury this message, ignore Lauren, and it would go away. Cordy didn't need to know. If she just pushed it down, Lauren might get the message.

Hannah made the decision, and in doing so, inexplicably fumbled her phone. Her fingers tried to grip it, but it was like they were greased with butter. Her phone fell from her hands.

What the actual fuck?

Hannah's eyes widened as she watched it sail through the air and spin, before continuing its journey downwards.

"Fuuuuck!" she shouted, just as a bike came into view on the path below pushed by Alan. "Alan, watch out!"

Alan looked up, then ducked. Her phone hit his shoulder, then bounced onto his delivery bag, where it settled. She held her breath – and she imagined Alan did, too – before they both stared at each other.

"I'm coming down, stay there."

Hannah turned, banged her leg into the table and her coffee sloshed over the top of her mug. She ignored it. She shimmied past her bike, out of the flat and down the stairs, skidding to a halt beside Alan.

"If you want to say good morning, I'd appreciate a heads-up before you launch a missile at me next time." He held out her phone with an eyebrow raised. "Good job I was wearing my helmet already."

Hannah winced. "I'm so sorry, are you okay?"

Alan patted himself down, then gave her a nod. "In one piece. Just about." He paused. "Are you okay, more to the point? You look a little ashen?"

"I thought I was just about to kill you, so that's probably it." She wasn't going to tell him of the missile her phone contained inside it, too. That was on a need-to-know basis.

Right now, Hannah had decided that nobody needed to know.

Alan seemed satisfied with her answer. "Bernice tells me Max is through to the semi-finals. Congrats! We're going to try to make this one. Promise." Alan nodded at his bike. "But now, I have to go and do my daily dice-with-death job so that people can have their Coke Zeros and protein shakes." He stopped, stared at Hannah, then leaned in and gave her a quick hug. "Despite me being on the end of your launch, you look like you could use that more than me today."

She watched him wheel his bike onto the pavement and away.

How did he know?

Chapter Twenty-Three

On Monday, Cordy took Hannah by the hand, and they got on the London overground to Whitechapel, then the Lizzy Line to Paddington. She wiped her seat free of pastry flakes – had the previous seat-dweller had a Gregg's sausage roll or a pain au raisin? – and moved a half-empty coffee cup from her feet. At just after 10am, the sun oozed through the windows like melted butter. Cordy congratulated herself for remembering to bring her sunglasses, especially now the weather was finally turning.

"What are we doing?"

"You'll see," Cordy told her, placing a quick kiss on her lips before they settled back into their seats. They'd just missed the morning rush, and now their fellow passengers on the train consisted of the non-9-to-5ers, kids late for school or bunking off, and the people like them, taking a day off.

"This almost seems decadent, right? Taking a Monday off and doing things while other people are at work?"

"Apart from I have every single Monday off."

Hannah gave her a smile. "There is that."

Even though they'd been sleeping together for a few weeks, they hadn't done anything that was vaguely like a date, which was one of the issues when you lived together. Also, they hadn't talked about what this was. Were they still just friends with benefits to Hannah?

Hence Cordy had requested that Hannah take a Monday off and had made sure they didn't just end up staying in bed. "We can do that any day. In fact, we did it until two o'clock this morning. My thigh muscles still hurt." She'd given Hannah a playful swipe then. "Today is about spending time together and having an adventure."

Hannah had told her they were just friends with benefits. For this to go anywhere, Hannah had to accept herself the way that Max did. Fully and unequivocally. If she didn't, Cordy knew this could crash and burn, taking with it her flat and the person who'd come to mean so much to her in such a short space of time.

When they arrived at Paddington, Cordy led Hannah out the side entrance of the sprawling station. She guided them past a few tall, shiny office blocks, across a bridge, and into Paddington Basin, a long, thin slice of water where two canals kissed. The expanse was surrounded by glinting apartment blocks, hip bars and cool restaurants. When she glanced at Hannah, she got an inquisitive look, but no further questions. It was only when they arrived at the GoBoat docking station that Hannah gave her a grin.

"We're going on the water?"

"We are. And you're the skipper, Hannah Driver." She reached into her bag and pulled out Theo's peaked cap. "For you to wear now." She raised an eyebrow. "And perhaps later."

"I can't believe you remembered that one of my dream jobs was to be a boat skipper and wear a peaked cap." Hannah shook her head with a smile. "Where did you get this?"

"I stole it from Theo. It's on loan, though, and the Captain wants it back. No dropping it in the canal."

Hannah stared at her, then kissed her lips. "You really do make my dreams come true."

"Yes, yes, I know. Again and again, over and over," Cordy told her with a wink. "This was easier than arranging for you to be a pilot for a day. My plan is to lie back and watch as you effortlessly glide us up the canal. And then back again because we have to deposit the boat back where we found it." She held up her phone. "And I'll be documenting it all for TikTok, of course. Max Girth, steering his ship to glory or some shit."

They listened to the bloke with an untamed beard tell them what to do, donned their less-than-sexy lime-green life jackets, and they were off. True to her word, Cordy relaxed beside Hannah, who sat with the peaked cap on her head, the tiller in her more-than-capable hand. Cordy was here for it.

They moved clear of the basin and out onto the canal proper. The smell of oil and salt mingled in the air, along with the promise of a day yet to be filled. The sun prickled Cordy's skin as she tilted her head back and soaked it in. Mondays normally involved cleaning, lesson-planning, or occasionally, visiting her gran. She and Hannah rarely spent quality time together out of bed. If they became more than just fuck buddies, perhaps this could become a regular thing. She smiled at the thought.

"When did you come up with this idea?"

A couple of ducks paddled by to their left. What kind, Cordy had no idea. She shrugged. "It just came to me in a flash of inspiration the other day when I was wondering what we could do as a first date." Cordy jolted. Shit. Had she said too much?

But Hannah only smiled. That sexy, sultry smile that Cordy hoped was just for her.

"This is a first date?"

Blood rushed to her cheeks as Cordy blinked furiously. "If you want it to be?"

Oh fuck, did Hannah want it to be? Yes, they were shagging, but did that mean she wanted more? Were they on the same page? She decided she didn't want the answer just yet.

"Anyway, you said you'd always wanted to skipper a boat. I thought, we've all got to start somewhere." Cordy's friend had just come back from two weeks in Croatia doing a skipper course, tanned and full of energy. For now, this algae-topped canal was a decent start. "I thought also, this is good practice for you taking control, navigating your way to success. What with the semi-final of the drag competition coming up."

Nicely smoothed over. Good work, Cordy.

Hannah frowned. "Since when did you become my life coach and manager?"

"Since I have a vested interest. The prize money is five thousand quid. If you win, you might buy me dinner."

Hannah grinned right back. "I definitely will. Maybe even a weekend away." Then her eyes widened as another GoBoat came into view coming right at them. Hannah veered left, but went a little too far, and couldn't course-correct in time to stop their boat smacking into the side of a stationery one. Luckily, it was a grey boat with no windows and nobody living there, rather than the row of houseboats beside it. Two blokes having their morning coffee on a nearby boat-top deck glanced their way and probably rolled their eyes.

When Cordy glanced over, Hannah's cheeks were red as she

pulled at her peak, then steered the boat back into the water, concentration full. Moments later, when the other GoBoat had passed, she looked at Cordy. "What were you saying about me navigating my way to success?" She frowned as she stared into Cordy's phone.

"I got it all on video, it's going to make a great outtake." She clicked stop, and grinned at Hannah.

"If that's what happens at the semis, I'm going to fall off the stage."

"Nonsense, you've got it out of the way early. Get the nerves out of your system. Besides, you've practised being Max far more than you've practised being captain of the Love Boat. I have complete faith in you on both counts." Cordy got up, wobbled, then sat back down. "I was going to kiss you, but I'll wait until we're on dry land."

They carried on gliding up the canal until they reached the junction Mr Beard had told them to turn at. Hannah skilfully manoeuvred the boat – Cordy made sure she got that on video, too – and they made their way back along the water. Out the window of one of the canal-side houses, Bowie's 'Let's Dance' floated into their senses.

"If that's not a good omen, I don't know what is," Cordy said. "Did I tell you one of my students played me a Bowie track this week? Ava, who writes her own stuff. Her parents are keen music fans, you can tell. She's going to play her own song at the summer concert, too. I can't wait for you to hear it. I gave her some suggestions for the chorus, but she's already a better songwriter than me. I'm looking forward to being name-checked on her first album. She's already promised me."

Hannah stretched out a denim-clad leg before she spoke. "Talking of your school concert..."

Uh-oh. Something was up. Cordy studied Hannah's face and waited for her to continue.

"Because of all the TikTok attention, ticket sales have spiralled, and they've changed the venue of the semi-finals and the final."

"That's great!" Cordy couldn't see the catch, but she was betting there was one.

"It is," Hannah agreed. "But more importantly, they've also changed the date of the final, and it's the same day as your school concert. If I get through – still a big if – I can ask Theo to put me last in the show so I can be at both. At least to help you out at first. I want to support you as you've supported me."

Cordy's stomach dropped. Dammit, that was the last thing she needed. Hannah had promised to help, and she needed her. Also, she didn't want to miss Hannah's big moment if she got there. But she had to suck it up. Her concert was just a school thing. Hannah's competition might be the start of the rest of her life. "You've got to put the competition first."

Hannah chewed on her lip. "I know, but I want to be at your concert, too. You've put a lot of effort into it. Plus, I said I'd help with the makeup, and I will."

But Cordy didn't want any grey clouds today. Up above, the sun was shining and the sky was blue. She wanted to keep it that way. "Let's not worry about it now. Let's see if you get through, and what happens nearer the time. Maybe you can still help out during the day, and I can make both."

"If it happens, I'm going to try my hardest."

"I know you will." And she did. It hadn't taken long for

Hannah to gain a foothold in her trust, but she'd done it. Cordy hadn't felt this pull to anyone in years. But she didn't want to speak it. Didn't want to jinx it. Rather, today was about showing it.

"But if you get through, win, and start a whole new career; and if I then play with Ruby O'Connell in June and she books me for her tour... what a year! Remember our dream jobs? You wanted to skipper a boat in a peaked cap and you're doing it. I wanted to play piano on a world tour. It could happen." *Unlikely, but it could.* "This year started off so rocky for us both, but now, the sky's the limit. We've got to grasp whatever opportunities come our way with both hands. Just you and me."

When Hannah looked at her, something crossed her face. Didn't she agree? Cordy wanted to make her see that they were young with the whole world in front of them. What's more, that if they stuck together, everything would be so much easier.

Hannah gave her a smile that didn't quite reach her eyes. "I agree. Just you and me."

* * *

After the boat trip, they walked the Great Union canal in the sunshine, past Little Venice and through Regent's Park, ending up in Camden. They sat on a bench near Camden lock, chicken kebabs wrapped in foil in their hands, watching the crowds drift by.

It had been the kind of day Cordy wanted to bottle: wholesome, romantic, couply. Not that they were a couple. But if they added Mondays like this to their roster, maybe that would come. Perhaps it was already here. But Cordy wasn't going to push Hannah. Even though she really wanted to.

Cordy bit into her kebab, and licked her finger as the garlic mayo dripped down it. When she raised her head, Hannah was watching her. Cordy's cheeks heated. If this was a first date, she wanted to present her best self, even though Hannah had seen her in the morning, sleep-creased and caffeine-deficient. Despite that, it still mattered. She wanted to be the person who could eat a kebab without getting it all down her hands and wrists. Small goals.

"I've loved today," Hannah said, not taking her eyes from Cordy.

Cordy wiped her mouth before she replied. "Me, too."

"We should do more dates."

"Hard agree."

"Maybe not just on a Monday."

"Less crowds." But Cordy liked where this conversation was going.

"Not in Camden," Hannah smiled. "But I guess Mondays are when those in the entertainment industries go out. We are in the entertainment industries now, aren't we?"

"Do you believe it now?"

"I do."

"Did I tell you I got another piano gig at a new bar in Dalston? High-end cocktail bar, and they want someone to play the classics once a fortnight. Next step on my scheme to take over the world, one piano bar at a time."

"Ruby O'Connell will be lucky if you can fit her into your schedule."

They gave each other dopey grins, and Cordy's heart swelled.

"I love that we're now in the entertainment industry." Hannah paused as two rowdy blokes walked by, shouting at each other. "You've turned my life around since we met, you know that?"

"I think you had a hand in it, too."

"I've definitely had my hands in a lot of places." Hannah grinned, then locked their gazes. "But it's not just about sex."

"I know." Cordy did. That's what today had been about. "You've opened up London to me, too. Introduced me to drag kings. One especially I'm particularly fond of."

"Sir Loin of Beef?"

"How did you guess?" Cordy grinned. "Is it weird that I feel like I've known you forever?"

Hannah shuffled along the bench until their thighs crushed together. "It's not. I feel the same. How could I not?"

Cordy's heart stuttered. "It's just, I know that Lauren did a number on you. I want you to know that you can feel safe with me. That this is real."

Hannah stiffened and gulped in a breath. "I know. I can feel that." She put down her kebab, and took Cordy's hand in hers. "I want every Monday to be like this from now on. Think of what we could do if we started every week like this."

"It would be fucking epic."

"Next Monday is the day after the semi-final. If we come back here, am I still going to be in the competition?"

"No doubt in my mind."

The skin at the side of Hannah's eyes crinkled as she pressed her lips to Cordy's, and Cordy's heart took off.

This was so much more than sex. They'd both caught feelings, and she knew that Hannah felt it, too. It was in the tempo of her mouth as it moved over Cordy's, the way she leaned into her, knowing Cordy would catch her. It was in the way her hand tightened in Cordy's hair. Hannah's kisses melted her like ice cream on a summer's day. They caused a delicious ache for more.

As she pulled back and opened her eyes, she dared to dream.

This was going to work out.

Hannah was going to win.

This story was going to have a happy ending.

Chapter Twenty-Four

The last-minute venue change messed with Hannah's mind. At the usual place, she might have moaned about the toilets they had to change in, and the tiny backstage area where you had to wait to go on stage, but after three performances, she knew what to expect. She understood the crowds.

Tonight was set to be different. On a Saturday night, the streets of Shoreditch were filled with bridge-and-tunnel people who'd made the trip to the hipster east to see what eccentricities they could find. Drag kings fitted the bill perfectly. The vibe was different. She knew this from her burlesque gigs. You never knew what might happen. However, she was a professional, and she had to deal with it.

As she sat in front of the mirror in the small basement room, she thought of her mum performing the Bowie song all those years ago. How she said the music made her come alive. Hannah got that completely.

Plus, as her makeup pencil grazed her cheeks, she thought of Cordy doing her original makeup that had now become her design. "Go bigger on the cheekbones. It's a big crowd. Everyone needs to see it." Tonight's crowd was going to be her biggest yet. Hannah leaned forward and made sure you could see her five o'clock shadow from space. Then she got to work on her stubble.

In half an hour, Hannah would take it to the Max.

***

"Beautiful people, you've now seen every act bar one, but I guarantee you he's worth the wait. Give it up for the TikTok sensation, the one, the only, Max Girth!"

Max strutted onto the stage, took the microphone from the Captain, gave him a salute, then put the microphone on its stand. "Hello Shoreditch! New venue tonight. I see we've moved down a notch from Dalston. Give me a holler if you're here from out of town and this is the first time you've seen such a gorgeous mobster in your life!"

A whoop from the crowd.

"You see, I'm here from the 1950s, a time where women are women, and men are men. There ain't no in-between, you get me?" A pregnant pause. "Although, I had a dream the other night where a dude came to me." More whoops. "I told him, in no uncertain terms, that my dreams were not this way. That I'd heard about dreams like that, but they weren't for people like me."

Max paused for laughter which duly arrived. He scanned the crowd, and caught sight of Cordy on his left, where she always was, with Greta by her side. His constant support group. They'd worked on this routine together. Treading the line between going too far, and pulling it back to show how times had changed, and how times simply get caught in a loop.

"You know, I don't mind what kind of dreams y'all have,

so long as you have them behind closed doors, and don't shout about them. But this dream guy, he was insistent. He told me about a future where there weren't just men and women, but there were in-between people. People who were both genders – or none. People who could change genders. And there were more than just two genders. That's when I knew it was a dream, you know what I'm sayin'? I was all set to wake up, but then this guy, he dropped a tune on me and I didn't want to wake up. But when I did, I couldn't shake it from my head. You want to hear it London?"

Whoops from the crowd, cries of "Yes Max!" from two women near the front of the stage. They'd been to every round. Max remembered them.

"Let's see if I can remember the words... Music, maestro, please."

Stage left, the Captain gave a grin, pressed play on the backing track, and Max strode to the front of the stage as the opening bars of Bowie's 'Rebel Rebel' kicked in. The crowd went wild, with twentysomethings revelling in a track they'd perhaps just heard, and the older punters wallowing as a cool, nostalgia trip washed over them.

Max pressed his teeth together and saw the lyrics flash up in his head. He wasn't going to forget them tonight. He sang the first line loud and true.

That was when he saw her in the crowd. Eyes the same dark, brooding nature as when Hannah had first fallen for her. An inquisitive, open look on her face.

Lauren. The woman Hannah had been avoiding ever since she messaged two weeks ago. Now standing less than ten feet away, staring at Max.

Who stuttered. Paused, on stage, in front of all these people. It was a split second, but it threw him off.

Max glanced at Cordy, who beamed his way. He eyed the oblivious crowd. He wouldn't let Lauren throw his life off course again.

More to the point, *Hannah* wouldn't let it happen.

Instead, Max strode across the stage, thrust his hips, jumped to the next line of the song and sang it for all he was worth. For all Hannah was worth. For every time she'd thought she couldn't do something and so she'd stopped. Max was the antithesis of that. Max just did it.

Hannah had learned to just do it, too.

As Max hit the chorus, he strode the stage like a lion, daring anyone to derail him. Nobody could. So long as he didn't look Lauren's way again. When he got to the end of that song, the crowd went berserk.

Max breathed in the acclaim, and turned to the space where Cordy was. She patted her chest with her hand and mouthed "ba-doom". Their sign. It gave Max extra fuel. Something he needed now, without the music to get lost in.

"I dunno, London, this guy, he was like a spaceman, you know?" Still not looking Lauren's way. Anywhere but there. "But then, his friend joined him. This guy, he wore crazy-cool threads, and he told me he was from Mars." Max scanned the crowd, and then stuttered again.

What the actual fuck was going on tonight?

Because there, looking directly at him with her mouth wide open, was his sister, Betty. Her dark hair corkscrewed around her face. Her red lips formed an O. Her friends that Hannah had once met at a party – she couldn't recall their names – stood either side of her, faces expectant. But none of them shared the same look that Betty did. One that told Max he was busted.

He took a deep breath, glanced at Cordy, then the judges, and ploughed on. There was nothing more he could do. He was a professional, the crowd was waiting, and this was a competition.

But holy fucking shit, what had Hannah done in a past life to warrant her whole current life turning up en masse to watch her give the performance that mattered most? This was pressure of a wholly different sort. But Max was equal to it.

To that end, he took a gulp of air, gripped the mic, and finished his pre-song banter. "Not only was he from Mars. He was from a planet called Bruno Mars. You know it?" He glanced at Theo in the wings, gave him a nod, and the opening bars of 'Uptown Funk' flowed into the air.

The crowd went wild.

Max gave a grin. Ignored Lauren, but looked directly at Betty.

"This one is going out to the woman with the shocked look on her face."

And then, he started to sing, ignoring the quantum firework display that was taking place in his very soul.

* * *

Max walked off stage, crazy applause ringing in his ears, but he didn't know which way to walk. Any path seemed dangerous. One led to Betty. The other to Lauren. The other to Cordy, who had no idea that Lauren had been in touch. Suddenly, from being the venue where his dreams might take one more step into reality, it now appeared to be one giant tripwire. A place where his whole life might blow up.

Where *Hannah's* life might blow up.

Max smoothed back his hair as the Sir Loin of Beef approached, sporting a wide grin. He held out a hand. Max shook it, marvelling at his impressive stomach, contoured into a six-pack with some clever makeup.

"Dude, you killed it." He motioned with his head. "Can you hear the crowd out there?"

Once Max subdued his fight-or-flight instincts, he could still hear the crowd's appreciation and excitement. He'd felt it humming through his veins when he was on stage earlier. But first Lauren and then Betty had thrown him into another realm.

The only people who knew about Max were those who'd been present at his birth. It didn't include Hannah's family or her ex.

It did now.

Or maybe not, if Max could get out of here avoiding them all. One thing he knew: he was desperate for a pee.

"Thanks dude, I appreciate it."

"I always knew you were my biggest competition," Sir Loin added. "That still stands. May the best kings get through tonight, and in a few weeks' time, may the best king win."

Max squeezed Sir Loin's arm as he walked by, and headed for the loo, which was thankfully fairly empty, due to the show still going on. Max heard the Captain on the microphone as he walked in. There to greet him was Cordy.

"C'mere, you stud."

She wrapped her arms around a particularly stiff Max.

He tried to loosen his shoulders, but nothing was giving. Did Cordy detect anything?

When she pulled back, there was a question in her eyes as she rested her gentle gaze on him.

Max didn't deserve her.

Hannah should have told her about the messages.

But what were the chances of Lauren turning up at Max's show, of all the venues in London? Max scrubbed that thought from his brain. He had to focus on the here and now.

"You okay? You're giving off really weird vibes for someone who just smashed it out there."

Max glanced over his shoulder at the person coming into the loo. Not Lauren or Betty. His shoulders were still clenched.

"Just still coming down, you know?" *Lies.* "Did I do okay?"

"More than okay, you have to know that. You fucking rocked it!" Cordy leaned in and placed a kiss on his lips, careful not to smudge anything. "Sir Loin was incredible, but if you don't get through after that deafening applause, something's up with the judging."

Max nodded. "Fingers crossed. Two to go through. Hopefully me and Sir Loin."

The door opened and a woman walked into the loo. It was Betty.

Max's spine locked up. He held his breath and tried to blend in with the tiled walls. He was pretty sure it wasn't going to work.

Betty stopped dead when she clocked the pair of them.

"I knew it was you as soon as you opened your mouth up there." She shook her head. "I cannot fucking believe how incredible you were." She shook her head, a grin spread wide on her face. "Max Girth. I also cannot believe how saucy you were! I was blushing on your behalf. I think you might have turned the head of one of our hen party, and she's already married. To a man!" She pulled Max into a hug.

"Watch the makeup," Max told her, and she obediently pulled back.

"Sorry, sorry. Just so excited to see my sister on stage doing brilliant things." She paused. "Or are you my brother, Max?" That idea clearly tickled Betty. "I always fancied having a brother. Having one called Max Girth takes the biscuit."

"I'm glad you enjoyed it, but can you not tell Mum and Dad?" Max's ears tingled as panic strode around his body. "I will eventually, but I just wasn't ready last time. It's still very new."

"It didn't look that way, you were incredible. Mum would love to see you perform. So would Dad and Amy. We need to invite them."

Max nodded. "I will. But just let me do it, okay?"

Right then, a woman wearing jeans and a tight black shirt walked in the door. She stopped when she saw Max.

Max froze. It was Lauren. Their gazes locked and he knew he'd been rumbled.

"Hannah?"

Shit the fucking bed. Max's mouth opened, then closed.

Cordy looked from Max, to Lauren, then back. "Are you going to introduce me?"

Max stared at Lauren, then at Betty whose eyes were like saucers, before slowly nodding Cordy's way. "You could say that. This is Lauren. My ex."

The penny dropped as Cordy gave a slow nod. "Nice to meet you." She was nothing if not polite. "I'm Cordy. Hannah's... new flatmate."

Lauren raised an eyebrow. "You've got a new flatmate." A pause. "In our old flat?" She gave Cordy a once-over. "But I can see that things have changed a great deal since I left. Then, you were swinging nipple tassels. Now, you're a drag king."

"A lot can change in six months," Max countered.

"Apparently." Lauren paused. "Is that why you haven't returned my messages?"

There it was.

Max winced, glanced at Cordy, then back at Lauren. "I've just been busy."

"I can see." Lauren's gaze slid from Max to Cordy to Betty. "Nice to see you again, Betty."

Betty's features were taut as she nodded. "You, too."

Lauren leaned left. "Anyway, I need the loo. Maybe we can chat later?"

Max nodded. "Cool."

"I need the loo, too." Betty held up a finger. "But stay right there. This isn't finished."

Max watched them both disappear before turning back to Cordy. "I can explain."

"I'm sure you can." Cordy took hold of Max's tie and led him into the corridor.

Max remembered when Cordy had grabbed his tie before. The first time they'd fucked. He much preferred that time to this. He scanned the corridor, and nodded his thanks at a couple of passing punters who told him he was great. He only wished Cordy thought so, too.

"It's not what it looks like."

Cordy nodded, but the look in her eyes told Max she didn't believe a word he said. "Are you talking as Max or Hannah? Because I feel like one of you says one thing, while the other says something completely different." She kept her voice low.

"I don't want to have our first argument in a public place. Not while you're still dressed as Max Girth, and ready to slay the world." She shook her head. "The thing is, you told me what we were at the start. Friends with benefits. I pushed it, and maybe I didn't listen because I wanted us to be more. But you're still not ready to commit. You're still not ready to come out fully as who you are. Or maybe this is the real you. Maybe I've been blind all this time. Maybe you've been keeping your options open."

"It's not like that."

"What is it like, then?" Cordy hissed, throwing her hands up. "I really want to think the best, but Lauren just turns up at one of your shows and you've been messaging…" She pursed her lips and looked away, trying to compose herself.

If she cried, Max would lose it.

She turned her head back. "I said I don't want to do this here, and I meant it. But how does this look?"

Max frowned.

This was not how tonight was meant to go.

"I haven't been exchanging messages, please know that. Her turning up is a coincidence. And we are more than friends with benefits. I told you that last week."

"I thought so, too, until a few minutes ago when your past hurtled back into your life."

"Can we talk about this later? This is all coincidence, you have to believe that. But right now, I have to go to the loo and get backstage for the final judging."

She reached over and took Cordy's hand in hers. She really hoped she believed her, but she could see how it looked. "Please trust me. What I said on Monday still stands. I want to be your girlfriend. I know I never said the words, but it's true. I haven't been lying."

"Maybe not. But you've been omitting facts. I'm not sure which is worse."

Chapter Twenty-Five

Last night hadn't turned out at all as Cordy had expected. She'd anticipated Max getting through to the final, them snogging when he walked off-stage and her being the envy of all the queer women in the club because she was the one who got to go home with the superstar.

Instead, Max *had* gone through, but after Lauren and Betty showed up, his attention fractured, and their lust bubble got its very first puncture. They'd walked home with Theo and Greta chattering away, but they'd been quiet. When Hannah took her makeup off, she'd wanted to talk, but Cordy was too tired and confused about what had gone on. There was a splinter in their trust now. And all the while, playing in the background of her mind was a particular song on repeat. Its title: 'Never Get Involved With Your Flatmate'. For the first time since they'd got together, they'd slept in their own beds.

When she woke up this morning, Hannah was still asleep. Cordy had intended to spend the first part of the day in bed with Hannah, and the second half preparing for her week's classes. But after last night, she made the decision to go visit her grandparents.

When she got there, the house was full. Six women –

including Kate and Meg and a few others she recognised from the wedding – sat around her gran and Joan's table.

Cordy got herself a coffee, then was introduced to the others. She plonked herself on the piano stool. She'd taught Finn his lesson here yesterday morning. She tried to cover up how she was feeling, but apparently it didn't work. Her gran had a sixth sense. She guessed she looked the way she felt: gutted.

"What's going on with my favourite granddaughter? Last time you were here, you were glowing and hinting that things had moved on with Hannah. But something's changed since then, judging by your face." Her gran exchanged a look with Joan.

"Can we not do this in front of guests, Gran? It's been a difficult weekend as it is."

"These are not just guests, Cordy. These women have been at the coalface of queer life for decades. My darling Joan is the leader, of course." Gran lifted Joan's hand to her lips and applied a kiss. "But you know Kate and Meg, and although you don't know their friends Jess, Lucy, Tanya and Sophie quite as well, they all know a thing or two about surviving in the world of lesbian dating. Am I right?" Gran gestured to each woman as she said their name.

Cordy looked around as all six nodded.

"I mean, I survived Tanya, and if I can do that, I can do anything." Meg winked in Tanya's direction.

Tanya, in response, rolled her eyes. She was an imposing figure with intense green eyes. The wedding band on her left hand glinted in the afternoon sunlight beaming in through the kitchen skylight. "Then you had kids, and you realised the pain I caused you was a piece of cake, right?"

"She has a point," Kate agreed.

Cordy glanced at Meg and Tanya. "Wait, did you two used to go out? I've only ever known you with Kate."

"Believe it or not," Meg said, before placing her palms over her wife's ears, "Kate was not the first woman I slept with."

Mock outrage overtook Kate's face. "There was a time before me?"

Cordy had to hand it to Meg, she had good taste. Tanya was a tall drink of water, and Kate could easily have graced the covers of the magazines she once worked on. But Cordy wouldn't have put Meg and her together.

Then again, she wouldn't put Tanya and Sophie together: dressed head to toe in black, Tanya looked like she might work as a spy, whereas, in her jeans, hoodie and an undercut, Sophie looked like the poster girl for cool urban living. However, the loving look she threw Tanya's way showed they worked well.

"It was all approximately one million years ago," Tanya replied with a wave of her hand. "And yes, I admit, I might have done some things wrong, but I was young. Sue me."

"I would have tried, but you were a lawyer," Meg grinned. "I didn't fancy my chances."

Tanya threw back her head and chuckled. "If I hadn't been a terrible girlfriend, you wouldn't have found yourself hooked up with Kate, so you should be thanking me, really."

"Is that right?" Meg leaned over and kissed Kate's cheek. "It's true, our lives could have been very different. Everything happens for a reason."

"And I assume something has happened with you?" Gran asked Cordy.

Unease twisted in her stomach. She didn't want trial by lesbian jury. Then again, they did know what they were talking about. She hardly saw these women much, so what could it hurt? "We've been together for a few weeks, but not calling it anything. It's still new. No labels."

"This generation hate labels," Joan lamented. "But sometimes, sticking a label on something makes it more solid. More real."

Gran wrapped her fingers around Joan's hand. "Let her continue."

Cordy threw her hands up. "I don't know! You've met her, she's amazing. And she was doing her act last night—"

"Hannah is the drag king who's going to be performing at your party," Gran told Kate and Meg.

"Max Girth or Captain Von Strap?" Kate asked.

"Fab names," Lucy added.

"Aren't they?" Kate agreed.

"Max Girth," Cordy said with a sigh.

"Hopefully she still will be?" Kate added.

"I hope so," Cordy replied. "But then, last night was a little weird, because her ex turned up. Who she only split up with six months ago. They've had no contact, but I think she was pretty broken up at the time. However, now I find out the ex has been messaging her. Hannah swears it's only one way, but she never told me about it. Yet she's told me we're just friends with benefits." She glanced up. "Sorry, Gran." She shrugged. "So now, I don't know what to believe."

Her gran looked at her with soft eyes. "The fact you're here shows how much this means to you. Even though it's only been a short space of time you've been together. When I met Joan, I knew something was different. When we slept together for the first time – remember that, it was after you made me dinner? – I knew I never wanted to let her go. Feelings can happen quickly. The length of time is irrelevant."

"I just don't know where we're going, that's the problem. One minute we're fuck buddies, the next we might be more, but only on her terms. If we're going nowhere, I might need to find a new place to live. Hence, I'm spiralling a bit."

Okay, spiralling a lot.

However, she also felt a swell of sympathy in the air. All eight pairs of eyes following her every word sat above kind smiles. The type that told Cordy they understood. Despite that, it didn't change the fact that Hannah should have been honest about her ex.

Maybe that's why she didn't want to call Cordy her girlfriend. Because she was weighing up her options. Cordy had thought it was Hannah's old insecurities rearing their head. She'd never dreamed it was something more sinister.

"You know, admitting you like someone is hard at any age." Sophie's cockney accent was loud and proud. "Just because you're in your 20s doesn't mean it's any easier. If it helps, I was a hot mess in my 20s. I'm far cooler in my 30s."

"She is," Tanya smirked. "Hotter, too."

Sophie gave her wife a wry smile. "I had a terrible ex who strung me along and was still stringing me along when I met Tanya. Sometimes, the person who's been dumped is happier in the long run. However, it can take a little time and if the ex comes back, it can mess with your head. Perhaps the messages were one way, and your partner just needed time to sort out her reaction."

"This time just felt different. *She* felt different." Cordy leaned over and stuffed a Jaffa Cake in her mouth.

"Did you talk about it?" Gran asked.

Cordy shook her head and swallowed. "A little, but we slept in our own beds last night. The first time that's happened since we shagged. She says she didn't know her ex was going to turn up last night, but she's been messaging and that seems a little too coincidental, don't you think?"

"From what I saw of Hannah at the open mic, she likes you, too," Gran told her. "If her ex has been out of the picture, maybe her showing up is just a bump in the road. Maybe you need to be more assertive and fight for her. Only you know if you want to do that."

"I agree with your gran. Hard as it is, you need to sit down and talk it through, see where you stand," Meg added. "Communication is always key with these things. When will you see her next?"

Cordy put her head in her hands. She knew communication was key. But if it was as easy as that, she'd have done it. She couldn't face it last night or this morning. Maybe in a few days' time, she'd feel differently. "She's working tonight, but hopefully one night this week."

"Do you want it to work?"

A definite nod. "I thought it was." She looked around the room. "I was falling for her." Why was she telling all these strangers this? Maybe because it was easier than telling Hannah. Than facing up to the truth that Hannah didn't feel the same. "She gets me, and we just click. But she's broken my trust a little."

"Can you rebuild the trust?"

"I think so. Unless she's cheated. But then, we aren't a couple, so can she even cheat?" Cordy's brain spun so hard, it turned itself to dust.

"If you've both been in the same bed every night, you're a couple. You just haven't said it yet." Kate's clear voice sliced through Cordy's bewilderment. Was that true? It sounded plausible.

"We always were a couple in my head, and I thought we were in hers. I hate dating, did I mention that?"

All eight of her audience gave a sympathetic nod.

"It's the reason Lucy convinced me to marry her: she told me I'd never have to go out on the dating scene ever again. I signed on the dotted line there and then." Jess gave her wife a wink.

"That, and the fact that you love me." Lucy, a dead ringer for Heather Peace, rolled her eyes.

"Of course, that, too," Jess replied. "But the thing is, if you click, it's worth sticking around. Exes can pop up when you don't want them, just ask Lucy. My ex came all the way from Australia to tell me she wanted me back, but Lucy believed me when I told her I didn't know she was coming. She could easily not have. If she's worth it, give her a chance to explain."

Cordy couldn't argue with years of relationship experience. "I just feel really vulnerable, you know? Like my heart's on the line. I hate it."

"That's what happens when you fall in love," Joan told her, years of unrequited love written into every crease of her face. "You have to trust that the other person treats your heart with care. The catch is, you don't know until you try."

"I worry she's still not totally available." Cordy sipped her coffee, then wrung her hands. Was she? She thought Hannah had made so much progress with her life and her family, but why the lies? It didn't add up.

"She sounds very much like Jess when I met her. Maybe you'll be the one to change her mind, make her change her ways. But you might have to be patient. Just like I was."

Jess leaned over and kissed Lucy. "She really was. Now my mum loves her more than she loves me."

Would that be the case for Cordy and Hannah?

Right now, she had no clue.

Chapter Twenty-Six

Hannah met Lauren on the Southbank on a freezing May 1st. She'd chosen this spot because it seemed safe. With the London Eye in the background and the river Thames by her side, it was public enough for nothing significant to happen. If Lauren wanted her back, she was less likely to make a scene when Hannah turned her down. If Lauren wanted to tell her some home truths, she was less likely to shout with hundreds of tourists in her lap. She'd expected it to be hotter, but that was the British weather. She'd put on her big coat again today.

She saw her ex before Lauren spotted her. Hannah took the liberty of giving her a once-over. When she saw her at the club, she'd only taken in a few details, too shocked to document Lauren six months on with Cordy and Betty in the same room. Now though, she had a chance to evaluate.

Lauren still looked fabulous. Her blonde hair moved in the river breeze, she wore new jeans that fitted her perfectly, and she was giving off an energy that told everyone she was not to be fucked with. That wasn't new. Lauren had always had that. When she split with Hannah, she'd told her she'd dulled her energy, made her doubt herself and who she was. It seemed like she'd got it back over the past half year.

When Lauren turned her head, she saw Hannah approaching

and smiled. Hannah had woken up wondering what to wear, until she snapped herself out of it. She wasn't here to impress. She was here to clear the air and move on with her life. "Closure" is what Lauren had said on her message.

"Hey, good to see you."

Lauren's words sounded sincere. Hannah wasn't sure what she'd expected, but it was a good start. "You, too."

"You want to get a coffee, or walk and talk?"

"Both? There's a great coffee truck near the Oxo tower."

"Lead the way." Lauren gestured with her hand, and they fell into step, the Thames choppy to their left. "I have to tell you, before we talk about anything else, you were amazing the other night. Your voice? I've heard you sing before, but it was on another level how good it was. You had the crowd in the palm of your hand. Great makeup, too. If I hadn't heard you talk, I wouldn't have presumed it was you in a million years. The old Hannah would never have got up on stage dressed as a man." She bumped her elbow to Hannah's. "This new Hannah is far more evolved."

Hannah's brain took a few moments to compute the elbow bump. On the one hand, Lauren didn't have the right to make such an intimate connection with her. She gave up that right when she walked out. On the other, what she said was right. Hannah had come a long way since she last saw her.

"Thanks."

"I mean it," Lauren continued, glancing Hannah's way. "You know my thoughts on burlesque – it's for the male gaze, despite what you might say. But drag kings are definitely for the queer gaze. If you'd become a drag king while we were together and been more open about who you were, who knows what might have happened?" She held up a palm. "And don't worry, this isn't a pitch to get you back. I'm happier than I've been in a long time. From what I've seen, so are you, if the other night and your new flatmate are anything to go by."

Hannah dug her hands into her coat pockets and studied the floor. She didn't want to react or say the wrong thing. The last time they'd spoken before Lauren left, there had been a lot of accusations flying around. Now life was different. Hannah was ready for a relationship, and had a new career on the horizon.

They arrived at the outdoor food court, an ornate stone arch at its front. A black-coloured coffee truck stood at the front, and Hannah gestured to it. "Best flat white this side of the river. Can I get you one?"

Lauren nodded. "Yes please."

They took their steaming drinks to the river wall and perched there, resting them on the wide slab of concrete. It was low tide, the river barely a quarter of the way up its banks. Below them, on a huge square of sand, a man was carving intricate sand sculptures, and advertising his Instagram details where people could leave tips. He was just putting the finishing touches to a sand dragon, replete with flames arcing out of its nose.

Hannah shivered as the breeze got under her coat.

"Why don't you do up your coat now it's got buttons? I'm amazed you finally got them sewn on."

"I didn't," Hannah replied, before glancing down and seeing them there, plain as day. "What the..." she began, then realised.

Cordy. She'd sewn on her buttons for her. She'd seen the sewing kit out the other night when she was doing some outfits for her summer concert. After their boat date. Before the semi-final, where things had spiralled out of control. She must have done it then.

A rush of love sailed through Hannah, warming her skin all over. She did up her coat, then stroked the buttons. Cordy had thought of her, and acted out of kindness, and perhaps something more. It made Hannah feel cared for. Loved. It also made the riverbank a whole lot warmer, too.

"Anyway," Hannah crashed on before Lauren could say anything else about the buttons. Hannah gripped them tight. "You know a little about how things are with me. I'm a drag king, still doing burlesque, and I'm a delivery rider now, too. Portfolio career, isn't that what they call it? What about you? Still in the same job?"

It felt like they were on a really weird first date. The conversation was polite, stilted. A year ago, they'd lived together, shared their lives. Now, they were trying to remember what connected them. It was still there somewhere, but the past six months had buried it. Or perhaps it had been buried for far longer than that, which was why Lauren had left in the first place.

"Yep, still in the same corporate career, so you can still hate me for that."

"I never hated you."

Lauren's mouth quirked at the edges. "You kinda did. You told me it reminded you of your family. Of what you were supposed to do."

"Did I?" Maybe she had. It sounded like something she might have thought, but she couldn't recall. "I'm sorry if I told you that; it was out of order."

Lauren shrugged. "Water under the bridge. I wanted to

meet up just to let you know I'm back in London, and I don't want it to feel weird if we bump into each other. Like we did the other night." She raised an eyebrow. "I've moved on. I recently met someone."

Hannah's stomach lurched, but she wasn't sure why. She didn't want to be with Lauren; she'd moved on, too. Still, this was all new. This mature chat about their lives. She was navigating it on the fly.

"I wanted to let you know. Not to rub it in, but so we could be okay. You were important to me, and you still are. I just had to get away when I did. You were spiralling and you wouldn't listen to me. I had to look after myself."

Hannah sipped her coffee, the sting of Lauren's words fresh on her skin. "You left very abruptly, though. It felt pretty harsh. Plus, it could have made me homeless."

"I knew you'd work something out, or your family would help. They were lovely when I met them, albeit briefly. They were more available than you for most of our relationship. It was meeting them that made me see something had to change. If it wasn't going to be you, then it had to be me." She winced. "It wasn't easy to leave, but it was the right thing to do."

"But you just disappeared off the face of the earth."

"I went home, then I went abroad. My employer said I could work from anywhere. My cousin has that place in Spain, and offered it to me."

"You couldn't have let me know where you were?"

Lauren sighed. "At the time, I didn't see the point. I left you that note explaining why. It seemed enough. But I know it was abrupt. I apologise for that. I wasn't at my best. I hope you can forgive me."

When Hannah stared at Lauren, something lifted from her shoulders. She felt lighter. Brighter. She suddenly realised there was nothing to forgive. Whatever remnants of their relationship she'd been carrying around had just flown away. She shook her head.

"Let's call it even. I know I was a pain to be in a relationship with. I know I wasn't who I should have been. I held myself back, and by association, you, and us. I was a bad girlfriend, someone who couldn't even say the word. I think you could have handled the split a little better, but do I blame you? No."

A glimmer of a smile ghosted over Lauren's face. "Who are you, and what have you done with the real Hannah Driver?"

For the first time since they met up, Hannah laughed. "I'm hoping this is the real me." The one Cordy had chiselled out of the old her.

"And your new flatmate is your girlfriend, I assume? Otherwise, it's a tight squeeze."

Hannah rolled her shoulders. "We haven't exactly put a label on it yet."

Lauren frowned and fixed Hannah with her dark, arresting gaze. "Have you learned nothing? I assume you like her?"

Hannah nodded. "I do, but it's early days."

Lauren rolled her eyes. "I say this as a friend, but wake the fuck up. What did I always tell you? Life isn't a rehearsal. You were always waiting for a better day to get things done. Always putting things off. But that better day is today."

She held up her coffee. "If that coffee truck had waited to perfect their flat white, we wouldn't have walked past a handful of coffee shops to come here. But we did. Because that coffee truck put their all into perfecting exactly who they were and what they wanted to produce." She pressed her index finger to Hannah's arm. "You need to be that coffee truck."

Hannah let out a small huff of laughter. Lauren had always been bossy. But sometimes, it had been necessary. Perhaps today was one of those times, too.

"If you haven't told her you want to be her girlfriend yet, what else are you holding back on? Holding her hand in public? Telling her how you really feel? Introducing her to your family? Don't make the same mistakes you did with me because you're carrying around some weird shame on your shoulders. Your family love you. You need to remember that."

"She's met my family," Hannah countered.

"As your girlfriend?"

Hannah bit the inside of her cheek. "Not quite. I was waiting for the right moment."

Lauren lifted her palm to her forehead and let out a strangled laugh. "We didn't work because of many reasons. But a key one was that you weren't invested in us. You weren't fully out. You weren't your true self, who I knew you were inside.

Seeing you on that stage the other night, I thought, 'fuck, she's finally embraced who she is'. But now you tell me it's only on stage, not off it. If you want to be happy, you have to be you in every aspect of your life. Tell your family. Call her your girlfriend. Kiss her in public. You'll be amazed how freeing it feels."

The skin on Hannah's scalp prickled. She and Cordy needed to have a conversation. She and Lauren were in the past, but Cordy could truly be her future. She just had to tell her. Was she scared Cordy wouldn't feel the same way? But then Hannah thought back to that day in Camden. What Cordy had said. She felt the same way. Hannah had just been avoiding it.

She was glad she'd come today. Lauren had given her the nudge she needed.

"You're right: I haven't fully committed. I just hope it's not too late and she'll still have me."

"If the way she looked at you – and the evils she gave me the other night are anything to go by – you'll be fine. Just do it soon, promise me?"

"I promise."

"Plus, you look way hot as a drag king. She'd be crazy to let you go."

Hannah laughed. "Did you fancy Max until you realised it was me?"

Lauren rolled her eyes. "Of course not," she replied, nodding.

Chapter Twenty-Seven

"Okay, let's do this once again from the top." Cordy rearranged her bum on her piano stool in the school auditorium. Today, it smelt like fried fish after a fish-and-chip lunch, her least favourite smell.

"Romilly, please focus on hitting the right notes. Ava, you need to come in at the right place for your solo. Jamal, you're doing great, just pick up the pace a little more towards the end of the second verse. The rest of the chorus, please watch me for instructions on the big number. Trust yourselves. I trust you. You can all do this, and you're going to be great."

If she said it enough times, she almost believed it. She wasn't sure why all her star pupils and chorus alike were choosing today to fuck up their performances, with only two weeks to go to the summer concert. Maybe they were picking up the vibes she was giving out.

That she didn't believe in anything much anymore. That she thought her life was going well, until Hannah threw in a roadblock that had tripped her up in every other part of her life. Because if she wasn't happy at home, and didn't have Hannah sleeping in her bed, her life was no longer smooth sailing.

She looked down at her fingers on the keys, which today seemed like they weren't attached to her body. When she started to play the end song – Take That's 'Never Forget' – her fingers moved but her mind did not. It was elsewhere. Still wondering why her life had turned into a quagmire of doubt. Wondering when and if she was going to have a chance to sort it out. She hoped later on, after the note Hannah left her this morning. It had been short and to the point.

1. I'm really sorry I didn't tell you about Lauren being in touch.
2. I'd like to talk to you about it and other stuff, too.
3. I've got someone to fill in at the club for me tonight, so I'll be back by 9pm tonight if you're around, too?

What did Hannah mean when she said she wanted to talk about other stuff, too? Was she kicking her out? Breaking up with her, even if they weren't officially together? Wondering if they could remain friends with benefits and have a review in three months?

Sometimes, she hated modern times and their fluid rules. Although as her gran always told her, the olden days weren't exactly a barrel of laughs and you had to go outside to wee. Perhaps Cordy's parents had grown up in the best times, although judging by her prude of a dad, you'd never be able to tell. Gran said he took after Granddad. But Cordy was sure Granddad would have been far cooler about her queerness than her dad had been. Maybe it was because they shared the same piano gene. The same yearning to express themselves. Granddad had expressed himself through piano and cricket.

Tonight, Cordy had to make sure she expressed herself through her words.

The group muddled through to the end of the rehearsal, then Cordy wished her students a good evening. Ava stopped by the piano as she left, a concerned look on her face.

"Miss," she said, touching the top of the Yamaha upright and not meeting Cordy's eye.

"Yes, Ava?" She winced internally. That was probably a little more curt than normal.

"Is everything okay, Miss? You just seem a little… I dunno, like my mum when she has a big case on at work." She searched for the right word. "Preoccupied."

Cordy's students constantly surprised her. Especially Ava. "I'm fine, but thanks for asking. Great job today."

Ava gave her a weak smile. "It'll be all right on the night, Miss," she replied, then patted the top of the piano, and left.

Cordy was just turning off all the lights when Greta arrived, bag over her shoulder and ready to leave.

"You're here late." Cordy gathered up her things, checking the clock. It was just after 5.30pm.

"I was getting some marking done. I'm going around to Theo's for dinner. I'm walking back now, and I wondered if you were, too?"

They walked out of the back school gates together, and Cordy was glad she hadn't brought her jacket to school today. The sun was still up, and the air felt fresh. A complete contrast to earlier in the week when it had felt like winter again. She loved this time of year when it behaved appropriately. When there was so much possibility in the air.

"How are rehearsals going?"

Cordy stepped over a large pile of dog shit as she replied. "Today, patchy, but I think that was the energy I was bringing. Note to self: don't bring your own issues into school."

"Easier said than done sometimes," Greta replied. "I know when everything was going wrong with Lucas last year, my lessons weren't the best." She stopped walking. "Are you and Hannah okay?"

Cordy had no clue. When she got back from speaking to the wise lesbians at her gran's house, she'd felt like she had a clear plan. However, once she was back at the flat and Hannah appeared to be avoiding her, the whole situation had spiralled again, feeling oppressive and heavy. She wanted to get it sorted, but simultaneously, she was scared of getting it sorted if it didn't turn out the way she wanted it.

"I don't know, which is why I'm slightly off my game. The kids were annoying me today when they hit bum notes, and that never happens. Hannah's ex and her sister turned up at the show at the weekend, and she didn't know they were coming. Neither of them knew she was doing drag, or that we were together. Plus, it turned out her ex had been messaging her beforehand."

Greta nodded. "Theo mentioned they were there, and that you'd had words."

Hannah had confided in Theo. That was unexpected news.

"I want to believe Hannah when she tells me she didn't message her ex back because she didn't want her back in her life again, but it's hard. I've had people cheat on me before."

Cordy sighed as they stopped to cross a road. She went to step into it, but Greta put a hand across her front. A car slammed on its horn and beeped as it whizzed by. Cordy's heart leaped in her chest. Getting run over would just about have topped off her day. But if she had, at least she wouldn't have to sit through Hannah telling her she was kicking her out.

"Slow down, please. If you die before Hannah lifts the Kings R Us trophy, both Theo and Hannah will kill me."

"I think you overestimate my importance." They moved left on the path to let a skateboarder past. Greta turned to watch as the woman sailed by. "I find skateboarders insanely attractive. All that balance and panache." She grinned at Cordy. "Anyway, back to you and Hannah. If you're doubting it, you're crazy. She likes you, you like her. End of story. You're having great sex, right?"

Cordy's whole body flushed with lust. "The best."

"That's the start. You're also living together without killing each other. You've got it all worked out too early, that's all, and neither one of you can believe your luck. I bet you any money she hasn't said anything because she doesn't want to jinx it. She's not getting back with her ex. Not when she's having crazy wild sex with you."

"You think?"

"I *know*. Plus, she told Theo she likes you, and coming from Hannah, Theo says that's almost saying she's fallen for you. She knows a good thing when she's found it." Greta linked her arm through Cordy's as they crossed the road. "You, my friend, are a good thing. Don't you forget it."

***

It was almost bang on 9pm when Hannah got back to the flat. Cordy heard the door close, and stood, waiting for her to enter the lounge. They'd talked about taking Hannah's bed out of the lounge and storing it at her gran's place. Hannah had even talked about buying a table and chairs if she won. That plan had been put on hold after last week. Now, every time she walked past Hannah's space, it was a stark reminder of where they were.

She heard Hannah prop her bike against the hallway wall, then she walked in, ruffling her dirty-blonde hair. She sat on the couch opposite and moved a cushion behind her. Her gaze didn't settle on Cordy. It didn't settle anywhere.

"How was your day?"

At last, Hannah looked at her. "Shitty. Yours?"

"Same." Cordy stared at Hannah. At her perfect lips she wanted to kiss. At the nervous flicker in her eyes. She wanted to be calm and rational about this. She took a deep breath.

But Hannah got there first. "I wanted to let you know, I met up with Lauren yesterday so we could have a proper chat."

Cordy's rational brain exploded.

"If you're kicking me out of the flat and getting back together with your ex, can you just tell me? I know we never promised each other anything. I know you've always wondered what might have been with Lauren. I get it, she's good looking, and she got here first. Maybe we tempted fate, and fate wasn't listening. But I don't want to sit here doing small talk if the outcome is going to be me having to find somewhere to live."

Cordy froze. Word vomit. That was not how she intended this to go down.

Hannah's face twisted as she shook her head. "That's not what I was going to say."

"It wasn't?"

More head shaking. "No. I should have told you all this beforehand. I should have been open, but there wasn't much to be open about. Lauren messaged me. I didn't know she was going to turn up at the show. She wanted to see me to explain why she left. That's all."

"She doesn't want you back? That's what exes generally turn up to say."

"In movies, maybe." Hannah tried a smile. "She doesn't want me back. She wanted us both to have closure. And to make sure it'll be okay if she bumps into me when she's out with her new girlfriend."

Cordy's eyes widened. "New girlfriend?"

Hannah nodded. "But even if she had wanted to get back together, I would have said no. Because of you and what we have."

"What is that, exactly?" Cordy's brain spun inside her head. "You've been luke-warm on commitment. You can't blame me for thinking you'd run off."

At that, Hannah got up and sat beside Cordy. She took her hand. It shook as she spoke.

"I know that, and that's all on me. I'm the one who wouldn't commit. I'm the one who asked you not to tell my family about us." She screwed up her beautiful face. "But I shouldn't have done that. That was me falling back into old patterns. Believe it or not, Lauren called me out on that yesterday. Told me not to make the same mistakes again. She made me realise I was in danger of losing you." Hannah paused, making sure she had Cordy's attention. "That really would be the biggest mistake of my life."

It was what Cordy wanted to hear, but it was taking a little while for Hannah's words to sink in.

"I need to change. I've started. But I need to finish. You don't need to change anything. Lauren left me because I was hiding. I'm still doing it, hiding behind Max. That stops today. I'm going home this weekend, I'm coming out as a drag king, and I'm going to tell them we're together." Hannah eyed her. "That's if you want that, too?"

Cordy was still processing everything Hannah had said. It took her a few moments to reply. "Of course I do."

Hannah exhaled a huge breath. "Okay, then. I need to start living life as the real me, on my terms." She wrinkled her nose. "I know I've said this before, but I finally realise it's true."

Of all the things that Cordy had expected to come out of Hannah's mouth, that speech hadn't got top billing. She'd expected Hannah to dump her. Tell her she'd been sleeping with Lauren for the past month. Because that's what happened before. But it turned out, her history was not repeating. Perhaps fate was on their side, after all. "Your note this morning made me fear the worst. It's never good when someone tells you they want to talk."

Hannah gave her a slow smile. "Sometimes it is." She stared at Cordy's face, then her gaze dropped to her lips.

Cordy followed it, too.

But then, Hannah shook herself. "Are you on-board? Can you forgive me for being stupid and can we start again?"

"You're really going to come clean to your family?"

She nodded. "I might even invite them to a show. At least then Mum can see her Bowie and my Bowie are a little different."

"Are we saying we are in a relationship, then? More than just friends with benefits?"

"You were always more, I was just scared you didn't feel the same way."

Greta's words echoed in her head. "She hasn't said anything because she doesn't want to jinx it." She'd been right all along. "Well, fuck."

"Fuck? I can do that, too."

Cordy finally let herself grin. "Oh, I know that, too. That contributes to my decision an awful lot."

"Back at ya." Hannah eyed her. "I can give you another three things if you want."

"Go on, then."

"One. I've never felt this much so soon for anyone in my life. Two. That kinda scares me. Three. That kinda makes this the best thing that's ever happened to me."

Cordy had no words to reply. Instead, she closed the gap between them and slipped her lips over Hannah's. This time, the kiss was a mix of heat and relief.

She hadn't lost Hannah. She wasn't homeless. They could perform at Kate and Meg's big party without it being totally awkward. It was a heady mix.

When she pulled back, she shook her head. "Can we talk to each other a little more about how we're feeling, though? Not just have sex, and hope for the best?"

"As long as we can still have sex."

Cordy put a finger under Hannah's chin and moved her head level with her own. "You wait until you see my plans..."

Hannah's grin nearly split her face. "Plans are good. As is talking more. I want this to work."

"We're on the same page. Finally."

"We are." She paused. "And by the way, thanks for sewing on my buttons."

Confusion crossed Cordy's face, before she let out a strangled laugh. "I completely forgot I did that with everything that's happened since." She blew out a raspberry. "You're welcome. Although you were meant to find them when we were together. I thought it would be a nice surprise. It's what girlfriends do. I want to sew your buttons on. I hope you want to do that for me, too."

"Every single one," Hannah replied. "So long as it doesn't involve actual sewing."

Chapter Twenty-Eight

"You're a what?" Her mum's face scrunched as she tried to take in what Hannah was telling her.

"A drag king. Like a drag queen, but instead of a man dressing up as a woman, it's the other way around. I'm dressing up as a man."

Even saying those words to her mum made Hannah cringe inside. Old Hannah would have clammed up now, reached for a biscuit, changed the subject. But new Hannah wanted to have these conversations.

Needed to.

She owed it to herself, to her family, and to Cordy.

Her mum's frown deepened. "You're dressing up as a man?"

"She looks absolutely wicked, too." That was her sister, Betty, a wide grin on her face. She'd told Hannah she'd be at their parents' to back her up. Also, that it was going to be a piece of cake. Oh, to have the unshakeable confidence of straight siblings.

"You've seen her?" Her mum couldn't quite take all this new information in. "When did you see Hannah dressed up as a man?"

Hannah winced. She still couldn't quite pin down Mum's

tone. Was she disgusted? Curious? Proud? That last one might be a bit of a stretch.

Betty nodded. "Last weekend. By accident. I was at Hannah's show, and I wasn't sure it was her before she opened her mouth. You wouldn't recognise her, because she's got a moustache and a beard and she's dressed in a suit. But even though she was putting on an accent, there was something very familiar about her voice. When she sang 'Rebel Rebel', I was sure. But you should see the way she had the crowd eating from the palm of her hand. She's a natural."

They were sat on tall stools around her parents' big island. Her dad passed tea around to her mum, Betty, and Hannah. Amy wasn't here as she couldn't get childcare, and Steve was playing football. Hannah had messaged her to say Betty would fill her in. Right now, though, she blushed at Betty's words.

"I didn't tell you before because it's a pretty new thing. I only started this year. But it's going well, people seem to like it, and I'm through to the final of a drag king competition. If I win, it might become more of a thing. Plus, there's a £5,000 prize." Hannah figured she might as well throw in the prize money, as finance had always been her mum's concern.

"But the main reason I'm telling you this is because I want to be honest with you. Tell you things. Let you in. I know that since I came out, I've retreated and not come home enough. I'm really sorry about that, but I plan to do better. I want you to know that as well as cycle couriering, I also do drag king and burlesque performance." She tapped her fingers on the white quartz island.

When she looked up, Betty gave her a 'keep-going-you're-doing-great' smile.

Hannah gave her a less confident one back.

"And where are you doing all of this?" Mum asked, her voice tight.

"Drag king stuff is mainly local, east London, but it might get bigger. The burlesque is more Soho cabaret clubs, but some locally, too."

Her mum sat back and surveyed her. "There was me thinking my biggest worry was you falling off your bike in London traffic. I didn't look at what burlesque was until recently." She exhaled. "That was an experience. But dressing up as a man, like they used to do in the London music halls? That one will take a little while to get my head around."

"You're not going to try to talk me out of it?"

Her mum shook her head. "What's the point? My concern was that you'd face rejection. You still might, but I can't protect you forever. Plus, Betty says you're good, so maybe you'll be the exception to the rule. But if you're not, I hope I've armed you with tools to deal with it."

To her left, Dad cleared his throat. "I'd love to see your act if what Betty says is true. And who doesn't love Bowie?" He bit his lip. "Do you look like me when you dress up?"

Hannah smiled. "A little, but I wear far more makeup than you ever have."

He ran a hand over his beard. "Maybe it's something I need to consider."

Hannah was grateful for his bad dad joke. It broke the slight tension that hovered in the kitchen.

"I need to ask this, Hannah, and don't get upset with me. You dressing up as a man..."

Hannah waited for Mum to get her next words out.

"... Is that the start of something else? Something bigger you want to tell us? Are you transitioning?" Her mum didn't wait for an answer, just sat up straighter, then looked Hannah dead in the eye. "Because if you are, I've read up about it, just in case." She put a hand over her dad's and gripped tight. "It wouldn't be a problem, we'd support you, wouldn't we, Greg?"

Her dad gave a firm nod. "Absolutely."

"It was one of the things I searched online when I wondered why you were avoiding us so much," her mum added. "I knew there had to be a big reason."

Hannah's heart lurched. Maybe she had underestimated her parents. Perhaps they were far better than she gave them credit for.

"I'm not transitioning, I'm just performing, and it happens to fulfil a part of me that's always been inside. We're all a bit masculine and feminine, aren't we?"

"It's true," Betty said. "Who goes to the gym and does all the DIY in our house? Me. Who does all the cooking? Ben."

"Gender is a made-up construct to keep us all in these strict lines. Being a drag king lets me step over the lines and do something else. It's quite a privilege, and besides that, it's a lot of fun." That part was definitely true. Ever since she'd started to embody Max, Hannah's life had only been on an upward trajectory.

"Let me get this straight," Mum continued.

"Or not," Dad said, deadpan.

Hannah blinked. Sexuality jokes. This was new.

"You're not transitioning, but you might have a masculine side."

"I might. And I might come out as non-binary, which is far more likely. In fact, very possible."

"I read up on that, too," her mum told her with her serious face on.

Hannah wanted to hug her, but it wasn't what they did. Instead, she ploughed on. "I just want you to know, I'm sorry for being distant, but I had a lot of things to work out. Things that Cordy's helped me to work out. Max has helped, too."

"Who's Max?" Dad asked.

"My character when I'm a man. But Max doesn't care about rules because he doesn't have to. Playing him has helped me to understand that I should loosen up a bit, too. Play with the rules. Rip them up."

"And Cordy. Are you together?" Mum asked.

"That was the other thing. Yes, we are. It's early days, but I can see this going somewhere. I *hope* it goes somewhere. More than I've ever hoped before. Plus, I want you to get to know her better."

"I do, too. She seemed lovely," her mum said. "If it helps at all, being clandestine about relationships might run in the family. You know that my parents were very strict, and wouldn't allow me to be on-stage? Thought it was uncouth. I didn't tell Granny I was seeing your father until we'd already been dating for nine months."

"You never told us that!" Betty trilled at a screech that might have the power to break glass.

"Why would I?" Mum turned to face Hannah, then reached over and put a hand over hers.

Hannah stared at it. This wasn't their relationship. They weren't tactile, not like she was with her dad. He was a hugger. Her mum was not. This was akin to a bear hug from her mum.

"When I had children, the one thing I said to your dad was that I wanted to bring them up to be whatever they wanted to be, and whoever they wanted to be. For you to be free of rules, because I grew up with scores of them.

"However, somewhere along the way those plans got a little blurred. If either of you become parents," she placed a loving hand on Betty's now, giving her a warm, sympathetic smile, "you might understand. You have plans to do things differently, but then you end up copying some of what happened to you, and not always the good parts."

But Hannah shook her head. "You didn't do too bad, Mum."

Mum took her hand away, then shook her head. "We could have done better, but we did the best we could." She eyed Hannah. "I hope performing brings you success. But more than that, I hope it brings you joy. I know it did for me." She paused. "One final thing."

Hannah waited.

"When can we come and see your drag show?"

***

When Hannah got back from her parents' place, she went straight to Doyle's. She pushed open the white-panelled glass front door, and recognised the song as soon as she did. 'Still The One' by Shania Twain. One of Cordy's favourites. Now one of Hannah's, too. She spotted her girlfriend – that was still going to take some getting used to – sitting at the white baby grand at the side of the room, an adoring crowd gazing her way as she played and sang. She was drawing a large regular audience here now.

What Hannah did with Max and her drag was cool, but she had a costume to hide behind. A persona. Whereas Cordy had none of that. When she played bars like this, it was just her and her talent fronting up, showing the world what she had.

Sure, she had a sparkly top hat which was currently sitting on top of the piano, but other than that, she was stripped back. A flash of glitter on her cheek. A strong calf flexing on the pedal. Capable fingers caressing the keys, and a voice that really should be in the charts. But Cordy wasn't in it for the fame or the adulation. Cordy was purely in it for the love of music. Hannah admired that, along with so much else about her.

She walked up to the bar and ordered a glass of red. Then she sat on a bar stool, and stared at Cordy. At her eyelids, currently closed as she hit the chorus for the third and final time. At her shoulders, not that broad, but oh-so-strong. They'd carried Hannah and her fears for the last couple of months, and then Cordy had showed her the way. Her and her indomitable spirit. She'd told Hannah to go for it. To tell her family who she was. To be who she really was. She'd been right all along.

As Hannah sipped her wine, she knew today couldn't have gone much better. Her mum hadn't been thrilled at first, but she'd come round, and as Hannah had left, she'd promised to send them some show dates. Just to see Max for now. Maybe even the final of the drag competition? The burlesque might have to wait until she was ready for her parents to see her almost naked. Which might be never.

Having told her parents, she did feel lighter. Her spirits lifted. She hadn't truly realised how much carrying around all those secrets and shame weighed you down. Now she did.

As Cordy launched into another song, she looked around the room and caught her eye.

Hannah beamed.

Cordy mouthed, "Hi!"

Hannah shaped the space between her hands into a heart and flashed it Cordy's way.

Cordy's smile made Hannah's chest ache.

Now that it was all out in the open and Hannah didn't have to waste her time and energy on emotions that didn't get her anywhere, maybe she could turn the spotlight on the emotions that did matter.

Like love. Which was exactly what she felt for Cordy.

She'd fallen for her.

Hook, line and sinker.

Chapter Twenty-Nine

"Can you pass me the Sellotape again?" Cordy tilted her phone to get another look at how the woman on YouTube was making this particular decoration, shaped like an ornate crystal chandelier. Even though it was actually made out of toilet roll inners, foil and a whole lot of ingenuity. She moved her head and frowned. "Why doesn't mine look like hers?"

Hannah reached for the phone and watched the clip again. Then she took the foil, wrapped it around the other end, sliced the tube and slotted it into the main chandelier frame.

Cordy leaned over and kissed her full on the mouth. "That's what I need a masc girlfriend for. Among other things."

"Get a room, you two!" Greta said, as she and Theo grinned from the sofa.

"Is that jealousy I hear?" Hannah cupped her ear, then turned back to Cordy. "And I think you're doing just fine on your own. My only question, as it has been from the start, is why you decided to do a themed summer concert, make a set and have everyone involved dress up for it. I've watched you tear your hair out getting the music and performance right. This could have been avoided."

Cordy had been asking herself the same thing for the past

few weeks, but it was what she would have wanted when she was younger. Someone to show her what a concert could truly be like. Someone to put their heart and soul into it, to inspire the students. She hoped she'd done just that.

This concert was shaping up to be fantastic, and if that happened, she'd be glad she provided the foundation for her students to shine. That didn't mean it wasn't currently the bane of her existence. Especially these chandeliers. She'd spent half an hour in bed last night contemplating buying a cheap one, until Hannah had ripped the phone from her hand and told her to go to sleep. Between Hannah practising for her drag show final, and Cordy making the set and doing rehearsals, they didn't have a lot of time to spare.

"When these chandeliers are done, I need to make 50 paper flower bouquets. Are you two sticking around for a little while?" Cordy glanced up at Greta and Theo, making paper bunting. Theo's time on the cabaret circuit bootstrapping most of their costumes and shows had turned them into an expert crafter, perfect for this job. They'd even started coming into the school to help with rehearsals alongside Greta, which Cordy was thrilled about. She'd told Theo if they ever wanted a job teaching drama, Cordy could put in a word with the Head. Theo was thinking about it.

"We're here as long as you want us," Greta told her. "You've ordered pizza, we have beer, we have everyone we love in one room, and we have glue that makes you high if you sniff it hard enough." She held up the tube of super-glue. "What more could we want in life?"

Cordy grinned. Greta was right, though. The people in this room had come to mean more to her than she thought possible. Last year, she wondered when her London life was going to take flight. Now, she wondered when it was going to calm down. She knew which extreme she'd rather have.

"I'm still worried about the concert, though. I can't believe it clashes with your final, too."

Hannah reached out and put a hand on Cordy's arm. "I told you, I'll be there. I can help with makeup during the day. I don't have to get to the venue until 7pm."

"But I don't want to distract you."

Theo laughed at that. "Coming from someone who knows, distraction is probably the best thing that could possibly happen. Prepare beforehand, then don't think about it. You can't do much on the day. If I'm free, I can come, too."

Cordy gave them a smile. "I'm not going to turn down offers of help if you can." She turned to Hannah. "Are you working the morning of the concert?"

"Of course," Hannah grinned. "It's a Friday. There's always hangover food and booze to deliver when most office workers go out after work on Thursday and work from home on Friday. It's almost as busy as a Saturday." Hannah paused. "You know what else? Distraction will be good for me, because my parents confirmed they're coming, too. Mum and Dad. In the audience of a drag show where I'm performing. Coming to support me and not to heckle. These are words that I never thought I would ever hear coming out of my mouth."

"I'm proud of you," Theo said. "Look at where you are now to where you were when I met you."

"A wreck with a lot of oranges?" Hannah asked.

Cordy grinned. "Don't knock it. Those oranges gave me the first glimpse of your knockout tits when you had to bend over on the tube to get them. I will forever be grateful to oranges. Plus, they also supplied the world's best marmalade, courtesy of Theo's mum."

"God bless Amanda. Who's made more marmalade and I've got a couple of jars for you upstairs. Rindless, of course. By the way, she's coming on Friday, too. To see you and me. She hasn't come to one of my shows in a while. She can't wait."

"At this rate, we might have more parents in our audience than you have at your school concert. Wouldn't that be a thing?"

* * *

When Greta and Theo left, Cordy rested her head on Hannah's shoulder. She appreciated them all making the effort, giving up their evening to help. Hannah didn't have much choice, she lived here. But Greta and Theo were treating her little show like it was a West End production. She loved them for that. Think big. Shoot for the moon. It's what she always told her students.

She'd always thought the same about her love life. Always thought that somewhere out there, there was someone waiting for her to show up and change their lives, and vice versa. She'd learned it through her parents and her grandmother, even though her story was heartbreaking. After a 60-year gap in their romance, did Gran and Joan lie in bed and talk about what-ifs? She doubted it. Her gran had always instilled in Cordy that what-ifs were pointless. Live your life now, with the people you want to live it with. Tonight had proved it beyond doubt.

Now, she sat on the sofa with her one. The one she'd been waiting for. That thought didn't even scare her. Hannah and what they had didn't scare her. That was new and exciting.

She definitely wasn't scared when Hannah took her hand and led her to the bedroom. Their bedroom. Hannah had even moved some of her clothes back into the wardrobe, although they'd agreed they might have to buy another. It didn't matter right now. What mattered was they were a couple. Sharing space, sharing dreams, sharing bodies.

Hannah's whole body was a soft, sensual delight, but especially her nipples. Cordy went to take one in her mouth, but Hannah shook her head, slowly stripped her naked, then pushed her onto the bed.

When she lowered her naked body on top of Cordy's, a ripple of desire shot through her, quickly followed by a slow wash of contentment. Was it possible to be turned on and content at the same time? She was living proof as Hannah's lips bruised hers, as Hannah's fingers skated across her skin. Cordy never thought of herself as beautiful, but Hannah thought she was. She told her now. The more Hannah told her, the more Cordy thought it was true. She was beautiful. Somebody thought so. Somebody called Hannah. Sometimes Max. But today, very much Hannah.

Their time together so far had been desperate, clawing at each other's clothes, thirsty for action right away. Tonight was different. Electricity still crackled in the air, but in a more sensual way. Charged, but slow. Tonight, she could already feel the intensity of Hannah's stare. The press of her muscle into Cordy's. The slide of her thigh between her own.

Hannah kissed her in long, drugged waves, pausing only to catch her breath. But as their eyes locked and their breath caught, Cordy gripped Hannah's arse, and it already felt like she was inside her.

Which meant when Hannah's hand slid between Cordy's thighs, Cordy bucked and gasped, then opened her legs wider. Hannah's grin was a lightning flash as she slipped her fingers inside.

Cordy's mind went blank. She'd found her person. She could allow herself to think that now. Before, it had been a hope. Now, it was reality. One that pressed into her, showed her how to feel, made her insides run hot with every touch of her hands and her lips.

As Hannah's fingers played Cordy just as she played her piano keys, she grabbed the back of Hannah's neck and pulled her down into a scorching kiss. One Cordy hoped told Hannah what she meant to her and how much she wanted her in her life. How much she'd changed her life. How the lights shone brighter when she was in a room. How proud she was of her for finally facing her family, revealing everything, and becoming who she truly was.

Cordy felt who Hannah was every time they kissed. Every time she curled her fingers inside her, like she was doing now. Every time she slid the tip of her thumb over her swollen clit and gave Cordy exactly what she wanted. Cordy's spirit roared as the intensity ramped up. Their bodies slid and clicked into place as her orgasm ripped through her like a wild tornado, spinning Cordy's mind and body out of control. She gripped Hannah and the bed sheets as she crested and fell, once, then twice, falling further into the bed, a rushing in her head and through her limbs, until she landed, soft and sure.

When their eyes met, Cordy knew she was right where she was supposed to be. That this was a journey they were only just beginning. She felt it in every inch of her bones.

"I love you," Cordy gasped, the words out of her mouth before she could think about them. She didn't care. Because the words were true. She did love Hannah. Every side, curve, and breath of her.

Surprise washed over Hannah's features, quickly followed by a flicker of a smile.

"That's good," she said, leaning in until their mouths were close enough to touch. "Because I love you, too."

Chapter Thirty

"Next!" Hannah waited for the next kid to sit on the plastic chair in front of her, foundation pencil in hand.

"Hi, I'm Ava." A perky teenager with queer energy stared back at her. This was one of Cordy's favourites. Hannah smiled at her. She was going to make sure Ava's makeup was the best yet.

"All ready for your show?" She smeared the foundation on her face and applied the brush to smooth it in. She could do with better lighting, but Hannah was used to this. She'd got ready for shows in shoddy loos and ill-lit corridors many times before. She could cope applying makeup in the school canteen.

Ava nodded. "Ms Starling has made sure of it. Plus, this is what I want to do, so I've practised. I've already got nearly 300,000 followers on TikTok. This concert is like a live showcase for me. Once I'm old enough to play in bars, I'll be doing it for real."

Hannah raised an eyebrow. "Now I'm sorry I can't stay to see the show."

Ava frowned. "You're not staying?"

"I have my own show tonight." She paused. Did coming out as a drag king extend to telling Cordy's students, too?

She eyed Ava, who was waiting for more. "I'm a drag king, and I'm in the final of a drag king competition tonight."

Ava's eyes lit up at that news. "Oh wow, I love drag kings. I've watched tons on TikTok, and I follow a few. I'm desperate to go to a show, but my mum won't let me until I'm 16." She paused, grabbed her phone, then showed Hannah a timer that showed 1 year, 1 month and 4 days. "That's how long to go until I can officially go to a show. Even then, I need my sister to come with me. Being young sucks big time."

Hannah laughed as she selected some rouge to adorn Ava's cheeks. "Enjoy the moment, you're only 14 once. You're already doing so much. You're going to smash tonight's show. I can feel it in my bones."

"What's your drag king name?"

Hannah hesitated. "Let's focus on getting your makeup done." If someone had spoken to her when she was Ava's age about being a drag king, she'd have been thrilled, but she wasn't sure if she'd already crossed some lines.

Ava pulled up TikTok as Hannah applied her makeup. She scrolled through a few London-based kings she followed, asking Hannah, "That you?" as she got to each page. On her fifth try, Hannah's cheeks flushed as she saw Max staring back. She couldn't lie. She gave Ava a grin and nodded.

Ava snorted. "Max Girth. Good one," she said, watching one of Max's videos with the sound low. "I've watched these before. Your videos are pretty good, but you need to do more. Post more content. I can give you some tips if you like. With your unique angle, we could easily make you go even more viral."

That sounded like the perfect plan. A teenager giving her TikTok tips. "I would absolutely love that."

Ava grinned. "In return, you can teach me drag makeup. Maybe I can do that when I'm 16, too."

Hannah gave her a smile. If only she'd been this composed, this in charge of her future at 14. Who knew what she could have done? But it wasn't too late, as Cordy always told her. She was only 27. Years to conquer ahead of her. Plus, she didn't have to ask her mum permission to do what she wanted.

There were plus points to not being a teenager anymore.

* * *

Hannah got on her bike two hours later, full of hope for the youth of today. If this was the generation coming up behind her, the world was in good hands.

Before she left, she'd found Cordy and pulled her into a supply cupboard to give her a searing kiss.

"Good luck tonight." Cordy had pressed a hand to Hannah's chest. "You're going to win. I have a good feeling."

Hannah had given her a don't-count-your-chickens look. "I'm going to do my best. That's all I can do." She'd paused. "But if I don't win, I might cry."

Cordy had grinned. "You'll win. I just hope I'm there to see it."

Hannah did, too. She'd wished Cordy luck, too, but she knew this concert would be a smash-hit.

"I wish I could see your triumph, too."

"Don't worry, one of the kids is recording it. There is no escape."

Hannah knew that Cordy's students were well drilled and ready, but could Hannah say the same? She'd practised hard this week, but you never knew what might happen on the night.

She might forget her first line, or see her parents and freeze. But hopefully the shock of seeing Lauren and Betty at the semi-final had prepared her for that. Plus, the difference was, she knew her parents were coming. Tonight, there would be no shocks or surprises. And if there were, hopefully only good ones.

She pushed off into the Friday night traffic, replete with a number of buses and big vans ahead. She briefly considered riding on the pavement. However, a quick glance told her the pavements were clogged with people, too, all heading home or to the pub after work. For most, this was just another Friday night. For Hannah and Max, this was the biggest Friday of their life. She wished Cordy could be there, but hopefully she'd make it for some of the night. With or without her, this had to work. Max had to win.

She cycled down the main road, past yet another fried chicken shop with the queue stretching out the door, the smell so strong, she could almost taste the first crunch. Next to it, the neon sign above Petra's Pizza Place flashed on and off, but nobody seemed to want pizza as much as they wanted fried chicken. A white van passed her too close for comfort, and she took a breath.

Hannah was going to try her best not to die on the way to Max's show. Although, now her whole family were coming, that was one way she wouldn't have to face them. Hannah brushed that thought to the back of her mind. Tonight, she was Max. Tonight, she was going to slay.

She stopped off at the bagel shop, getting a stern semi-smile from Sylvie as she paid for a salt-beef bagel.

"Good luck tonight, yes?" Sylvie's accent hung from every word. "Break a foot, or whatever it is you English say."

Hannah was going to try and avoid that. "Thanks, Sylvie."

She put the bagel in her bag. "This is going to fuel me to get through the show. You've basically provided most of my sustenance over the past year. You've kept me alive."

Sylvie walked around the counter and embraced Hannah, who stood stock still. Ever since that night she'd shown up as Max, Sylvie had become far more tactile.

"Someone needs to make sure you eat. Although I think Cordy might be doing that, too, no?" Sylvie gave Hannah a knowing look, raised her index finger, then stepped back behind the counter. "In fact, I'm going to give you more food, because you probably haven't eaten all day, yes?"

Hannah didn't have to check a mirror to know her face spelt 'rumbled'.

Sylvie walked around with one of those thin blue carrier bags that were slowly killing the planet, and presented it to Hannah. "A few more bagels, and also a custard slice so you can have a treat. You need treats in your life. You can't just live on bagels and Cordy." Then Sylvie winked at her. Actually winked! Who was this woman? "On me. Now go win the trophy. I don't want you coming in to see me next time empty-handed." She gave her a stern look. That was the Sylvie she knew and loved.

"I promise," Hannah replied. The she leaned in and kissed Sylvie's cheek.

In return, she got a slight blush.

Hannah walked out, a spring in her step, and mounted her bike. She didn't put her helmet on as it was only ten minutes to the venue. Plus, she didn't want to flatten her hair. She went to push off, looking over her shoulder to check for traffic. There was a double decker bus coming, but the light was red.

She had plenty of time to get ahead of it before it came around the corner.

However, that didn't account for the bus sailing through the red light, and Hannah pushing off into its side as it rushed past her. Its very strong, very immoveable side.

The impact was like hitting a brick wall.

A brick wall sprinting by at 30mph.

The collision crunched through her. Her brain spun wildly, trying to compute what was happening and how to ensure she didn't die. Yes, she'd had the thought earlier, but she didn't *want* to die. She wanted to kiss Cordy. Hug her parents. Win the competition. Eat her bagel. She couldn't let this bus win. She willed herself to stay upright, but it was a losing battle.

Hannah and her bike glanced off the bus and arced towards the pavement, which rushed up to meet her like an old friend.

As she went down, screaming inside, the bag of food Sylvie had given her swung upwards from the handlebars, and hit the pavement just before Hannah's shoulder. Crack. Then her head. Thud. Her bike's frame slammed against her knee, and pain skittered up her. Her mum was never going to forgive her for not wearing a helmet. She could feel something wet on her face. Hannah raised a hesitant finger. Was it blood? Was this the end? She tensed her muscles as she pulled her finger level with her eyeline, but all she saw was something white. She licked her finger. Sugary, custardy cream. Her finger explored for the source and met the crackle of plastic. The bag of bagels was under her ear. Had Sylvie's custard slice and bagels saved her?

The screams in her mind mellowed, replaced by the sound of traffic and Friday night, along with someone nearby shouting loud. "Fuck! That bus just hit her. Is she dead?"

She wanted to assure them she wasn't. But no sound escaped from her mouth.

Moments later, Hannah heard hurried footsteps, followed by a familiar voice.

"Hannah!" Sylvie's voice crackled into her senses. She moved her head, but Sylvie shrieked. "Don't move! You've got... cream on your face."

She was aware.

"Are you okay?"

Hannah heard other voices mingling with Sylvie's now.

"We're going to lift the bike off you. Let me know if you want us to stop," said a male voice.

They moved the bike slowly. Hannah flexed her toes. Still there. She moved her fingers. All good. She went to push herself up. Damn, her shoulder hurt. But her head didn't feel too bad. Slowly, she sat up. She glanced down. Her bag was still on her body. She could wriggle her hips. But there was something up with her head. It felt weird. She moved her head and felt what was there.

"Sylvie, have I got a custard slice stuck to my head?"

Sylvie looked at her, and finally cracked a smile. "Yes."

"I think it might have saved my life."

***

After just nearly dying and being saved by a custard slice, Hannah didn't need extra motivation to win. She knew what it was to look death in the eye and stand up with a custard slice stuck to her face.

Now it was his shoulder that throbbed, so did Max.

Yes, he was currently running on adrenaline, and by tomorrow, he'd likely be very sore. Yes, he was glad he hadn't done his makeup first, otherwise his five o'clock shadow might have ended up somewhere north of midnight. But he was still here. He was still breathing. And while he still had breath in his body, he was going to go out there and give the best goddamn performance of his life.

All those doubts he'd been having about winning? He knew now they didn't matter. It wasn't about the winning. It was about the performance. It was about the journey, and what he'd learned. He stared at himself in the mirror.

"All right, hot stuff? Ready to storm the stage?" Captain Von Strap took off his peaked cap and grinned at Max.

Max gave the Captain a firm nod. "Born ready, you know that."

The Captain assessed Max, then reached over and smoothed down his lapels. "I know we don't usually do this, but if you're nervous, that's normal, and I want you to channel that energy into your performance. Max Girth means something to people now, something he didn't at the start. That's all down to you. Take all your nerves and energy, and mix it with how far you've come. Max Girth is so far removed from Orange Lady who turned up at my door, curious about drag kings. You've taken control of your own destiny, so get on that stage and give the people what they want."

"You think I can beat Sir Loin? He was on fire tonight."

"I know you can."

The strains of the penultimate drag king's song came to a close amid huge cheers and applause, and the Captain gave Max a final nod. "Three minutes, ready?"

Max nodded. "It's a good job you're not a judge. I get the feeling you might be a bit biased."

The Captain grinned, and then put a finger to his chest. "Me? Never." Then, with a wink, he disappeared to the stage.

Max sat back on the red plastic chair, and looked in the badly lit mirror. His whole left side screamed, but he was going to get through. He had an audience to please. Including his family, Kate and Meg, along with some of their friends, Lauren and her girlfriend, and most of all, Cordy. If she made it.

Damn, Max hoped she made it.

Moments later, the Captain was on the mic introducing him.

Max's heart thudded in his chest like an incision. Raw and hot. He'd never been this nervous before. But then, there was more on the line. Not just the competition. More than that, this was where he got to impress his mum. The Captain called his name and as he stepped out, the heat and noise of the crowd came at him like a wave. He already knew he'd be sweating through his makeup in minutes.

He glanced left, and Greta beamed up at him. Cordy wasn't there. Disappointment sloshed inside. His momentum hung for a moment in a holding pattern before he pushed that thought away. Cordy would make it if she could. He had a whole room full of people waiting to be entertained.

"Hello motherfuckin' London!" Max yelled. "How you all doin'? Surviving the heat? I gotta tell you, I was nearly killed on the way here tonight, so for these next two songs, I want to hear you make some noise like this might be the last night of your motherfuckin' lives. Are you ready to do that?"

Screams from the crowd, who were all standing, jostling for space. Then he ran through his opening patter, just as he had on all the other nights. He found Lauren front and centre of the crowd, beaming up at him. He was pleased she'd come back, and that they'd worked it out. Alan and Bernice grinned up from a similar spot, too. He couldn't make out his parents or anyone else, the crowd was too thick and boisterous.

It was only when his gaze swept to the left at the end of his monologue, that he saw her. Someone elbowing their way through. Someone with dyed red hair that you might be able to see from Mars. Cordy. His Cordy. When their gazes connected, Cordy gave Max a stellar grin, then placed her hand over her heart, and patted her chest. At the same time, she mouthed "I love you."

Max's heart popped like a slingshot in his chest. He might be hurting, but having Cordy in the audience gave him wings. He grinned, raised an eyebrow, then turned to the Captain waiting just off stage. Max gave a nod, the Captain pressed play, and the backing track started.

"Sing along if you know it. Especially my mum, who's travelled through time and space to be here tonight. I hope I do it justice. This one's for you."

***

When Max finished his two-song set, he was pumped. The crowd were still going berserk when he got a hug from the Captain, before he went back onto the stage to announce the break before the judging took place. The audience had a sway with their cheers, but the judges had the ultimate final decision.

Max blinked hard, then strode into the crowd, where Cordy rushed over and grabbed him in a hug. The wrong side, where Hannah had fallen. Sometimes, it was hard to recall they shared a body, but not today. Max jumped and let out a small scream.

Cordy stepped back. "What's wrong?"

Max shook his head. "Nothing. I'll tell you later. Got in a fight with a bus on the way here. The bus won." Alarm streaked across Cordy's face, but Max put a hand on her arm. "Nothing a kiss won't fix."

"That," Cordy stepped forward and placed her lips on Max's, "I can do." When she pulled back, she eyed him. "Did you fall off? You sure you're okay?"

"I'll survive," Max said, shaking his head. "I'll fill you in later. More to the point, how was your concert?"

"The kids smashed it. Just like you. I've never seen you perform it better. If you don't win, it's a travesty."

"Says my girlfriend." Max raised an eyebrow.

"And the crowd."

Right then, Max's parents appeared at his side, with Betty grinning like a loon. "You were fucking A. May. Zing!" she squealed, clutching Max in a manner that was no good for his side. Pain screamed through him, but he said nothing. He was already waiting for his mum's verdict. He didn't need her to know Hannah had been knocked from her bike, just like her mum always feared.

Max turned an expectant face to his parents. He knew how this went down. If people loved something, they told you. If they hated it, they said nothing. If this silence kept up, it would crush him.

"Betty's right, you were amazing." Mum reached up to cup Max's cheek, but then thought better of it. "I don't want to smear your makeup." She waved a hand in front of Max. "This whole charade is so convincing, I have to say. You're gorgeous as a woman, but you're terribly handsome as a man, too. But it was your performance that really did it.

"You can sing. I'd like to say you get it from me, but I think you get it from yourself. Your confidence in your ability, even when your parents tried to knock it out of you, shows how incredible you are. I never managed to get over that when it happened to me. You did. I'm just sorry we weren't there to support you from the start. But I can't tell you how glad we are that we're here to see you star tonight." She shook her head, her eyes shiny. "Win or lose, I'm so proud of you."

Next to her, Dad nodded. "I saw a side to you tonight I've never seen before, and I'm beyond proud." He paused, then gave Max a grin. "Also, I think you're the best-looking man in the family, and that stings."

Max never thought a moment would arrive where his parents told him they were proud of his performance. Neither did Hannah. But the past few months had taught them both that nothing was set in stone. Things could change, and sometimes for the better. Max had just performed drag, and done it so well, his mum was crying.

Whatever the outcome of the judging, he'd already won. So had Hannah.

From the kernel of an idea, to this moment, Max had changed Hannah's life.

She'd be forever grateful.

"One last thing," Cordy added. "Now you've seen Hannah perform as Max, will you come to my open-mic night and sing the Bowie song with her?" She looked at Polly, then Max. "I know Hannah would be thrilled. It would mean a lot."

Max blinked. As did Hannah. They had no idea what their mum was going to say.

Polly dabbed her eye, then nodded. "I would love to. It would mean a lot to me, too."

* * *

Half an hour later, Max's heart pounded in his chest. He was normally unflappable, knew exactly what he wanted and how to get it.

However, this situation was the most stressful in Max's short lifetime. The finale of the Kings R Us competition. Of the eight drag kings stood on stage, it was impossible to tell who'd won. If Max had to guess, he'd say Sir Loin of Beef was his biggest competition. But a couple of others had wowed the crowd, too. However, he and Sir Loin were the only two to sing live. To hold the crowd that little bit more. Max hoped one of them won.

"Thanks everyone for coming tonight, for supporting London drag kings, but most of all, to the drag kings themselves for putting on a terrific show." Captain Von Strap swept an arm to the line of drag kings at the back of the stage. "Show them some love!"

The crowd went wild, which only made the tension coursing through Max's body ramp up more. He wasn't sure how people at major awards shows coped. His whole body burned like it was on fire, and about to combust. Next to him, Sir Loin gave him a tight smile. Max returned it.

"But there can only be one winner, and this was a really close-run competition. So much so, the judges have decided to award a second-place prize of £1,000. Please give it up for our runner-up, the fantastic Sir Loin of Beef!"

Max watched as Sir Loin hugged the Captain, took the applause of the crowd, then stood to one side.

"Now I'm thrilled to announce that the winner of the

Kings R Us drag king competition, winning £5,000, a regular booking at a major venue for the next six months, and all of our hearts is..."

The Captain paused for far too long. Max gazed into the crowd, then closed his eyes. It was the most silent it'd been all night long as everyone held their breath. Max squeezed his eyes tight shut and his fists into balls, willing the Captain to say his name.

"Max Girth!"

Max jolted as hands slapped his back, but he didn't move. The crowd roared their approval, and he glanced at the Captain, just to check his ears hadn't deceived him. Had he just won? The Captain beckoned Max forward.

He'd done it! As Max stepped to the front of the stage, his knees almost went, but he managed to stay upright. When he reached the Captain, he held Max's arm aloft. "Beautiful humans, your winner, Max Girth!"

A cannon of confetti exploded on stage, showering Max and the Captain in glittery multi-coloured shapes. Tears welled in the back of Max's throat as the crowd began to chant his name. He had to hold it together. The Captain presented him with a gold trophy, then hugged him tight, before presenting him to the audience again.

This time, sure he'd actually won, Max held the trophy high above his head, and scanned the crowd. He picked out his family and friends at the front, hugging each other, and to his left, Greta and Cordy. All the people who helped get him here today, and make him what he'd become. He stared at Cordy and shook his head in awe. He held up his free hand, punched the air, then blew her a kiss.

Cordy grinned his way, tapped a hand over her chest, then formed a heart shape with her fingers.

What a spectacular night this was turning out to be.

Chapter Thirty-One

Cordy walked out onto the old wooden stage and stared across the bar. The place smelled of a thousand debauched nights well spent, all pressed into the fabric of the red velvet seats, trampled into the wooden floorboards, baked into the glass of the chandeliers. She glanced up. Those were the real deal, not like the paper ones they'd made for the summer concert. She couldn't wait to play here later. To accompany Ruby O'Connell, who was a chart-topping act. That was definitely the weirdest thing to happen to her in a very long time.

At the bar, Kate and Meg were joined by Jess and Lucy, arranging photos of their years in the capital. As Cordy had pointed out to them, they weren't actually leaving London, just moving to zone six. Meg had given her wife an 'I told you so' look. Meanwhile, Jess and Kate had spluttered, and looked at her like she knew nothing.

She would never live in zone six, but then, she wasn't married with two kids. Her priorities were to be as close to as many bars who'd have her play. She was perfectly happy exactly where she was. *More* than happy. With Hannah by her side, her students to keep her grounded, and her career on the up. Hell, she was even in a relationship with a prize-winning drag king. If you'd told past Cordy that would happen this time last year, she'd have laughed in your face.

She walked over to the foursome, pointing at a photo and laughing hard.

"What do you think, Cordy? Does Lucy look like a young k.d. lang in that photo?"

Cordy gritted her teeth. "I'm not sure I know what a young k.d. lang looks like?" From the frowns, she wasn't sure that was the right answer. "If it helps, I think she looks cute." She smiled at current-day Lucy. "Still looks hot today, too."

Jess crossed her arms over her chest, a playful smile on her lips. "Back off, or I'll tell your girlfriend you're flirting with my wife."

But Lucy slung an arm over Jess's shoulder with a grin. "It's been a long time since a twentysomething flirted with me. Let me have it just this once."

Jess laughed, then checked her watch. "Enough reminiscing, we've got to get these boards in place and set up. People are arriving in less than an hour."

Behind the bar, a couple of cute bartenders chopped citrus fruit and chatted, in preparation for the night ahead.

"How many have you got coming?" Cordy asked.

"Just shy of 100," Meg told her. "We'll have a Spotify playlist to start, then the drag kings, then Ruby is going to perform, and then you're doing your songs and requests. We thought Max was incredible at his show. Thoroughly deserved to win. I saw Hannah and Theo arrive already. Are they getting ready?"

Cordy nodded. "Putting the war paint on backstage, transforming into Max and Captain Von Strap."

"I'm still not over Captain Von Strap." Kate smirked.

"Or Max Girth," Meg added. "I think you're all going

to gain a lot of new fans tonight." She clapped her hands. "We still need to decorate the tables, and Rachel and Alice are running late with the final bits of catering. London traffic triumphant again."

Right at that moment, Tanya and Sophie walked in carrying stacked plastic boxes. They were followed by two other women, all four red in the face.

"Talk of the devil!" Meg said.

She and the rest of the gang greeted the newcomers, and Meg introduced them to Cordy. "You remember Tanya and Sophie. This is Alice and Rachel – Rachel is the caterer." Meg tilted her head Cordy's way. "This is our very talented pianist for the night."

"You're teaching Finn!" Alice said, shaking Cordy's hand. "He played me 'Rocket Man' the other night. Very proud of it."

Rachel put the boxes down. "Can we get a couple more hands so we can get the food in and I don't get a ticket?"

The group hustled, just as two more women walked in. "Becka and Cleo!" Rachel turned them around and walked them out the door. "Just in time to help."

***

Two hours later and the party was underway, the room filled with balloons, bonhomie, oodles of queers, and a few bemused-looking relatives. Cordy had already been introduced to Jess's mum, who'd arrived alongside Kate's mum and her husband Lawrence, who was Meg's dad. Kate also introduced Cordy to her sister Vicky, who was married to Jess's brother, Jack.

"That's a lot of family connections," Cordy told her.

"I know," Jess interjected. "Everyone wanted Kate and I to

get together, but we defied the odds. That would have been a bit too much."

Their nephews, Luke and Freddie, sat in the corner, cokes on the table in front of them, heads lowered to their phones.

"Remember when I got back from Australia, and Luke and Freddie were tiny?" Jess said to Vicky, reminiscing.

Vicky gave her a wistful sigh, as Cordy admired her sparkly earrings. "I sometimes wish those days were back, but time moves on. Back then, they loved us so much. Now, that love has been passed onto their phones." She paused. "Although Freddie is excited to see the drag kings. I think Luke is, too, but he's far too cool to show excitement for much these days."

"Not true." Jack ran a hand up the back of his dark close-cropped hair, greying near his ears and round the back. "He was excited when I told him tonight was a free bar."

Vicky rolled her eyes. "Of course he was. He's 16. Remember us at our family gatherings at that age?"

Kate's smirk was wide. "We were a nightmare. Good luck if he does the same." She shook her head. "I still can't quite believe we're moving. When I was in my early thirties, I never thought we would. But times change."

"They do," Jess agreed. "I remember when you rescued me and took me in. Now I'm over 40, live in zone three, all grown up with a dog and a wife."

"Not sure about the all grown up bit." Lucy grinned.

"Artistic licence," Jess replied. "But I'm looking forward to the next phase of parties in Kate and Meg's massive kitchen with doors to the garden. You're going to be living the Sunday supplement lifestyle now. Especially with the money that Kate's getting for her flat."

The photographer, Heidi, all dressed in black interrupted their chat and asked them all for a few photos. Meg gave her a hug, as did everyone else.

"Cordy, this is Heidi, have you met?"

Cordy nodded. "Heidi took all the great shots of Gran and Joan's wedding. Big fan."

"Thank you," Heidi replied.

"Are Eden and Maya here, too?" Meg asked.

Heidi pointed to the back of the room. "We left Maya with my mum. Means we can have a night together once I've done the photos. We've even booked a hotel nearby, so we're making the most of it."

"Good for you!" Meg said, giving her a high five. "We had to pay through the roof for a sitter tonight, with all our family here. But we decided it was worth it. Otherwise, Luna would have been tearing around the place wearing me out."

"I know the feeling," Heidi replied. "Eden's over there with India and Gina, on the same table as Joan and Eunice."

"I didn't see Gran and Joan turn up," Cordy said.

"That's because they're very popular," Heidi replied. "India and Gina were just telling us they've been approved for adoption, so they might get a new child any day soon. Maybe two. How wonderful is that?"

"Fantastic. I'll have to catch up with them. They can join the parental club and be exhausted like the rest of us."

Just then, a ripple of excitement went through the room, and the volume got that bit louder. Cordy twisted her head to see what the noise was about. That's when she saw Ruby O'Connell coming through the crowd, led by media star, India Contelli. India had become a close friend of her grandparents after orchestrating their meeting, and she was lovely. However, even though Cordy had met her a few times, she still got starstruck. That only magnified ten times in the presence of the chart-topping folk star, Ruby O'Connell. If she did end up asking her to play her piano on tour, it might take Cordy a few weeks to speak to her.

"Hello everyone!" If charisma could be bottled, India would be a very rich woman. She oozed it, along with style and glamour. Cordy had met her wife, Gina, and they were definitely a case of opposites attract. Gina had charisma and charm, too, but she was far quieter than India. Cordy guessed that's what made them work.

Were she and Hannah like that? Hannah had told Cordy she'd brought her out of herself since they met, so maybe they were. Hannah, too, had introduced colour to Cordy's life, and she was far happier than she'd ever been. She hoped they'd got it right, just like all these couples surrounding them. Perhaps in 20 years' time, they'd have a crew like this lot, and they'd be leaving London, too. Although Cordy didn't think so. She might have only been here less than a year, but she was tethered in a way that felt just right. Maybe it was her gran's influence. She wished she'd never left. It seemed Cordy's roots were here, after all.

"Ruby, this is Cordy, she's on the piano tonight. I believe you've exchanged emails, but not met yet."

The whole room pulsed as Cordy shook Ruby's hand.

"I'm really sorry I had to duck out of our zoom. Blame my girlfriend, who hadn't told me about an interview she'd scheduled." Ruby put an arm around a smiling brunette next to her. "This is Fran, by the way."

Cordy shook her outstretched hand, and focused on making sure her hand didn't shake. Yes, she'd just shaken hands with Ruby O'Connell and her partner, but she wanted to appear cool, calm and collected. Even though rampant panic screamed through her at meeting such a big star.

"But you got the notes I sent through?" Ruby added. "Obviously I brought my guitar, but any backup you can give would be appreciated." She smiled warmly at Cordy. "India tells me you're a great singer, too, so maybe we can do a duet to finish my set?"

That internal panic she'd been trying to contain screamed the house down. A duet with Grammy-award winning Ruby O'Connell? Could tonight get any better? Cordy nodded like it was every day an international star suggested a duet. "I'd absolutely love that."

***

The night couldn't have gone better so far if Cordy had scripted it. Max and Captain Von Strap had kicked things off with their usual songs that went down a treat. Cordy was in the audience, and heard exclamations from those who'd never seen a drag king before, but definitely wanted to see one again. The pair also rolled out two special duets for the night. First, their version of The Clash's 'London Calling' brought the house down. Then, Estelle's 'American Boy', rewritten as 'London Boi', had taken the roof off. Cordy had never been prouder.

She and Ruby had performed a duet at the end of her set, too: one of Ruby's biggest hits, a duet she sang with country superstar, Cam. Ruby asked Cordy to sing the Cam part, which she knew well, but it didn't stop her internal chatter, or her inner peace taking a coffee break. It was one thing singing along to this mega-hit on the radio; it was quite another to perform it with the star.

However, Ruby had taken the time to run through it a couple of times back stage, and she'd complimented Cordy's voice and playing, making her feel like she *could* do this. When the time came, Cordy had thrown herself into it the way she'd told Max to, wringing out every note she sang for all she was worth. The applause at the end told her she'd done a good job, and Ruby made her take a separate bow too, much to Cordy's embarrassment. Hannah recorded the whole thing. It was a pinch-me moment for Cordy, one she was still getting over. One for the showreel.

When the performances were done, Kate took the microphone and thanked all the performers, and outlined the piano karaoke to come. Then she got misty eyed as she reminisced about her time in London before Meg, meeting her, getting married and having their kids.

"London, and more specifically, Shoreditch, has been home for so long, it's going to take some time to dislodge it from my psyche. But I know it's time to move when I'm not willing to queue for the latest food trend, get annoyed when I can't get a seat in a bar, and find them all crowded and loud. They tell me the pubs in zone six always have seats."

"That's because they're shit!" Jess heckled from the back of the room.

"You'll have to come visit and find out." Kate narrowed her eyes at Jess, and the crowd laughed. "But seriously. To everyone we've met, to all our friends, old and new, I want you to know that Meg and I consider you family. Yes, we've both got family who we love dearly, but we also treasure our found family too. London is a great place to live, but it's nothing without people you love. We're all nothing without the people we love. Thanks for being here with us, and for making the past 25 years an absolute treat." She took a deep breath. "And now, let's get the wonderful Cordy on the keys before I start to cry."

Cordy kicked off the karaoke with her Shania fan-favourite, and followed it up with some Taylor Swift that got the crowd on their feet, singing and dancing. When the requests started pouring in, she knew the night was going to roll smoothly. What's more, Kate and Meg's friends weren't shy, something Cordy loved.

Joan got up again, to huge cheers, Jess and Lucy did a duet, and Meg crooned a Fleetwood Mac stunner, with Kate swooning at her throughout. Meanwhile, India's partner Gina silenced the crowd with her soulful voice, Heidi snapped the lot, and Becca, who didn't look much older than Cordy, dedicated Nat King Cole's 'Unforgettable' to her wife, Cleo. "Remember that night in Boston?" she asked before she started to sing. Cleo's face told Cordy she remembered it well.

At the end of her final set, just before half-eleven, Cordy got on the microphone. "For my penultimate song, before Kate and Meg sing us out with their final choice, I want to invite my girlfriend back to the stage. You'll know her as Max Girth, but underneath the makeup, she's also my Hannah. Come on up, gorgeous."

Max accepted Cordy's offer of the mic, giving her a kiss on the lips, too. "Perks of shagging the pianist," she said, to a huge cheer from the crowd.

"We thought this song probably summed up Kate and Meg's experience in London. I know it speaks to our past six months, ever since we met. Thanks for having us tonight, and if we meet as many witty and wonderful people as are in this room over the next two decades, we'll be lucky."

With that, Cordy broke into the opening bars of '(I've Had) The Time Of My Life' from the 'Dirty Dancing' soundtrack. "I finally got Hannah to watch this recently, and now she sees its majesty. Get on the dancefloor. I want to see a few lifts at the end!"

As Cordy sang the opening lines, the crowd went wild. Even her gran and Joan got up to dance. Cordy wasn't joking, either. The past six months had taught her so much. She'd had the time of her life. It'd been a rollercoaster, but if she had to ride it with anyone, she was glad it'd been Hannah. And Max.

When Hannah hit the chorus for the final time, she eyed Cordy, tilted her head, and put a hand over her heart.

Mad happiness flowed through Cordy.

When the song finished, she gazed out at the crowd, soaking up the wild applause. This was the most epic gig she'd ever played, and she was so thankful to be doing it with Hannah by her side, her grandparents close by. She wanted to frame this moment. Remember it. Hold it close to her heart.

Because for some, this was a London farewell.

But for Cordy and Hannah, this was just the beginning.

***

When they arrived home, they walked to the kitchen, the start of all their best and most unwise adventures. Cordy plucked the bottle of Veuve Clicquot that Hannah's parents had bought her for winning the Kings R Us competition.

"You've been saving this for a special occasion," Cordy told her. "We just performed the gig of our lives. I can't think of anything more special than that."

Hannah took the bottle, unwound the wire around the cork, popped it, then got two wine glasses from the cupboard. They didn't have champagne flutes; these would have to do. She made a mental note to buy some. Maybe that's what people did as they approached their late twenties? After buying a new table and chairs with her winnings, champagne flutes were next.

As she placed the glasses on the counter, Hannah saw the latest decorated orange by the tea cannister. She let out a howl of laughter. This time, the orange had a silver lightning flash drawn on its belly below a pair of dark eyes. "You made the orange into Bowie."

Cordy kissed Hannah's lips. "Today seemed like the perfect day. I don't know why I never thought of it before. Plus, Amy had seen better days."

"RIP Amy." Hannah held it up. "I think this might be my favourite."

Cordy wrapped an arm around her waist. "That's what I like about you. Easily pleased."

They took their drinks to the balcony, and as Hannah sat, she cast her mind back to the first time they'd done this. "Remember sitting here on Valentine's Day?"

"How could I forget?" Cordy grinned. "Greta and Theo met, and it was my first drag-king show." She pointed a finger. "It was also the first time I asked for three things about you."

"I recall."

"Do you remember they were all negative?"

"I remember. Yours were all about music and marmalade." Hannah sipped her drink. The bubbles went up her nose and she sneezed. She still wasn't sure if champagne was her drink.

"Tonight, I want you to give me three more. But with a more positive spin."

Hannah puffed up her chest as she thought. "Three positive things in my life? It should be easier now." She held up her thumb. "Max Girth, about to crush London's cabaret circuit."

Cordy snapped her fingers and held them above her head. "Yes, King!"

Hannah grinned, then held up a second finger. "My family. Who the fuck knew they were all drag-king fans?" A third finger. "My girlfriend. Because she's quite simply the best."

"I'm honoured I made the list." Cordy sat back, beaming. "You've come a long way, baby."

"*We've* come a long way." Hannah got up, pulled Cordy to her feet and pressed her lips to hers. It never failed to give her a thrill. "Me, you, Max. Watch out London. You ain't seen nothing yet."

THE END

Would You Leave Me A Review?

If you enjoyed this slice of sapphic London life, I wonder if you'd consider leaving me a review wherever you bought it. Just a line or two is fine, and could really make the difference for someone else when they're wondering whether or not to take a chance on me and my writing. If you enjoyed the book and tell them why, it's possible your words will make them click the buy button, too! Just hop on over to wherever you bought this book — Amazon, Apple Books, Kobo, Bella Books, Barnes & Noble or any of the other digital outlets — and say what's in your heart. I always appreciate honest reviews.

Thank you, you're the best.

Love,
Clare x

Also By Clare Lydon

London Romance Series

London Calling (Book One)

This London Love (Book Two)

A Girl Called London (Book Three)

The London Of Us (Book Four)

London, Actually (Book Five)

Made In London (Book Six)

Hot London Nights (Book Seven)

Big London Dreams (Book Eight)

London Ever After (Book Nine)

Standalone Novels

A Taste Of Love

Before You Say I Do

Change Of Heart

Christmas In Mistletoe

Hotshot

It Started With A Kiss

Nothing To Lose: A Lesbian Romance

Once Upon A Princess

One Golden Summer

The Christmas Catch

The Long Weekend

Twice In A Lifetime

You're My Kind

All I Want Series

Two novels and four novellas chart the course of one relationship over two years.

Boxsets

Available for both the London Romance series and the All I Want series for ultimate value. Check out my website for more: www.clarelydon.co.uk/books

Printed in Great Britain
by Amazon